THE LITTLE COFFEE SHOP OF HORRORS ANTHOLOGY

PAUL CARRO & JOSEPH CARRO

TETHER FALLS PRESS

CONTENTS

1. INTRODUCTION: HOW ABOUT A SECOND CUP? 1

2. STARBUCKS 4

3. THE HANDOFF 6

4. FORAGE MARKET 57

5. POPSICLE KIDS 59

6. COFFEE & MILK 79

7. SHIRTS & SKINS 81

8. STARBUCKS 102

9. ANKOU 104

10. UNURBAN COFFEE SHOP 121

11. STRANGE   123

12. ALFRED'S   142

13. KOPI DARAH   144

14. JAHO COFFEE ROASTER & WINE   176
BAR

15. SALEM   178

16. BOARDHOUSE COFFEE   196

17. CUL-DE-SAC   198

18. STARBUCKS   229

19. OUTBREAK   231

20. PEET'S COFFEE   255

21. OLD BONES   257

22. CARPE DIEM COFFEE & TEA   297
COMPANY

23. YOU CAN'T GET THERE FROM HERE   299

24. 10 SPEED COFFEE   324

25. THE CANDY HOUSE   326

AFTERWORD   346

ABOUT THE AUTHOR   347

ALSO BY PAUL CARRO   349

Roots of All Evil   351

About The Author   352

INTRODUCTION: HOW ABOUT A SECOND CUP?

Y ou have seen us, maybe even now, as you sip your coffee in your favorite cafe while reading this. We are legion in coffee shops across the world. Those of us with laptops plugged in while plugging away on projects. Most are unlikely to be authors, the majority only there for free wi-fi, a caffeine fix, or the lonely hoping to score.

Coffee culture is a social affair. If you look around, really look, you might find just that—an affair. Sometimes people meet for coffee as a pretense to connect with someone other than a spouse or a current lover. How many couples sit with their true partners? How many are stepping out on the love of their lives? It is impossible to know unless one sits close enough to eavesdrop, close enough to overhear whispered confessions. People with secrets are also legion.

And there they are, those with secrets, typing away on laptops. What is it that these people on their laptops do all day? Are those in a corner with screens turned away from crowds, up to nefarious deeds? Do they plot to hack identities? Perhaps glean adult materials in the most inappropriate of settings? Is it unfathomable they plot a murder unbeknownst to a cadre of witnesses who are simply there to get a beverage topped off with whip cream to help them get through their day?

No matter what the laptop people do, it remains mysterious despite them operating in plain view of the public. What occurs as multitudes of fingers type away will affect some lives, will change courses of history for certain individuals. Even if one is innocently completing a work report hoping it will lead to a raise, or at least ensure they survive the next round of job cuts. Make no mistake, something is happening at the hands of people with their faces buried in screens while the world goes on.

You hold in your hands one result of such typing. In this case—this one singular case—two laptop people authored a book of horror short stories, each one crafted in one of twelve different coffee shops across Southern California and Southern Maine. The tales of terror do not all revolve around coffee or the cafes that serve it up. Joe and I created these tales while sitting next to you. Right next to you. A whispered breath away.

The stories are born from the locations we consumed coffee in. Whether involving ghosts, goblins, psycho-killers or witches, the locale inspired the tales. Perhaps something you said, or did, influenced us to twist a story a certain way, to change the course of the original idea. Perhaps your entry into our key tapping orbits inspired something far worse than we ever could have created on our own.

This is *The Little Coffee Shop of Horrors Anthology* and maybe you have seen us. Maybe we are next to you now while you read this, maybe we are waiting to observe your reaction to this book. Maybe we are close enough to breathe down your neck. For if you are in a coffee shop, so are we, listening to all your secrets...

STARBUCKS

SANTA MONICA, CA

In a book written in coffee shops, it would be near impossible not to write at least one in a Starbucks. This one, in Santa Monica, California, stands out from many I have frequented. First off, it is distressingly loud. The music blares at a level that will overpower any noise cancelling headphones one might wear. People often shout to be heard in the tight confines. It does not lend itself well to writing unless chaos is one's go to for studying.

The location lives at the lower level of an apartment complex which made news a few years ago for arrests related to a prostitution ring within the complex. The crowd is heavy on local industry types and apartment dwellers. It was during one trip to get my caffeine fix that I noticed an event which spurred my inspiration for this story. I saw a divorced couple taking part in 'the handoff' of their child for the weekend. The parents were far from happy seeing one another. Was it easy to write in that environment?

No, but I like to think it was worth it. While this book is filled with all kinds of horrors, this story is filled with a little Hope.

THE HANDOFF

PAUL CARRO

"Jerry, you're not meeting my needs, Jerry," Stella Collins whined into the cellphone cradled against her neck. She searched an immaculate living room for the one thing that might be out of place. "Specifically, how? You want to go there? I do not say Siri this or Alexa that. I pay you well so I can say Jerry do this or that and you are letting me down."

Stella fluffed the cushions in search of the seemingly unattainable, a move normally left to the work of a housekeeper. The housekeeper, Rosa, legal, (as far as she knew, Jerry took care of such details, leaving her with plausible deniability) would not arrive to work for another hour. That left Stella only one person to vent to.

"Okay, let us go down the list. Your swipe right version of a date you set me up with last night was a bust." Jerry pleaded his case while Stella took a much-needed breath. "Okay, fine, I agree he was good looking, but the man plays for your team. Oh, please, do not give me that. I don't care if you are gay, I can tell if someone else is better than you. Your head gets in the clouds when you see a pretty smile, alters your judgement."

It felt the perfect time to throw the cushions back onto the couch in the manner of a hissy fit. She did so while Jerry raised his voice on the other end of the phone.

"Okay, fine, I concede. Maybe you know better than me in that department. You think I am being offensive? Obviously. Have you met me? Oh, that's right, you work for me Jerry (she lingered on the 'e' so it came out Jeeeeeeeery). Back to the problem at hand, you refused to do the handoff with my daughter to save me seeing my shit show of a husband."

"Mom, I can hear you up here, God!" Hope, eight, with long blonde hair in equestrian shape dressed in Polo, leaned over the banister in a spot where the chandelier did not block her view. She let loose on her mother before storming back to her room.

"Gloves! No, not you Jerry. I am not asking you to buy me gloves. I'm asking since you did not help me avoid the handoff to at least help me with my other pressing need." Jerry snarked a reply on the other end of the line. "Oh, please, I have a vibrator for that."

"Mom, you're upsetting me times four!" Hope repeated her objection stance, this time wearing snow boots, a getting dressed work in progress.

"Look Jerry, you've upset my beautiful child. Now listen, part of our court battle centers on my ex never spending time with Hope on their weekends. When dropping Hope off, Danny should be there, but he never is. That forces me to interact with the bitch, Nikki."

"Upsetting times five!" Hope slammed the door behind herself for good measure.

"Close your door, honey, the adults are talking!"

Hope opened the door and yelled from within. "I already slammed it if you would pay attention! Times six, Mom!" She slammed it two more times for good measure.

"I swear Jerry, I don't know where my daughter gets it from. So, as I was saying, if you take my picture from ten years ago, that bitch Nikki looks exactly like me. How sick is that? She is so uneducated, into all that namby-pamby healthy living crap. No, I have not forgotten that I partake in hot yoga classes. But she is into all that organic, vegan, gluten stuff. I worry my daughter might fade away to nothing after a weekend eating their squirrel food. Yes, I remember you too are a vegan, Jerry. Still, you are a much different type of bitch and I love you for it. I would trust you with my daughter's life and do whenever you babysit. But Nikki? She is a kid herself. Jerry, the earbud for my phone, you must help me find it. That is the reason I called you. Yes, I have a mirror."

Stella stepped to one of several in the room, an ornate wood carved floor mirror centered on one wall adjacent a vase and an antique chair, a creative use of space for a seldom used part of their mini mansion. Stella gazed at her image. While many considered her a beauty at forty, she always searched for the younger version of herself at every glance in a mirror. Stella smiled, bringing her appearance down another decade. She had a charm, a fun-loving air underneath the designer clothes, if she would only show it more often.

Time wears down the soul faster than the flesh, Stella thought. Jerry, her assistant, the true current love of her life, where other men had failed, came through for her once again. Using the mirror as a guide, Stella touched the ear bud in her ear and tapped it on.

She released the phone at her neck, pleased to discover releasing the shoulder scrunch de-aged her the tiniest bit more. Maybe there was someone in there after all. The old Stella, right? She spoke into the air.

"You're right, Jerry. It was in my ear, the whole time. You're the best, Jerry."

· · · ● · ● ● ● · · ·

"A new study confirms last year to be the warmest on record. The results raise concerns about the tipping point for global warming having already passed. Politicians who still argue both sides of the science appear no closer to consensus. Recent reports of underwater volcanic activity have only added fuel to the global fire," the radio voice said.

"Mom," Hope said, bundled warm in the passenger seat of their Lexus SUV, despite the vehicle's climate controls.

Snow melted on contact with their heated windshield.

Stella fumbled with her phone in the media dock on the console until finally turning off the local news. She looked to her daughter, now occupied with watching the snow on the far side of the vehicle. Stella caught her daughter's gaze in the window's reflection.

"Does hearing that kind of news upset you?"

Hope nodded.

"We do it on purpose. We know it will affect the future, will affect all you children, so we're holding the Earth hostage."

Hope turned to her mother frustratedly furrowing her brow from within the confines of her faux fur-lined Burberry coat hood.

"See, we're waiting until you all learn to clean your room. Once you do, we'll set the environment free."

"I always clean my room. Release the hostage please," Hope said, leaning back into her window, her world.

"Sorry, there are less diligent kids in the world. How about I release a part of Miami, just as a show of good will, then you spread the word to other kids?"

"I hate Miami."

"Oh, so you're selective in what parts of the planet you want to save? I see how it is. Our home in Maine or nothing?"

"No, I want to save even Miami."

"Even though you hate it?"

Hope nodded against glass. Stella rubbed her daughter's arm.

"Please never get jaded. We need more like you, kiddo."

"Music please."

"Let me check my playlist, some songs from my spin classes. How about a little *Funky Cold Medina*?"

Hope continued leaning into the window and used the reflection to eye-roll her mother. "Please."

"Oh, come on, that was funny, admit it."

"Times two," Hope said.

"Only two? I need to work on my material. Fine, Miley Cyrus?"

Hope shrugged. "She's fierce."

Stella rubbed her daughter's shoulder again as Miley launched into dreams of Malibu. "So are you, kiddo, so are you, times ten."

Hope managed to smile.

············

For the sake of her daughter, Stella drove at a mall walker's pace along the snow-covered dirt road. The narrow road was barely navigable even during the all too short summers on Tether Falls Lake. The town had never widened roads designed long before SUVs entered the consumer marketplace. Locals had no desire to make the drive into their secluded stretch of paradise any easier. Residents preferred tourists flock to the public beach portions of the waterway. Homeowners voted down any proposed upgrades year after year.

The road ran through a deep forest so thick that the only gaps in foliage were people's homes. Many front yards were yards in name only, with many acting as an extension of the surrounding forest, with massive trees fronting their homes. The more affluent residents cleared trees and planted grass. Tree removal costs were prohibitive for many. A workaround for some locals was to cut front yard trees down to stumps, a cost-effective solution, better than nothing. Stella considered the half-job stumps the equivalent of the home in every small town littered with junkers but minus an actual working vehicle. Those stumpy yards saddened Stella, though she was uncertain why.

There was little traffic to worry about on the lake road in winter. Most folks abandoned their places for the season and traveled to Florida as if they were migrating birds. The roads were slick with snow. Take a curve too fast and one was apt to slide off-road to make the acquaintance of a local pine or birch, many of which displayed trophy marks on their trunks of past meet and greets. The trees nearest the road collected vehicle battle scars like Pokémon cards.

Stella felt the urge to speed up, chance a foliage face-to-face as she neared a singularly distressing location. Ahead to her left (the side facing the lake) was Old Man Hennigan's house. The man had been old for as long as Stella could remember. The large unkempt local often walked through the woods, following the edge of the lake even where it did not beach. He crossed property after property on his strange walks while poking at the ground with twin ski poles, which he used even during the summer months. Many a time when Stella sunned herself on their dock along the water, she felt his eyes before noticing his presence. How long he watched before she spotted him, she could never be sure.

It kept her on edge, never fully allowed her to relax when she was alone at the cabin. The man never seemed to leave the area, staying year-round, and no one really knew him. Creepy. Stella felt a chill so she voice-activated the vehicle to heat up another ten degrees. She stiffened at the wheel. Hope noticed the change in her mother's demeanor as they approached the house. A beat down pickup with a plow attached sat in the yard. Smoke drizzled from a chimney which took up almost half the front of the tiny house, more of a shack really, a beach house not designed for winter living.

"Nikki says he is nice," Hope said.

"Who?" Stella asked.

"Mr. Hennigan."

"Mister?" Hope nodded. "Yeah, well, so was Ted Bundy," Stella said.

"Who is that?"

"Never you mind. You stay away from Old Man Hennigan, you got me?"

"Why?"

"Why do I ask you to do a lot of things? Because I can. Stay away from him, you hear me?"

As if sensing their presence, the gray thermal onesie wearing old man, white bushy beard yellowed under nicotine, stepped out onto his tiny front stoop. Stella leaped in fright at the man's sudden appearance. Her discomfort transferred to Hope, who reacted likewise. Stella sped past. Once clear, the two turned to one another.

"You're right, he appears quite nice," Stella said.

The pair giggled, though Stella stopped upon realizing she would have to drive back again on her own shortly. They rounded a curve into a straightaway. Their destination eventually came into view.

"Dammit, he's not here!"

"Mom, language."

"Sorry, honey, but do you see a Mercedes?"

"You know he works a lot."

"But it is his weekend. I expect him to spend time with you, otherwise I would."

"You work a lot too."

Stella looked through the windshield at the cabin up ahead, a familiar sight, a home once hers, their second one. She spent most summer weekends there, often hosting parties where she and her ex closed several business deals. Stella and Danny sealed plenty of their own deals under the sheets as well. Something about the location prompted the couple to be more primal in bed than when home in the city. Strange that, Stella thought, blushing warmly at the memories of a time before her betrothed asshole became her ex-asshole.

The lake house was modest compared to the home she received in the settlement, yet the location proved painful to let go. Stella was happy Hope would get to enjoy it since her husband did not sell it after the divorce. It still hurt to be an outsider looking into that which used to be hers.

It was a one-story house if one did not count the twin dormer windows jutting out from the attic as a story (and she did not). The modest A-frame structure had a heavy oak door as an entrance and picture windows on either side. A living room centered the house. The kitchen branched off to the right and two bedrooms branched off to the left. Their love shack became less so after Hope was born because of the proximity of the sleeping quarters. But whenever Hope visited Nana for a weekend, all bets were off and bacchanalian shenanigans ruled again.

"Should I call him?" Stella asked.

"So that I can hear you two argue?"

Stella sighed. How her daughter remained so normal given the tug of war over custody which her 'adult' parents constantly engaged in remained a mystery. Stella often fought her worst instincts in front of her daughter regarding Danny and his place in both their lives. Still, there was the whole part about dropping Hope off in the hands of the bitch.

"I'm sorry things are the way they are, honey."

"Everyone's parents are divorced. I'm used to it."

"A, that's sad, and B, you should not have to be used to it."

Her daughter appeared to ponder the world again, looking away from her mom, out into the falling snow.

"What is it?"

"I like Nikki, I wish you could too, she's fun."

Stella felt the ice outside slip into the car and throat punch her heart. She gripped her daughter's shoulder.

"Honey, when you get older, things get complicated."

"You hate her."

"Okay, so maybe complicated is the wrong word."

"She's funny, she's nice, and she never says bad things about you."

Stella felt the ice melt a little before realizing she was likely being played. Nothing makes a victim more a victim than being such a nice person. No, her competition was probably playing a long game for her daughter's affections.

"Is that so?"

"She likes stuff I like."

"I watch your equestrian competitions all the time, honey."

"I love horses, I don't like competing, you never listen."

"Honey."

"Nikki listens, always. Sometimes I don't have to say what's wrong, she just knows."

Stella fought the urge to hit the gas and crash into the house. The young woman—key word being young, ridiculously so—had no responsibilities which left Nikki all the time in the world to listen, not to mention Stella's ex-husband was never around on the father's weekends. Stella always felt she was leaving her daughter in an enemy camp, no true adult supervision in sight. Next thing you know, her daughter would pine for tattoos or piercings.

"It upsets you when I talk about her?"

"Times six."

"I'm your mother. I reserve the right to worry about who my daughter spends time with, but I promise I will try harder. Deal?"

Hope nodded, hugged her mother then stepped out of the vehicle. Stella popped the back allowing her daughter to grab a bag.

"Remember, you can't see the ice under all the snow so no going out on the lake are we clear?"

"But it's fun," hope said.

"And dangerous. No ice, now go, I'll wait until we know she is there."

The hatch lowered itself as Hope rushed to the front door on bouncing steps. Too giddy for Stella's liking. Nikki answered on the first knock. Hope dropped her bag and hugged the woman. Nikki wore yoga gear, ridiculously underdressed for the weather, showing off what her ex was getting regularly. The toned blonde let go of Hope to wave at Stella. Stella responded in kind.

"Hi there, you back-stabbing bitch. Turn my daughter against me and I'll end you," Stella said aloud while smiling and waving.

Nikki raised a finger and disappeared from the doorway. Hope tapped on her phone.

Stella's phone binged. The text read: 'She has something for you.' Nikki reappeared in a pink Michael Kors fur-lined jacket which hugged her tight body while the most adorable Ugg boots encased her feet. The ensemble somehow accentuated the yoga pants which emphasized a too tight derriere. God, Stella hated the woman.

The woman trudged through the snow and tapped on Stella's window twice before Stella bothered to remote control it down. Nikki held up a paper plate filled with cookies, covered in red holiday cellophane.

"I made these for you. They are a healthy treat without all the calories. Everything is organic," Nikki said.

"I'd expect nothing less of you. Danny isn't here?" Stella looked around as if possibly her ex was playing hide and seek. Nikki bounced excitedly, not reading the room.

"Oh please, you remember how much he works. He will be here. He loves Hope, you know that. I can't shut him up heading into his weekends."

"You might suggest he show up for a handoff occasionally."

"I don't mind so much. I enjoy catching up with you. I'd really like you to stay for supper sometime."

Stella scrunched her face. Raised in New York, Stella moved to Maine only after meeting her husband. Dinner was the proper term. Supper in the conversation meant Stella was talking to a hick from the sticks. Stella wondered what Danny saw in the woman. Ass and more ass, she figured, furious that Nikki owned an undeniably fine one.

"Sorry, I'm all 'suppered' out. Have a big date myself," Stella lied.

"Oh, that's great! You are seeing someone, that's awesome! Maybe we can double date sometime. Hope would love to see the two of you in a room together," Nikki said.

"Well, thanks for the cookies. Might want to step away before I roll you under the tires."

Nikki laughed. "Wouldn't want that now, would we?"

Stella shrugged. Nikki smiled and stood like a dork as she waved, an adult-ish version of her own daughter who mirrored the wave from the front porch. Stella had to wonder whether the woman was that nice or that ignorant. Nikki finally returned to the house where the two went inside.

The driveway remained snow covered. That meant he did not plan to be home soon. Even if Danny planned to be absent the entire weekend, he should have shoveled it off for Hope's benefit. Making the poor girl carry her luggage much further than necessary. Infuriating. As it was, Stella could not turn around in the driveway. She knew the drill. They used to close the cabin for winter and never worried about plowing or shoveling, but they checked on the property from time to time in the off months. On those days it meant parking in the street and when finished driving to the road's end almost a mile down. There was a turnabout in which to circle before heading back the way she came.

Stella did just that. As she neared her old home from the opposite direction, Stella pulled over by a snowbank opposite the house and opened the window. Checking to make certain no one watched, she dropped the plate of cookies into a snowbank. The plate sank, the crinkly red cellophane barely visible in the white blanket. A pleasant surprise for Nikki when the snow melts in Spring, Stella thought.

Then she drove away, trying not to think about passing the old man's home again. And how she would have to do the same again in two days. She passed the residence without the old man making another appearance and for that she was grateful. Soon she reached the end of the road. It merged with the primary thoroughfare. As expected, she never encountered her husband driving by on the way out of the lake road.

· · • •• • • · ·

"Jerry, listen, I know it's Sunday. I understand it is your day off except I pay you salary not hourly so suck it up buttercup, the hockey game and your boyfriend du jour will wait. I need you," Stella said as she made the return trip to pick up her daughter.

Two days of shopping and a spa treatment had taken the edge off. One road trip back toward Old Man Hennigan's House brought the edge back. Other than a few texts over the weekend (where her daughter too gleefully announced she was having fun) Stella had not had contact with her daughter. Now, as she drove closer to the old man's house, she felt a sense of foreboding, something off kilter. *There was something in the air and it weren't no good*, which was why she called Jerry, who was watching a sporting event on TV with a new mystery man. She planned to ask for details later, but for now she needed to hear his voice.

"Jerry, please, no, do not hang up. It's hockey. I dated a player, semi-pro, so I know the game. You have about an hour of scrimmage in between goals. It is an obnoxiously low scoring sport; you will miss nothing. If your boyfriend loves you, he will be there when you finish with me. I need you on the phone as my earwitness for when I go to court again to update visitation. You can be my proof Danny will not be there when I arrive. I do not want my daughter staying with this immature tight-assed woman any longer if my husband is not around."

The bend in the road that would lead to the old man's place appeared. Stella stiffened, unnerved for no good reason. Jerry took advantage of the sudden silence to remind Stella that her usual complaint was how the woman had too much fun, but now was tight-assed? He asked which it was.

"She is fun, according to Hope. Annoyingly so, like a cheerleader. I mean tight ass in the literal sense. If I didn't hate her so much, I'd beg to find out who her personal trainer is. But if it turns out she has none, I might have to drive my car straight into the lake, don't think I could take it."

Smoke rose above trees, signaling the Old Man was home, always burning that stove, or always burning something. The unease gripped her tighter. She pleaded with Jerry as the hairs on her arm lifted and gooseflesh rose on her skin despite the climate-controlled cab.

"Please, just twenty more feet, stay on the phone for…"

Stella hit the brakes, slid into a skid but settled quickly given how slowly she was driving. The angle turned her towards the Hennigan home. From there, she noticed a red cellophane covered plate on the stoop. Had that naïve participation trophy wife visited the crazy coot's home with Hope in tow? Or had the man dug up that which she deposited roadside earlier? Either way, it meant a crossing of paths.

"Jerry, I've got to call my daughter. Call you later, bye."

Stella told her phone to dial Hope, panicking when it went to voicemail. A curtain parted from inside the house. The burly man appeared bare chested (fully naked?) in the window and grinned. A lascivious smile? She did not wait to identify intentions before flooring it, but the wheels skidded in place on the snow.

The man vanished from the window. The door cracked open just as the tires found purchase. Stella fishtailed towards a massive pine with branches reaching into the road like witch's hands. The hands missed their target as she regained control and sped off.

She dialed her daughter again, straight to voicemail. How could Nikki allow Hope anywhere near the creep? Stella occasionally suffered disgusting objectifying attacks from the male persuasion. With Nikki being objectively annoyingly hot, Stella figured the young woman must receive the same treatment, should understand the creep factor behind unwanted advances. All it takes is one infatuation, Stella thought.

"Come on, answer, sweetie."

Stella parked in the street in front of her ex's house and got out. She approached the bank where she dropped the cookies. It had snowed since the night of the hand off so she could not remember the exact spot. She trudged through the snowbank, her Timberland boots absorbing the sticky snow. Perfect to make a snowman. Perfect for Hope and her to play in. Never mind they had not done so together in so long.

She failed to locate the red prize but was uncertain whether Old Man Hennigan had absconded with it or not. Stella still felt something was 'wrong' about the forest. Sensed a difference in the air, a change in nature that suggested the times they were a changing. Hope had to be okay. She just had to. Stella marched toward the house, dialing as she did so, cursing that the driveway remained unplowed. Had Danny never come home or had fresh snowfall covered both the driveway and the batch of cookies?

The familiar Katie Perry song sounded within the home. Hope's ringtone. That meant the phone was inside. So why wasn't her daughter answering? Stella peered through a window and noticed Hope's bags ready just inside the door, a planned handoff, at a designated time. *Where could she be*?

A toilet seat dangled from a bent nail center of the door. In poop brown lettering, the seat read: taking a meeting. Stella always hated the stupid thing, but it served a purpose. The novelty sign communicated that everyone was down by the water.

Behind the house, past a narrow backyard, the land dropped precipitously into a steep hill, difficult to navigate without face planting. At the bottom of the hill, the ground settled from forest loam into a narrow dirt beach leading straight into the lake. A perilous staircase of creosote covered railroad ties anchored deep into the landscape on a portion of the hill served as the bridge between the home and the dock. Across the yard from the staircase, a rope swing hung from the branch of a massive tree rising along the edge of the lawn. The massive trunk leaned toward the water as if it too wished to swim. The tree also served as shade for the picnic table in the backyard.

The rope swing was lengthy and dangled over a narrow runway, allowing space for a brief run before ground would vanish from underfoot. From there, the rope took over, doing the heavy lifting. Swimmers swung high over the lake where they would often somersault (or do the belly flop Watusi as she did far too many times before, often drunk, once landing so hard she worried she ruptured a boob) before splashing into water.

Riding the rope was a great way to avoid the tricky stairs, which were dangerous when wet. And they were always wet. The rope was relatively safe unless one refused to let go once in the air. The return swing without a dismount often resulted in serious scrapes as soon as riders returned to ground. Worse was when someone collided with the tree on the swing back. That often led to a tumble all the way back down the hill. Injuries were common and multiplied when beer entered the picture. Of course, it being winter, the entire summer fun world of the backyard remained blanketed under snow.

Stella assumed the toilet seat was being used properly, so she headed to the rear of the house. Her daughter screamed from the backyard. Stella gave chase but slipped and banged her head into the side of the house. Bouncing off, she fell onto all fours. Instantly her gloves filled at the wrists with wet snow.

Groaning, she quickly pushed herself up and rushed forward. She rounded the corner. A picnic table in the backyard served as a great jumping off point for the rope swing for those more daring. The launch required a leg lift to avoid immediate ground contact but gave a better push off with a higher arc above water. The picnic table was where Stella spotted Hope.

Hope sat perched atop a toboggan, screaming in delight as Nikki battled to keep the sled in place atop the snow-covered table. The sled threatened to drift sideways off its perch. Nikki muscled it straight as best she could. The battle for control of the sled revealed itself as the source of the child's screaming. Hope screamed anew before falling into a nervous giggle. Stella missed that part earlier, too concerned over the initial outcry.

"Go!" Nikki yelled.

Nikki released Hope, who hurtled straight down the slope, riding the steep incline alongside the stairs. Stella's heart skipped a beat, watching her daughter jet down the perilous blanket of snow. The stairs ended in a cedar dock which extended well out into the water. At the base of the hill, perilously close to the path of the rope swing, stood a storage shed that held gas cans for their motorboat and housed a canoe which they used well into the fall months. They kept the motorboat stored off property at the end of every summer. Hope's sled path cut cleanly between the pair of obstructions.

"You go, girl! To the moon! Ha!" Nikki cheered even while she recovered from the push off and bumped into

Stella.

Stella stiffened, crossing her arms, nerves still on edge despite finding her daughter safe. Then Stella noticed the lake below and how someone plowed an immense section all the way to clear ice. Snowbanks rose high along the borders of the open space. A narrower strip of cleared ice ran from one side of the plowed area to a wide path in the nearby woods. That was the slipway Danny and Stella used to launch their boat from. Whoever cleared the lake must have entered through the same spot.

Stella bit a thumb through her glove. "Ice, didn't want her on the ice..."

Nikki could not make out Stella's muffled gripe but isolated the word ice. "Mister Hennigan plowed it for us. It is safe. He had his truck out there. Holds a truck, it holds us. Go Hope!"

Screaming for joy, Hope rocketed down the slope, picking up speed as she hit the lake. The wax bottomed sled sluiced over the ice. Hope shot across the frozen clearing until the sled collided with the furthest snowbank, launching the toboggan high into the air. The contact tossed Hope off the ride. Stella screamed in concern over her airborne daughter.

Hope tumbled in the air, leading with feet and butt before spinning and landing on her back, buried under snow. She quickly rose to her feet, raising her hands in celebration. Hope noticed her mother and waved. Stella breathed deep before waving back.

"Hi, baby," Stella whispered.

Nikki finally turned to Stella. "Are you okay?" Stella nodded, but Nikki noticed the woman's appearance. "You sure? Your face is kind of red. Wait, is that a bruise?" Nikki reached for Stella's forehead. When Stella flinched, Nikki got the message, smiling awkwardly. "Wouldn't hurt to put some snow on it, just saying. Sorry, she's packed, ready, just she loves sledding here, wanted a couple more runs before you got here, guess we lost track of time."

"Danny allows Hope to do this?"

"I do this. It's fun. Does it matter who says it's okay?" Nikki squared off with Stella.

Stella noticed that even bundled the woman was too lovely, which was infuriating. This homewrecker got to play the "cool Mom" card, could get away with anything. Let her daughter do that which she as the child's actual mother would never allow her to do.

"I don't want my daughter out on the ice, you marriage wrecking bitch, and don't want her in your house, which should still be my house, understand?" Stella thought before saying, "No, as long as she's having fun."

Nikki smiled, nodded. Far below Hope retrieved her sled from the snowbank, struggling with its size but finally wrangled it. She dragged it by its red nylon rope leash across the open ice. Midway across the expanse, Hope stopped and looked down.

"Mom?"

Stella eyed Nikki, wondering how the woman could be so oblivious to how she felt. Was she daft?

"Mom!"

The change in tone immediately drew both women's attention. Hope pointed at her feet.

"Fish. BIG fish."

It took a moment to register, but even from atop the hill Stella could see—what? Something. Furious motion swirled beneath her daughter. Something was moving. More accurately, several things were moving beneath the exposed ice.

They circled as if corralling prey before an attack. They appeared massive, larger than a man. Stella counted roughly half a dozen (a school?) moving in a fluid circle with her daughter serving as the epicenter.

Hope observed the creatures swimming in concentric circles. The aquatic oddities moved with grace at a speed one would not expect of anything immersed in frozen liquid. Hope's heart kept time with their lightning-fast movements. Light refracting off the frozen lake obscured the child's view. What she saw clearly were flashes of orange and blue. Coral? Hope remembered the crayon from one of her Crayola packs which she used in a mermaid coloring book.

The things moved too quickly for Hope to get a good look, but the colors were enticing, hypnotic and kept her rooted in place despite the unnerving size of the odd figures. One creature dropped from the pack and took up a stationary spot directly below her. It swam closer to the surface and pressed its grotesque face against the ice! Hope screamed.

Its face thrashed briefly in the chilled water. The stuff of nightmares. The beast's prominent wide eyes (too large for its head) appeared to watch her despite being covered in a white sheen suggesting blindness. A heavy full bottom lip hung so low it held the crescent-shaped mouth open in a snarl, which displayed jagged, translucent teeth. A line of disease ran diagonally across the creature's face, white crusted spots clumped together resembling barnacles.

A strand nearly a foot long jutted from the creature's forehead like a partial umbilical cord originating from the elusive third eye position. It bobbed in the water's undercurrent. The creature reached for the ice. Its arm length fell in line with someone over six-foot-tall and culminated in a bony fin. The 'fin' spread open to reveal razor-sharp claws jutting out at the tail end of the Geisha fan style hand. The creature displayed seven claws versus five digits.

The creature tapped its claws from its position underneath the ice lazily, like a bored student on a desk. The dangling flesh extending from the creature's forehead stiffened and glowed orange. Light from the protrusion cut through the wintery deep as the beast thrashed its head again, more violently. It gnashed transparent yet solid teeth while jabbing claws into the ice. The powerful blow caused the surface to crack.

Startled, Hope lost her footing, causing her to run in place to keep her balance on the slick surface. The resultant move would have been a comical dance under different circumstances, the image something to laugh about later with friends from the safety of a cell phone screen. While the one creature sought her out, the others continued swooping in wide arcs. Hope screamed again but could not wake herself from the nightmare. Her legs finally splayed in different directions, bringing her down painfully onto all fours.

"Mom!"

Time stilled the moment the underwater dance revealed itself to Stella. The reflective orange and blue underwater ballet floated in the distance as something so unnatural, so unexpected, it forced her to examine the landscape of what was surely a dream-world. Stella figured there would be something to latch onto, an anchor which could deliver her back into the other world, the waking one. Upon waking, images such as those in the water would vanish from memory in the time it took her to tap the snooze button.

Hope's scream was the catalyst that woke Stella from thoughts of sleeping nightmares. This was a real one. Her child was in danger. The same concerns that rose in her chest upon passing the Hennigan home came back tenfold to clutch her guts. The 'wrongness' she felt earlier finally revealed itself.

For Stella, the world tilted into slow motion, sound dredged to a halt. Her own frantic breathing faded leaving nothing but the voice of a daughter needing a mother. Stella sensed more than saw Nikki grab another toboggan off the back wall of the house and place it on the packed snow trail. Nikki climbed aboard and reached towards Stella.

"Stella, get on!"

But Stella was already moving, destination child. Stella sprang towards the railroad tie steps, launching herself through the snow, kicking it up in wide sprays. Nikki pushed off with the toboggan. The speeding sled quickly passed Stella.

Stella glimpsed the movement, understood in a small lizard part of her brain that there was another human being next to her, one planning to help, but Stella had only one thought—run! And she did, two steps at a time until she slipped and fell onto her back, suffering the jagged blow of a hard-edged wood corner. Cold air intensified the pain. Stella slid uncontrollably down the stairs, absorbing blows from each wooden edge along the way.

Nikki screamed for Hope to move out of the way as she bottomed out and slid across the ice. With no way to steer, Nikki rocketed toward the downed child. Hope leaned just far enough for a miss. Barely. Nikki rocketed over the snowbank and went airborne like the child before her. But Nikki hit the ground running.

Emerging from the snowbank, Nikki reached the ice and raced for the child. Hope remained on all fours, as frozen as the lake, while staring straight down into the icy abyss. Nikki yanked on the young girl's coat, only to scream upon spotting the beast for the first time. The creature thrashed anew, eager for a buffet. It struck the underside of the ice with enough force for its arm to break through.

The hole was modest, only large enough for its arm to extend through up to the elbow. The glistening blue-orange scaling appeared darker under sunlight. It splayed claws while trying to catch its prey. The forearm, scaly, long, and thick, (a closer view confirmed barnacles spreading like cancer) reached toward the two women. The furiously flopping arm mimicked the movement of a fish out of water.

Nikki pulled the frightened girl closer. Hope buried her face in the folds of Nikki's winter coat. The creature blinked, its eyes closing in two separate stages before flashing back to white again. Cracks formed, stretching out from the ruptured spot. Water flooded the surface, spreading toward Hope and Nikki's feet. The balance of underwater monsters stopped swimming to focus on the fragile barrier between them and a meal.

As they ceased their underwater motion, the headcount became clear. Five. All put their claws to work. Ice cracked like gunshots as water slicked across a large section of the surface. Hope tried to burrow further into her protector.

"Make them stop!"

Stella arrived and launched herself at Hope, lifting the child into her arms. Hope relinquished her hold on Nikki, gripping her mother like a lifeline.

"Mom!"

"I'm, here, baby!"

Stella noticed the illuminated protrusions rising erect from the beasts' foreheads. Memories of a boring ass nature documentary her husband watched on Netflix sprung to mind. Anglerfish. The subjects of the documentary had similar protrusions called illicium. During the show, Stella made a joke about their endowment only for her husband to scoff at the observation, dismissing her unsubtle attempt to proceed to the 'chill' part of the evening. Instead of going coital, Danny went cerebral, noting how the predator used the light as a lure. A fish who fished for other fish.

The creatures at her feet were not the fish from the documentary, they were far too big and far too humanoid. Still, Stella recognized the illicium meant that the scaly inhabitants were predators. The ice sagged as water bubbled to the surface, hastening a melt. The cracks spread ever wider and would not hold much longer. Stella released one hand from her daughter to grab one of Nikki's arms. The young woman seemed to be in a fugue, locked on the stunning sight below the ice. Nikki reacted to the older woman's touch.

"We need to go," Stella yelled.

Stella ran with her daughter in tow, using a strength she did not know she had. She ached from her thigh, into her hip, back and even shoulders, heavily bruised from the earlier fall. She felt immense pressure deep along her lower back suggesting kidney damage, yet she continued running with Hope.

They reached the dock, relieved to step onto the lifeline of red cedar. The dock extended twenty feet out from the beach and was cleared of snow. Whoever plowed the lake must have also shoveled the dock and steps Stella thought. She was grateful. Excess snow would have slowed them down. Stella considered the plowed lake. If the ice could withstand the weight of a plow, how strong were the monsters that ruptured the frozen enclosure?

Stella finally gave into the weight, lowering her daughter who fought off her mother's attempts to release the young child. Nikki reacted to Hope's fear, gripping the young girl's shoulder until both women had contact with the young girl.

"You're too heavy. We need to get up the hill," Stella said.

"We've got you," Nikki said.

Hope nodded. The dock rocked as the ice exploded somewhere behind them. The force dropped the women to their knees. Stella glanced back as a massive chunk of punched out ice ascended in a spin. It crested and crashed back down, smashing into smaller pieces. The hole from the strike stretched roughly five feet across, large enough for the creature to squeeze through. And that is exactly what it did.

The one with the barnacles, (*Cancer Face,* Stella thought) burst through rising high into the air, a seemingly impossible leap from submersion. The beast landed on feet mimicking those of its claw finned hands.

The monster stood nearly seven feet tall, covered head to toe in the colorful scales. A fin covered its back from tailbone to neck. Spindly sharp spines (venomous?) rang the length of the creature's arms. The barnacles which covered the creature's face circled across its chest to loin as if a beauty queen sash.

After rising and taking in the surroundings, the thing crouched and pushed off arcing over the women's heads. It landed midway up the snowy hill. The women screamed, frightened by the raw display of power and by being cut off. Cancer Face on one side and the others working their way through the ice on the other.

With a mournful hiss, the monster took a step only to lose its footing in the unfamiliar snow. The beast dropped into a split and shrieked as its legs went in directions not meant to go. *They feel pain,* Stella thought. The packed snow provided momentum to the downed beast which slid down the hillside. On the way the creature reached toward its prey, to no avail.

The women scrambled to their feet to take advantage of the sudden opening. Nikki took the lead up the steps, Hope in the middle, holding the hand of each adult.

"Be careful. We can't afford to fall," Stella said.

The three women ascended the ties. Despite their panic, they moved methodically, hoping to avoid a repeat of the creature's acrobatics. Stella glanced over her shoulder, watching with some satisfaction as Cancer Face slid across the ice toward the open hole. A second creature pulled itself free, but the sliding monster took the legs out from under its scaly compadre. The pair splashed back into the water.

Stella waved the others on. "Go, go, go!"

Nikki fell, her face slamming into the edge of a step. The impact split her lip. Blood flowed, but she quickly rose and ran. Stella understood. Time for pain later.

Ice cracked like gunshots behind them. One, two, three. Fresh fractures. Two more creatures leaped through the air, landing near the women on different parts of the hill. The beasts fought to adjust to the slickness of their new white world while hissing at their prey.

The women crested the top of the hill and rushed through the back door slamming it closed. The pursuers pounded the other side forcefully enough to knock Stella away, but the door slammed closed after striking her. It remained closed but not locked. Nikki leaped over and turned the latch before a second blow threatened to take the whole thing down. It held. For now.

"What are those things?" Hope asked.

"I don't know, Honey, I don't know."

"Angler fish," Nikki said. Stella eyed the young woman knowingly. "I watch the boring documentaries with him too. That's what they look like, right? I mean like nuclear reactor versions but that's them, right?"

Stella nodded. The door shook under an onslaught, followed by claws scrambling across the roof, partially muted by snow. The creature's weight shook the home with every rooftop step.

Both the adults reached for the knife block simultaneously, clasping the handle of the twelve-inch chef's knife. The ladies eyed one another in a standoff. Nikki released the blade and opened a drawer near the sink.

"Be careful, stainless steel handle, might get slippery if they have any kind of blood in them, and let's hope they do," Nikki said, pulling a meat cleaver from the drawer, waving it in satisfaction.

Claws penetrated the wooden door, becoming lodged in the slab. The door shook as the beast shrieked, trying to free itself from the other side. The rooftop claws paced, searching for an entry point. Hope screamed as a monster pressed its face against a small box window above the sink. Its illicium glowed orange.

Stella smashed her knife through the glass into the creature's eye! The creature yanked itself off the blade, bleeding a phosphorescent blue. It pressed a curled finned hand to the damage before scurrying out of view.

Behind the fleeing creature stood another fighting for footing on the slippery surface world. It face-planted but did not slide down the hill. The creature quickly recovered, revealing a face covered in a solid pack of white. It shrieked and gnashed translucent teeth in Stella's direction. Something about the white packed snow covering most of its face made it more terrifying if possible.

Nikki shoved Stella, bringing her back to the moment. The mother grabbed her daughter's hand, and the three rushed toward the living room as the kitchen door smashed into splintery pieces. Nikki yelped as wooden shrapnel sprayed into her back.

The women slammed the interior kitchen door and locked it, but the obstruction possessed nowhere near the stopping power the exterior one did. They had only minutes before the beasts would burst through. The creature on the opposite side went to work, providing a percussive soundtrack to the frantic situation. The two women circled tightly around Hope, blades raised. Glass smashed above them, an upper alcove window.

"The pull-down stairs?" Stella asked.

"Recessed," Nikki answered quickly, as if reading her mind.

Still, it would not be long before something that powerful broke through the ceiling. Stella examined the room, finding nothing but terror in the once upon a time quaint space. The flat screen TV, anchored to a far wall, originally offered fond memories of Disney movies during her daughter's sleepovers, but the device now took on the form of a menacing dark mirror reflecting the collective fear in the room. The rustic charm and warmth from the wood-burning stove in the corner took on the trappings of a prison from which they could not escape.

A tightness gripped Stella's hands, a slight arthritic tick she occasionally felt from overusing her cellphone. The pain gripped her as tightly as she did the blade in one hand and a clump of her daughter's coat in the other. A fresh thump sounded overhead. Even if the beast could not work the stairs, it could collapse them.

"My car," Stella said.

"Your car is outside. Those things are outside," Nikki said.

"They are inside too."

"I know. Not disagreeing, just…"

Stella looked at the young woman with such a life ahead of her and nodded in solidarity. *Life sucks, it is not fair kiddo, sorry, now suck it up buttercup and help me get my daughter out of here,* Stella thought. Nikki glanced at Hope before nodding back.

Dropping to her knees in front of her daughter, Stella noticed the young girl wince with every blow on the door behind them. Stella felt the thunderous pulses shaking the room but hid her fear for the sake of her child. "Sweetie, you've always been so fast, sweetie."

"Mom?"

"I can't carry you fast enough. You're quicker than me, maybe quicker than Nikki."

"Mom?"

"I need you to run. Run like the horses. You want to ride the horses again, right?" Hope nodded, sniffling. "Then I need you to run like they do, just for a minute. Once we reach the car, we can escape. Then we ride the horses, ride them together. I need you to focus. I know you're scared."

"Times nine," Hope whimpered.

"Times nine? Only times nine?" Despite everything, Stella laughed, proudly eyeing her daughter before pulling the girl into a hug. The door groaned as a hinge screw shot free and bounced near the women's feet.

"We need to go," Nikki said.

The ladies rushed to the front door, opening it right as the kitchen door burst off its hinges. Cancer Face appeared behind them, hissing and drooling. The creature's momentum carried it forward into the wood-burning stove. It screeched in pain and circled in terror before slashing at the vent in anger. Black acrid smoke filled the room.

Tossing the couch aside as if it weighed nothing, the creature turned toward the women. Hope exited first, followed by Nikki. Stella grabbed the front door handle as the beast advanced. The creature from above finally broke through, shattering wood framing and sheetrock as the monster rode the still folded stairs into the living room.

The commotion startled even Cancer Face, who turned and hissed at the intrusion. The fallen beast had a fully orange face with blue and green tinges kicking in only from the neck down. It scrambled to free itself from the debris while shrieking at Cancer Face. (A cry of help?)

Stella leaped onto the porch, pulling the door as Orange Face rose to an even taller height than Cancer Face. She felt the force as both slammed into the other side of the door. She prayed they would not figure out windows because she needed the time.

Hope reached the car first, but in her panic struggled with the door handle. Nikki was close behind the girl. Stella bolted towards the vehicle, which seemed so far away. A hiss sounded from above, announcing the second creature on the roof.

"Help her, get her in the car!" Stella yelled.

Stella watched in horror as the creature from the backyard, still half caked in snow, raced toward the vehicle. The two women at the SUV appeared unaware of the new threat while they struggled with the SUV's door handle. The vehicle's height off the ground seemingly an issue for the two petite and panicked women.

The ground shook under Stella's feet as the roof creature leaped down nearby. It ran an end run alongside her toward the other women. Its eyes did the double blink repeatedly. It seemed cognizant of the different opportunities, aware enough to form a cold calculation. Eat two now, save the big one for later.

"Nikki!"

Snow slowed both human and monster. The other creature neared the vehicle from the opposite direction. *Why could the ladies not open the door*? Right before Snow Face reached them, Nikki opened the vehicle, shoved Hope in, and followed. Snow Face reached an arm into the vehicle. Nikki slammed the door on the appendage. Snow Face shrieked, waving its forearm obscenely around the cabin, extending claws before retracting them down to folded fan style fin repeatedly.

Nikki fought to avoid the sharp claws while holding the door tight, using all her body weight to trap the arm in place. Stella reached the vehicle the same time as the roof monster. The two faced off. The creature hissed at her in a *dinner is served* timbre. Its forehead appendage went from limp to erect and burned orange. Drool dripped liberally down the creature's lower lip. Stella sliced off the erect protrusion.

The illicium flew in an arc over the SUV where it landed in a snowbank, possibly making the acquaintance of discarded cookies. The creature grasped both closed finned hands against a wound bleeding blue phosphorescent liquid. While it tended to its injury, Stella opened the rear door. The roof monster threw its arms wide in a raging fury. Before it could strike, Stella buried the blade into the exact spot where she previously cut off the organic lure.

With a startled grunt, the creature stiffened. One of its hands opened, all seven claws exposed, and it lashed out impossibly fast, swinging straight down at her, a clean slice. The move sounded as if her coat had forcefully unzipped. Finally, the roof creature fell straight back, thudding heavily onto the snowy ground. Its dead eyes remained open, more dead than before.

A world of white danced around Stella who felt lost in a cloud. Had it sliced her open? Ended her? It was too fast, its claws too sharp. She experienced a monstrous tug of her entire body when the creature swung at her, yet she registered no pain. She reached out a hand to discover not snow dancing around her, but feathers. Looking down, she found her jacket sliced open at the front, exposing her yoga gear underneath. But otherwise, she remained unharmed.

The world came back to her. Time returned to normal, and she watched as Nikki struggled to keep her monster trapped. Its awkward angle the only thing keeping it from having the upper hand. Stella leaped into the back seat and closed the door.

Hope cowered in the corner against the passenger door. The meat cleaver lay on the seat next to Nikki. Stella reached over, grabbed it, and swung at the arm in the cab. Stella felt a thunderous pain in her arms upon contact. The blade did not puncture the scaly arm, only echoed loudly within the confines of the vehicle. Waves of pain jolted through her arms. Blades would not get through their armor. She had been lucky earlier by finding a soft spot. Instinct had brought one monster down.

With Stella inside, Nikki released the pressure on the arm. The creature yanked free, falling away from the vehicle, allowing Nikki to slam the door closed. Hope screamed, drawing all eyes to the windshield where One Eye lay atop the hood. The creature struggled to remain on the slick, curved metal while scratching at the glass, but appeared to lack the footing necessary to break through. The glass pockmarked with every strike of claws threatening to crack like the ice earlier.

Snow Face rose from the white with a fresh look, its snow packed features shifted with every grimace and shriek. A monster as angry as it was hungry. It launched itself at the driver's side with such force the vehicle tilted.

"Drive, drive, drive!" Stella shouted from the back.

"The keys, where are the keys?" Nikki yelped as the vehicle shook again.

"In my purse, somewhere, it's push button, go!"

Nikki struggled, could not get it to go.

"Brakes, press the brake to start it," Hope said.

Nikki started the engine. One eye snarled anew at the warmth of the engine below its torso, slicing harder at the windshield, which finally cracked. Nikki floored it but Snow Face struck the side of the vehicle, causing the SUV to glide sideways. It tufted into a snowbank, leaning at an angle half on the road, half off. One eye remained on the hood during the short ride.

Nikki hit the gas. The rear tire spun wildly in the snow, failing to gain traction. Wham! Snow Face struck again, hard enough that much of the snowpack flew off its face. It snarled furiously, rearing back for another blow, a humanoid sardine trying to open a can.

Wham! Again. The vehicle tilted wildly. The spinning tire squealed as it spun through snow all the way to ice. Then one last body slam from Snow Face and their world turned upside down. The SUV rocked, tipped, then gave over to gravity, following a slope where the dirt road dropped into the snow-covered forest. The SUV rolled onto its roof.

The women tumbled inside the vehicle with no seatbelts to hold them in place. Stella's handbag made its presence known, slamming into Nikki's face, drawing fresh blood from her swollen lip. The butcher's knife hurled through the air and thunked into the fabric of the upturned roof inches from Stella. The trio crumpled into twisted, unnatural upside-down positions.

Stella's body throbbed in agony from all the pain brought on from her first stumble alongside the house until the present. The punishing blows rushed her nervous system all at once, threatening to shut the whole thing down. Stella's world shifted as white as the snow, leaving her on the verge of passing out until she heard her daughter moan. Stella turned to find her little one crumpled oh so small against the ceiling of the vehicle. Their eyes met. Stella reached over, no seat between them now, and gripped Hope's hand.

"I want to go home," Hope cried.

Stella nodded, suddenly aware of the tear streaking down her own face. Whether from sorrow or pain did not really matter. It rolled from a quivering eye on its own accord. Stella wiped the drop away wishing to convey nothing but strength in front of her girl. Stella found satisfaction in her daughter pronouncing where she considered home. Stella long wondered about her daughter's preference, but the panicked cry suggested it was with her mother. Stella felt some shame in finding any comfort in the blurted truth given their situation.

Nikki was closer to Hope so the two embraced. Hope gladly slipped into a hug with the other woman.

"Are you okay?" Nikki asked.

Hope stifled a cry in lieu of an answer, instead gripping the woman tighter and nodding into her side. Heavy footsteps crunched snow outside the vehicle. The passenger side faced the road. They had not rolled far, merely a foot lower than the street. Stella saw legs but could not determine whether they belonged to One Eye or Snow Face. One of them was marching on their position.

The others surely discovered a way out of the house by now, Stella thought. Heavy footfalls displaying a newfound familiarity with the wintery ground could have been from any of the remaining four. The legs stepped closer, unhurried, aware the food was bento boxed, ready to go.

As the ground rumbled again, Stella assumed the others found their way out, which meant an entire school advancing on them now. One set of legs appeared outside the street side window. One step away from their position. Stella pressed her hand onto the upturned ceiling of the vehicle to brace herself for the coming onslaught. She cried out and withdrew a hand that met shards of glass. She retracted her bleeding palm while noticing the shattered rear window. Wind swirled through the cabin.

Fresh pain from the cut brought Stella back to her senses. She grasped the butcher's knife and aimed it toward the single set of legs just out of reach. Wham! The legs suddenly vanished from sight. Gone, just like that. The whine of an engine and brakes slamming filled the air. Through the still intact front windshield, the group watched a snowplow skid to a stop in the distance. The truck took out the beast. But had it killed it?

"It's Mr. Hennigan!" Hope yelled.

Hope pushed the door open over Nikki, who fought to right herself and grab the girl.

"Hope, no, he doesn't know what's out there," Nikki said.

Too late. The girl ran. Nikki scrambled after her. Stella eyed the jagged remnants of the back window but chose instead to use the upturned rear door. She shoved it open and screamed. Pinned beneath the vehicle at the waist was One Eye. The creature slashed at her slicing her cheek so deep that a section of skin flopped over the side of her face. Her blood jetted across the creature's face. When her blood splashed into its mouth, the creature reacted despite the crushing weight. It shook violently chasing a hunger the little morsel of liquid inspired.

The motion bounced the vehicle, lifting Stella slightly in the air. When she and the vehicle dropped back into place, a crunch sounded accompanied by a screech from One Eye. The beast made no attempt to repeat the movement.

Lesson learned. Stella jumped as she could within the tight confines. Her landing elicited another screech from the monster.

Stella grabbed the butcher's knife and raised it over the creature's forehead. With both hands she struck. Blue phosphorescence splashed her face, leaving both covered with the other's blood. The creature flip-flopped, trying to shake the blade free like a fish caught on a hook. One Eye's clawed hands could not seem to find the handle.

Outside Nikki caught up to Hope, halfway to Old Man Hennigan. The man stood alongside his truck further down the road. Stella frantically worked on escape. She eyed the jagged remnants of the rear windshield (which looked all too much like the monster's translucent teeth). Deeming it the best option she rolled out the back of the vehicle.

She emerged from the wreckage and pressed the dangling piece of cheek skin back in place. The frigid air quickly froze the blood which held the wound roughly in place. She looked toward the house and discovered why the other beasts has yet to attack. The heavy oak door had burst off hinges but wedged sideways into the doorframe. The open gap at the base of the door proved too small for them to fit through. The opening at the top was larger but still too tight for the monstrous sized beings.

Orange Face and Cancer Face appeared too dumb to figure out they had windows available for a quick exit on both sides of the blocked passage. Their limbs swiped wildly through the cracked openings, seeking to free the obstruction. In the distance the man shouted to the two closest neighbors.

"What the hell is this thing? I heard your screams all the way down yonder. Are you ladies okay?" Hennigan asked.

"Mister Hennigan, thank God, there's more of them, they…" Nikki started.

A window in the house shattered. They figured it out. More precisely, Cancer Face did. The beast leaped through the window while Orange Face continued swiping around the blockage.

"It's out, get in the truck, run!" Stella yelled racing toward the group.

Cancer Face made it to the road in two leaps, landing between the women and the older man. It looked both ways assessing who to eat first. Hennigan reached into the back of his truck and pulled out a tire iron.

"Get away from them, you sorry son of a bitch!" Hennigan yelled. He raised the tire iron over his head and rushed the beast.

The women collectively warned him off. Hennigan continued running. Cancer Face spun, arm outstretched, an obscene reach, longer than any prize fighter. Its hand closed in the fan configuration swiped with deadly precision. Hennigan's head separated cleanly at the neck. The severed head spun through the air while the man's body continued running with wild, high steps. The body only made it a few paces before collapsing. Blood gushed from the neck, painting the snowy landscape red.

The creature pounced on the body, snarling while feeding. Stella raced to her daughter standing white in shock. Even Nikki stood transfixed, unable to comprehend the horror before them. Hennigan's face rolled to a stop in a position facing them, eyes still wide, as if asking, "what the hell?"

Stella lifted her daughter, found the strength, pulled her tight. Her injured cheek stuck to her daughter's hair and threatened to pull away from her face again. Stella grabbed Nikki's hand and they ran. The creature looked back briefly while it continued to feed. The women reached the truck, noting a dead creature trapped under the plow.

The women poured into the front of the pickup and slammed the door. The interior was spotless, despite the beat to shit exterior. Hennigan appeared to have been a clean soul, not a fast-food wrapper in sight. A 'world's #1 Grandpa' coffee mug sat in a console drink holder, the beverage still steaming with heat, the aroma incongruous to the bloody world just outside the truck doors.

Stella sat in the driver's seat while Nikki took the shotgun position with Hope between them. The girl looked to her mother and touched her own face, dragging an invisible line across her petite cheek.

"Mom, you're hurt," Hope said.

"Jesus, Stella, she's right," Nikki said, noticing.

"I'm fine. I'll be fine. I'm..." Stella froze upon finding the ignition switch empty. "Shit! Key, do you see a key?" Nikki frantically searched the glove compartment, also tidy. Both women flipped the visors. Then Stella noticed something about the truck. Looking down, she spotted the extra pedal. A clutch. She winced.

Wham!

The truck rocked. Orange face had escaped the house and smashed the side of the vehicle. The women grabbed the dash, trying to ride out the onslaught. Given how the truck centered in the road, there was no roadside slope to help the creature's efforts to overturn them a second time. Still, the creature slammed the vehicle repeatedly. It would not hold forever. The beast hissed loudly in a high-pitched whine as it sought a snack.

"The keys. They must be on poor Hennigan. I'll make a run for it, then you drive, drive like hell. We're facing the wrong way as far as getting back to town. There's no outlet, but the road has a culvert a mile down. You can turn around there. Don't look back when you pass by here again," Nikki said.

"I know. I lived here longer than you." Stella stopped herself from the display of misplaced rage. "No, I'll go."

Nikki shook her head and grabbed the door handle, ready to make a run for it. "Hope needs you, needs her mother. I'll keep them busy as long as I can."

Stella gestured to the center of the truck. "I can't drive stick."

Nikki released the door handle, even though the truck rocked wildly. Hope appeared to understand.

"Mom, no, we can stay here, someone will come, we can just stay here forever."

Stella and Nikki crawled over Hope, switching places. Nikki yelled at the creature through the window. It stopped for a moment, eyeing her, blinking in that fisheye way. Stella cradled her daughter's cheeks.

"Be good, huh? Ride those horses for me." Stella said.

"Mom, no. No, Mommy. I'm scared."

"I know, honey, that's why I have to go."

The creature smashed at the glass. It cracked. Would not be long now. Nikki grimaced, stifling a scream before looking at Stella.

"Take care of my baby!"

Nikki nodded. Stella opened the door.

"Mommy, I love you times ten!"

Stella touched her heart, then leaped out, slamming the door closed on her little girl.

"Hey ugly, like what I did to your brother? You know orange is a bad look on you!"

Orange Face finally broke through the glass before noticing Stella standing in front of the vehicle. It hissed wildly, looked towards the dinner in the can, then the dinner in the open. Checking the white ground below as if still unsure of its footing, it moved slowly towards the unpackaged meal. Stella tried not to move, but a single step brought the beast so perilously close. It took a second tentative step while Stella stood there ignoring her daughter's shouts from inside the cab. The whole time, Stella kept her hands behind her back.

Another step. Snow crunched loudly under the weight of the beast. Stella looked past the creature, saw Cancer Face still busy with its meal. Orange Face followed Stella's gaze, gauging where she planned to run. It stretched an arm out, protracted its claws to full length, and hissed. Its upturned crescent moon snarl almost appeared as a smile. Things were looking too easy for the beast. One more step from Orange Face. Crunch.

Splat!

The monster shrieked when Stella nailed it in the face with a snowball. It instinctively reached to clear the obstruction, only to stab itself across the face with extended claws. It shrieked in pain while repeatedly blinking eyes to clear the snow.

Stella ran towards the house. The creature recovered and gave chase. Orange Face cried out in a higher-pitched squeal than before. Cancer Face took note, looked up, its barnacles dripping red, its teeth pink where snow and saliva mixed. Cancer Face joined the chase. Soon the pair were nearly upon her.

As they reached for her, Stella leaped and slid through the gap below the twisted door frame. The same blockage that stymied her pursuers earlier proved effective a second time. Orange Face collided with the wedged slab, but the obstruction held. The creatures howled in fury at the frustrating obstacle.

Nikki jumped out of the truck, turning her head away from the full view of Hennigan's body. She attempted to keep him only in the periphery of her vision. The car keys were on a rounded fishing lure keychain. She grabbed them and ran, glancing back at the house. Orange Face burst through the broken window, shattering the last remnants of glass and stumbled into the living room. Cancer Face looked back at Nikki, who grabbed the truck's door handle.

Cancer Face followed Orange Face through the window and appeared far more confident in its movements than its ugly cousin. Nikki leaped in the truck, ground the gears and peeled out. Snow tires did their thing, the tires gripped the road. The vehicle drifted slowly at first, dragging along an obstruction. The now deceased Snow Face. Finally, the body dislodged from the plow, falling under the rear tires before rolling down the embankment on the side of the road. The truck roared away.

Stella rushed through the house where furniture smashed behind her as the creatures gave chase, right on her tail. She counted on it, but also hoped things were where she remembered. This place, once so familiar, had long since stopped being her home. She knew that now. She raced into the kitchen, heard their alien cries right behind her.

Open air greeted her. The missing back door had allowed in windswept snow which spread across the linoleum. She stepped around it and launched herself outdoors. Behind her, she heard Orange Face hit the slick and crash amidst their version of curse words. Cancer Face avoided the slick snow on linoleum combo by leaping straight through the doorway.

Cancer Face was learning. It landed on stable ground, aware enough not to leap too close to the sloping hill. Orange Face, conversely, stepped gingerly through the doorframe, dripping blue drops from the seven puncture marks on its face. How easily would those claws go through her if it could pierce their own armor?

Stella found that which she hoped for. The rope swing hung exactly where it always was. Some things never changed. She gripped the knotted handle, lifted her legs and swung down the hill. The creatures hissed in protest but remained on the crest of the hill while she arced out high into the air, over the icy water which was not the destination she had in mind. Instead, she swung partially back, hoping the snow would absorb the impact.

As she arced back towards the snow-covered beach, she dropped, landing on her feet before falling to her knees in the deep drift. Landing with a grunt, she absorbed the shock and rose quickly running to the boat shack. She looked up where Cancer Face raised one leg, then extended claws on its foot and planted it hard on the ground using the sharp protrusions to anchor itself in place. It did the same with its next step. Learning. They were learning. Orange Face watched and repeated the action as both took anchoring steps while slowly making their way down, arms outstretched at their sides for balance. *Like monsters from the old 'Thriller' video,* Stella thought.

She rushed into the boathouse. Gas cans were in place, kept year-round for the generator but used mostly during the summer for their motorboat. The cans would be full this time of year. The shed housed a canoe, a toolbox and a mini chest of drawers full of swimsuits and towels for guests who would invariably forget to bring their own. Stella hoped her ex never discovered her secret stash. She pulled the drawer of towels completely out of the chest and reached under the glide track to pull out a pack of cigarettes and a lighter.

A long-time closet smoker, she hid the habit (along with other things) from her ex, could give a shit about his feelings toward it now, but had remained smoke free for some time for the sake of her daughter. She rose and looked through a crack in the thin wall, watching the creatures descend slowly, halfway down.

Three cans of gas. She hoped it was enough. She stomped on the drawer, busting it to pieces, then yanked the canoe from the wall. Stella set to work, understanding she had only about a minute. Her plan in place, she kicked the door open and dragged the canoe by its nylon rope handle out onto the ice. The sections which ruptured earlier had partially refrozen but remained too thin to traverse. Stella bypassed the questionable area and staged herself in a solid, wide-open section.

The creatures neared her. Stella reached into the canoe and lifted a wooden slab from the broken drawer. She had wrapped it in gas-soaked swim trunks, a makeshift torch. Orange face reached the beach first. It snarled and made the leap, landing right in front of her. Stella lit the rag which 'foomped' to life, singeing her eyebrows. She pointed the fire at the creature, jabbing flame into its chest.

It scrambled away in pain, suddenly aware of the ice under its feet. It sunk claws into the frozen ground, planting itself before snarling in her direction, shaking claws, wanting to slice yet too fearful to get closer. Cancer Face understood and leaped higher than Orange Face had, arcing high above before landing assertively behind her. They closed in as she spun, waving the flames first in one direction, then the other.

Surrounded.

With her free hand, she scrambled and lifted one of the gas cans out of the canoe, setting it down at her feet. She had already opened it and stuffed it with a gasoline-soaked towel. She lit it and kicked the burning can. The makeshift missile glided toward Orange Face with the precision of Olympics curling. Stepping aside to avoid it, the creature hissed at the passing flame. The device came to a stop behind Orange Face, then exploded!

The force knocked Stella to her knees. Fire engulfed the creature, even as a hole ruptured in the ice behind it. The monster turned and burned, shrieking. Its face no longer the only orange thing about it as it danced within flames. The creature slipped into the water, leaving fuel burning across the surface of the ice.

Cancer Face roared in her direction, pure monstrous rage. Stella lit one orange towel and one blue (their beach motif was the same sea coral colors of the beings that stalked her). The last two cans remained in the canoe's belly. Stella rose to her feet.

"Hey, Cancer Face. Fuck you!"

She shoved the canoe, which slid across the ice. Stella ran in the opposite direction, parallel to shore towards the non-plowed portion of the lake. Cancer Face, howling in anger, leaped through the air intending to cut her off and cut her open when the cans ignited. A fireball shot into the air. Ice ruptured and massive cracks spread in all directions, threatening to break off an entire shelf of ice.

The creature burned as it landed, inches from the water, but still on solid ground. It advanced on her even while burning. She raced onward, close to unplowed snow over the lake. The crack spread faster than the creature who kept coming despite the burn. The beast stalked her with arms outstretched, its claws reflecting the flickering glow of flames dancing along Cancer Face's body.

With a loud snap the ice broke, swallowing the creature deep into the darkened waters. Stella ran, the crumbling surface chased after her, threatening to take her down.

· · ● ● ● ● ● · · ·

"We have to go back!" Hope yelled.

Nikki understood how frantic Hope was over her mother. They were mid-circle through the turnabout and about to return from where they came, but the fact was lost on the terrified girl. Hope had not even wanted to wait to reach the turnabout. The girl urged Nikki on the way to plow a driveway in which to turn around. Nikki ignored the pleas and drove to the end of the road. She was unfamiliar with the plow and unwilling to chance them getting stuck. Now they were heading back. Straight into the carnage.

"Hope, I need you to close your eyes when we get close, okay?"

"I can't. I have to look for Mom."

"I'll do that for both of us. I don't want you to see... Well, just don't look, okay?"

Hope nodded, and Nikki sped away, charging down the road with abandon. With her house quickly approaching, Nikki reached over protectively towards the girl, pressing her head down.

"Close your eyes."

Hope did, then Nikki hit the brakes. Stella stood on the side of the road, smoking the tail end of a cigarette, smoke puffing through the hole in her cheek. Hope slowly raised her head, looking directly at Nikki, who nodded permission for the girl to look. Hope turned and smiled. Stella flicked the cigarette at One Eye's body, then limped toward the truck. Hope tried to run out, but Nikki held her in place, looking around for signs of anything amiss.

Stella climbed over Nikki into the truck, where Hope hugged her mother tight. Stella hugged back, wincing at the effort. Nikki drove off as the three women fell into silence, the truck bouncing them gently.

Lights from an approaching vehicle filled their cab. Both vehicles hit brakes. A well-dressed man stepped from the vehicle.

"Are you crazy? Driving like that on these roads? You could kill someone!" Danny yelled.

Hope leaped from the truck and rushed to her father.

"Daddy!"

"Bean pole?"

Hope launched herself into his arms. Danny tried to spot the driver of the beat down truck, but his own headlights reflecting off the plow cast shadows so he could not quite see.

"Daddy, there were monsters!" She held him tight, so tight.

He pushed a lock of her hair away. "Monsters? You don't say." He looked back to the truck. "Hello in there?"

From inside the truck, Stella and Nikki looked out on the world. Stella took Nikki's hand and squeezed. They held hands as snow started to fall.

FORAGE MARKET

LEWISTON, MAINE

When I agreed to do this anthology with my uncle, I had little time before I'd begin my travels south. But one thing I did before traveling and disrupting my writing with that and with COVID was hang out with my brother Gary at a little coffee shop on Lisbon Street in Lewiston. He knew I was leaving and wanted to hang out with me as much as possible. I felt the same way, so we would meet most mornings when I had time off from work and spend the day writing there and, in the Lewiston Public Library. We both grew up in Lewiston, so it was very cool to spend time there with my brother as adults. He would blog and I would try to come up with ideas for horror stories, and one idea I had for a story and began writing there was this one.

A portion of the idea came to me a very long time ago in a nightmare, the first one I ever had. I still remember the man's face clearly and how he whistled. The image has haunted me ever since and I never knew eventually I'd author a story about him. This tale is a blend of fiction, locations, and personal events woven together into what I hope is a suitable little horror story that might creep you out a bit. Certainly, makes you think twice about entering dilapidated houses. Growing up in the 1980s was prime for those types of activities and now they are much better at sealing off dangerous areas to youths.

Forage Market is a local chain with another store in Portland. The interior is an old mill or shoe factory (I can't remember which) and has a lot of history. Back then, in the years in which I set the story, I often wandered past that location, although it has been different businesses over the years. Forage is a great place for getting bagels and coffee and absorbing the morning sun. It's also right near Kennedy Park and Simone's Hot Dog Stand.

POPSICLE KIDS

JOSEPH CARRO

When I was just a boy, it was the late 1980s and things were different from how they are now. For example, today the world has helicopter parents and people filled with outrage over bad things they see online (and good things, too, come to think of it. People hate on everything). But back then, it was like there were *no* rules. There was no Internet (*at least not in today's form*) and no social awareness either. Everything just sort of happened. If you survived, *you survived...* And we all seemed to survive, regardless of what happened. We stayed out until the streetlights came on; we didn't talk to strangers, and we checked our candy for razorblades on Halloween. Blah, blah, blah—I'm sure you've seen the memes on Facebook being passed around by an old person like, you know, me.

I lived in Lewiston, Maine at the time with my mother, Bonnie. Lewiston was packed with French-Canadians (my mom called them "Frenchies" because half of our family was French Canadian) who'd migrated there in the 1800s and early 1900s to work in the factories dotting the shores of the Androscoggin River. When I was a kid, the waters of the Androscoggin remained poisoned by those old factories and never recovered, even decades later, even *after* I moved away.

I'm forty now, and the water likely won't be safe for another five or six years, so maybe-maybe–by the time I'm fifty I could finally take a swim. But I still wouldn't dare to. Back then, we were told not to go in the water unless we wanted to become radioactive or get stuck full of needles or bump up against a dead body. I'm not sure any of that would have happened, but you can be sure none of us trusted the Androscoggin to look at, much less dip our toes in.

I bet you're wondering what any of this has to do with *anything* at all. Well, the simple answer is that my therapist tells me I should write about a specific event from once upon a time, and I'm struggling to work my way up to it. You get me?

My therapist's name is Judy Wolfe, and she's pretty great. Cute, too, but I focus on keeping it professional. I'm sure she's picked up on my attraction to her, but I fight to keep myself level, try not to focus on the attractive things about her. I try not to stare at her legs for too long, and that seems to help, but dang, she's got some pretty stems. Whoops. Well, Judy told me to be open, so here I am.

Anyway, back to my predicament. Judy told me that what happened back then is affecting me still to this day and she wants to help me treat it, but because I won't (*and can't*) tell her what happened, she asked me to face it on my own before our next session. She believes after that I can share it with her. Because she doesn't know what really happened, she seems to think I was abused. I read her notes one day when she answered an emergency phone call, (because I'm curious in that way) and saw she had written that I'd been molested. Not in those words, exactly. She wrote something like:

History: Mr. Langlois exhibited symptoms of possible sexual molestation and abuse. Neglect. Registered heavily in PTSD spectrum, acute anxiety, depression, and trouble sleeping. Possible Attachment Disorder. Disheveled in appearance, polite yet withdrawn. He stated he wished sometimes that he didn't exist. I repeatedly inquired about an event he mentioned from his childhood, but he refuses to discuss it.

You get the idea. She thinks I'm wacko. That sucks, because she sure is pretty, and I may not be one hundred percent together, but I'm sure not a wacko. I wish I could tell her, but it just won't come out because it sounds like something a wacko would say. And here I am rambling on still, avoiding the inevitable, so I guess I can't make it come out properly in writing, either. Whoever said that writers have it easy has never put pen to paper or fingers to keys.

It was hot on the day it happened, that much I remember. It was mid-summer. I was playing a difficult game called Rygar on our Nintendo Entertainment System (*NES for short*) in the living room. The game was a fantasy sword and sorcery game; I liked those best because they transported me away from my life for a time. My home was a sty with laundry everywhere. Kids ran amok through the apartment with food crusted to their faces and dirt caked onto the backs of their knees and between their toes.

The windows were all open and a dinky, bent little fan tried to blow the hot air from the apartment back outside where it belonged.

My mom was yelling at all of us. We were what my grandmother called *Popsicle Babies*. She laughed when she said that term, and I guess I kind of get it now that I'm older. We were always caked with dirt and Kool-Aid and gave off an odor like old popsicles. Occasionally, when I'm walking in the city in the summer, I catch a whiff of a kid like that, and it brings me back to my childhood in Lewiston. This all still seems like something a wacko would say. Ugh. Getting nowhere with Judy. Maybe she'll find my avoidance skills attractive. Unlikely.

So, anyway, my mom kicks me out and tells me not to come back until the streetlights come on. Yeah, it was literal. Maybe she didn't say those exact words, but she implied it. Being a kid, I put up a fuss, but back in those days, parents weren't afraid of Child Protective Services, so they could be rough. My mom was smoking a cigarette when she turned off the NES in the middle of my game (*meaning I'd have to start all the way at the beginning again... because that's how that damned game worked*) and hauled me up off the couch by my shirt collar. She may as well have lifted me by the scruff of my neck like a mother cat would a kitten.

"Dusty," she said, blowing smoke all over me with her exhale of exasperation. "Mom needs a break. Go out and play with your friends."

"But I don't have any friends," I said. I was angry at all the time I'd lost playing Rygar, and she just wouldn't understand and never did. Even if I had friends, I wouldn't have wanted to go outside to see them at that moment.

"You don't have any friends," she said, her scratchy voice rising, "because you just stay inside all damned day. Get some sun for Christ's sake!" I thought her eyes were going to pop out of her head. My grandfather had a thyroid problem and he often looked like that, too, now that I think of it.

With that, she pushed me out the door and slammed it shut behind me. I stood in the hallway nursing anger until AC/DC screamed over the radio from behind the door. *Hell's Bells*. It was Bonnie's time. Trying to get back in was futile. She'd be drunk in an hour, and most likely, into the early morning. It was kind of her ritual.

I'm a rolling thunder, a pouring rain, I'm comin' on like a hurricane, My lightning's flashing across the sky, You're only young but you're gonna die

Leaving the screaming behind, I went out onto the hot streets of Lewiston. AC/DC's words from the radio stayed with me as I tramped down the stairs and out the front door. I hummed and sang to myself as I walked, kicking rocks, and spitting on the street. I smacked a plastic milk jug filled with sand tied to the stop sign outside our place as I walked by. It was our makeshift tetherball. The milk carton swung around the pole while I wondered what to do for the next few hours besides cursing the heat.

Our apartment building was large and boxy, with the bottom half painted green in a terrible shade, like an olive on the wrong side of its expiration date. Classy place. When I was even younger, I was playing in the dirt alongside our unit when I discovered a needle sticking out at me. Bonnie (*my mom*) arrived at just the right moment and screamed bloody murder, swatting it out of my hand and hoisting me up by the arm. I didn't know what it was, but she made sure I understood it was bad and to never touch one again. She sealed it up in a plastic Ziploc bag and brought it to the police station with me in tow.

The cop appeared as disgusted as Mom, but it confused me when he asked her if she found anything else. He mentioned some other things I did not understand, but I picked up one word. Spoon. Wouldn't a spoon be good for digging in the dirt? (Okay, I do not want to talk about spoons. See? I'm not ready to talk about this. But Judy is both hot and my therapist, and so for her I will try. Back to my shitty apartment for now.) Every single day after that one, Mom came outside with me and made sure no needles were in the dirt before I played. I guess she was a good mother sometimes. Sometimes, I still checked the dirt out of habit.

Back to that sweltering day, I wandered the streets by myself until becoming lightheaded. I believe I would have sold my soul for an ice-cold can of soda in that heat. Come to think of it, writing this, I would almost sell my soul for a can of soda now. It's been years since I drank the stuff, but I used to drink it more than I drank water, at least when I had access to it. But I digress, again, on purpose. I really do not want to remember…

All I could think about was that soda, but I had no money. I did, however, have a lot of time to kill. Then I noticed a crushed Budweiser can on the curb, the sun reflecting off the aluminum.

Bingo!

I decided to hunt down some cans and bottles and earn enough in recycling for a can of soda. Maybe even a candy bar or a bag of Party Mix to go with it. I loved Party Mix because it had pretzels, corn chips, cheese tortilla chips, cheese curls, and more, all mixed in the same bag. Each can or bottle would earn me five cents. A buck fifty was all I needed to get everything I wanted. I started bottle hunting.

Soon I passed The Ritz (*where all the old people drank their beer with my mom*) and turned onto Maple Street. Guns 'N Roses blasted from within The Ritz. It was *Paradise City*. Hearing that song not long before the bad stuff is why I still feel anxious all these years later whenever it plays on the radio. I associate it with terrible memories. Ms. Wolfe would likely have something professional to say about that. I'll have to remember to ask her when next we have an appointment. But, let me get back to Maple Street.

Maple Street looped up toward Blackie's Market. Blackie himself, a thin old man, was what Bonnie would call a *Frenchie*. The man owned a farm on the outskirts of Lewiston and sold his crops at his convenience store. Inside the shop, one could find fresh corn and other veggies. But the town liked one vegetable above all others. Beer. Because people always drank in the park behind the store, I'd likely find most of the bottles and cans I needed people threw their trash anywhere.

Once I reached the top of Maple Street, Blackie's came into view on my right. It was a squat white building with a red awning shading an exterior icebox. A couple of kids were eating popsicles outside under the awning, melting red liquid dribbled down their pudgy arms like blood. (Not that I want to think about that. See how everything leads to the horrible event? See why I should not try to remember this, Judy?)

They were *Popsicle Kids*. One of them glanced at me as I walked past. He smiled at me in such an odd manner, like he knew something I didn't. Maybe I'm just projecting. That's what Judy would say. I walked past the popsicle kids, hoping they didn't pick a fight (*I was scrawny back then, so always ran from any sort of fighting, a fact known by most neighborhood kids*) but they paid me no mind. It was too hot, and they were too content with the treats. I reached the hill leading to the park below and tried to spot any metal or dark brown glass ripe for collecting. (Collecting means something so different to me now.)

The grassy hill rolled down into an asphalt and dirt playground, complete with a swing set and a basketball court with one net and backboard on a rusty metal pole. Beyond the basketball court, there was a chain-link fence which prevented stray basketballs from rolling into the woods. There was a small dilapidated white house in those woods and though some of the older kids would go into it from time to time to listen to music and spray graffiti, most of us stayed away. The house gave me goose bumps whenever I looked at it, much less went inside. I only entered once and rushed out like a chicken. I spotted a shiny can down by the swing set, half buried in sand, smiling at the thought of how many bottles and cans I would find in the park.

Making my way down the grass hill alongside the stone steps, I made sure not to drop the one can I'd found on the way. For some reason, kids never used the stairs. We always walked or slid or rolled down the deep rut, the same one we sledded on in the winter. Maybe it reminded us of those fun days in the snow. Once at the bottom, I approached the can. It glinted next to the swing set.

It was a Budweiser can. Picking it up, I poured sand from it and wiped it off. The aluminum was hot from the sun. There was an old plastic shopping bag wrapped in some branches behind the swing set. I grabbed it, careful not to tear any more of it than it already was, and put my returnables inside, happy to have something to carry them in. My fortunes faded when instead of spotting more cans, I spotted a group of kids biking toward me, grinning from ear to ear.

My blood went cold. I didn't dare run per usual because they'd likely give chase, and I couldn't outrun bikes, leaving me to stand my ground and pretend they did not terrify me despite almost pissing my pants. Funny how I was never afraid of other kids after that day, though. *Just of that house.* See Judy? I am making progress.

The kids spread out, all three boxing me in. I recognized one of them… Greg Libby. Once I gave his girlfriend a Valentine's card like an idiot, believing I made it anonymous enough, but she figured it out. Ever since he had it out for me and often called me "cowboy" though I'm uncertain why. What I understood is he always punched me in the gut as a greeting.

"Hey, Cowboy," Greg said. The other two laughed. "What're you think you're doing?"

"Nothing," I said, feeling vulnerable watching them descend on me. Greg was taller than me with blonde hair styled into a mullet. The two kids alongside him were roughly my size and were identical twins. They had a mean look about them, with hard eyes, dark brown hair, and freckles on the bridges of their nose. We'd all had rough childhoods back then, and some kids took a wrong turn before they could leave the city. I hadn't, but they had. They cycled around me in a circle and jeered.

"What're you staring at, faggot?" Said one twin, looking into my eyes. "Take a picture. It'll last longer." I looked down at the ground.

"Yeah, he's probably playing pocket pool right now," said the other twin. In my head, I labelled them as Tweedle-Dee and Tweedle-Dum. Greg just laughed along with their jeers, pleased with the situation. Their shirts were damp with sweat. Greg was the first to get off his bike, pushing it down into the dirt. I was shaking as he walked up to me and stood there, looking into my face, smirking. Tweedle-Dee and Tweedle-Dum circled like sharks, laughing.

Without warning, Greg ripped the plastic bag from my hand and tore it in half, the two meager cans falling into the dirt. He kicked them away. Then he punched me in the stomach, bowling me over as a surge of pain shot into my diaphragm, knocking my breath out of me in a big "WHOOF."

Tweedle-Dee and Tweedle-Dum laughed harder.

"What a pussy," Tweedle-Dum said.

"Lay on your back or I'll hit you again," Greg said, kicking me backward from my shoulder. I couldn't see any way out of the situation without a beating, so I did as he said, coughing, laying my back on the hot tar and sand, which crawled into my clothing and felt like fleas that were on fire.

If anyone believes I have made a breakthrough and finally arrived at that which I refuse to speak of, I have one word. Wrong. Once upon a time, this situation would have been the trauma I carried with me into adulthood like a piece of luggage. But no, the bad thing makes the rest nothing more than peaches and cream even though Greg was far from done.

He placed a foot on me to keep me down, not that I was going anywhere. Then he nodded to his friends.

"Now what they're gonna' do, Cowboy, is they're gonna' jump over you with their bikes. If you move, you're gonna' get wrecked. Got me?"

I didn't acknowledge what he said, only wiped tears from the corners of my eyes. Tweedle-Dee and Tweedle-Dum rolled away, hooting and hollering as they created enough distance to build up speed for their daredevil jump over my frail little body. Greg eyed me with this pure, evil satisfaction from above and then motioned to the twins. If I hadn't been so dehydrated, I would have pissed myself.

"Alright, guys… get to it!" Greg moved his arms over my body as if to clear the runway for flight at an airport. I closed my eyes. As I lay there, expecting to get a tire to the face or for the bike to land on my body, I tried to think of other things. My pet cat Blackie back home, named after the convenience store, and the adventures of *Rygar*, which I would no doubt get back to after this, forget the soda and the bottle collecting. Not knowing that soon things were about to get worse.

I heard Tweedle-Dum land, not on me, and give a little cheer. "I'm gonna' try again," he said, and my stomach fell. They were going to be at this for a while. I only had one chance to escape this. I opened my eyes.

"Stay down there," Greg said, balling a fist. "Or so help me, Cowboy."

I stayed down and waited. My heart pounded because I knew what I was going to do. Tweedle-Dee primed his bike and made a beeline for my body, aiming for my waist. As he approached, moving faster and faster, I brought up my legs at the last second. Tweedle-Dee screeched and tried to move his wheel, but I lashed out with both feet, striking the side of his bike and front tire. Greg could do nothing as Tweedle-Dee crashed into him and the two of them fell into a swearing heap. I bolted to my feet, scrambled on the tar as my shaky legs fought to move my body, and I grabbed a rock on the way, making for the woods and the old white house. I knew that Tweedle-Dum was right behind me, gaining fast, and he was furious.

"I'm gonna' fuck you up, you little shit," he screamed.

I turned, and I threw the rock as hard as I could. A look of surprise crossed Tweedle-Dum's face as the rock sailed home and struck him in the temple when he tried to move his head to the side. His bike crashed to the ground, and he hollered and clutched the side of his head. I knew then those guys were going to kill me. I noticed Greg and Tweedle-Dee untangling themselves before I turned and ran into the trees.

The air was cooler in the woods, and it would have been nice had I just gone in there in the first place. I ran down the rough path formed by homeless people and delinquent children and made my way toward the small white house with the chipped paint and the boarded windows. Once there, I slipped inside through a break in the boarded-up door.

The air was musty inside and so quiet I felt as if I'd stepped into another dimension. I'll never forget the moment of calm that descended over me inside those doors. I almost forgot that Greg and his friends would come after me soon. The genuine possibility of having the snot beat from me dissolved any fears related to the house itself. I crouched down by one plywood covered window that had holes poked through it. I watched from a corner hole as the three boys made their way into the 'front yard' of the old house. They seemed to hesitate there. Tweedle-Dum still clutched his head. A streak of red covered the side of his face from the beaning. My heart was pounding, and I shook with adrenalin. I could taste copper in my mouth.

"That little fucker… where'd he go?" Tweedle-Dum looked at the house and the surrounding area. He crouched down as if to examine the ground for my footprints. I held my breath until I realized he did not know how to read for my tracks.

"Think he went inside?" Tweedle-Dee asked, moving toward the window.

"Maybe." Greg said. "He's such a little pussy, though. I don't think he'd go in, but if he did it's because he knows he's going to get his ass beat."

Greg stepped forward and cupped his hands to each side of his mouth. I could see scratches on his forearms, a gift from when I'd kicked over Tweedle-Dum's bike.

"HEY, COWBOY," he shouted. "WE'RE GONNA' GIVE YOU TO THE COUNT OF TEN TO GET OUT HERE AND TAKE YOUR BEATING. IF YOU DON'T GET OUT HERE AND WE HAVE TO COME IN THERE, IT'S GONNA' BE TEN TIMES WORSE FOR YOU AND YOU'RE GONNA' GO TO THE HOSPITAL!"

I backed away at first, afraid to make noise, as Greg began his countdown. I turned when I reached the stairs and took them two at a time, my thighs burning with the effort. Upon reaching the top, I ran the length of the hallway toward a room I saw when last I dared enter. I looked back as I ran, checking for pursuers. Bad move. I collided with something solid, like a human body. Stumbling sideways into the railing, it snapped, giving way. I fell for what seemed forever until hitting the wooden floor. Everything went black.

When I came to, large rough hands held both sides of my head while large rough thumbs slid my eyelids open. Despite struggling, the hands held me tight. I could barely move, and my entire body throbbed with pain. My ankle was sprained, and I had a concussion, (though I didn't know that at the time). All I knew was I hurt, and a massive man had hold of me.

The face staring into my own was pudgy, with a round jawline. I'll never forget that face as long as I live. Stubble surrounded his jaw, and a porkpie hat rested on his head at an angle. The man's glasses were thick and round like the bottoms of Coke bottles and covered eyes like coal set in deep sockets. A large black turtleneck covered his throat while he also wore a black pea coat that reeked of wet wool and tobacco.

"Wot' we got 'ere," he grumbled, tilting his head back so that he could better examine me in the poor lighting. "Looks like y'hurt yer 'ead."

"I'm fine," I tried to say, but only let out a sigh of pain.

He seemed to ignore me while feeling around my scalp with callused fingers which felt like spiders scurrying under my hair and down the back of my neck. The odor emanating from his fingerless gloves smelled like a dead cat I found in an alley once. There was strength in his grip and his hands seemed to move too fast for how large he was. Maybe he was trying to help examine my injuries from the fall.

I was about to tell him I was okay when he pulled a spoon out of his pocket. A big one, all shiny and fancy. The spoon's handle looked like a clamshell molded out of the shiny silver, with gold inlay. He smiled and moved the spoon toward my eye. Then Greg and the Tweedles shouted from the front porch.

"ALL RIGHT, COWBOY – WE'RE COMING IN THERE FOR YOU. YOU'RE GOING TO FUCKING REGRET IT."

The big man let me go and turned his head toward the ruckus before placing one of his sausage fingers in front of his crusty lips. Greg and the Tweedles entered the front room, and the man disappeared into the darkness, spoon and all. His stench lingered. I held my breath and crawled on my elbows and the tips of my knees to an old television stand and moved my way behind it, hoping their talking would drown out my scuffling.

I thought for sure they'd heard me, but I became comfortable enough to rest, crouching, in case I had to bolt again. My heart was racing, and my head throbbed, as did my ankle. But the bigger issue was the man. As my head cleared, I wondered what he was even doing there, why he had such an interest in my injuries, and what was with the spoon. (If I hadn't eventually seen what he used it for, I might have thought him a crackhead given his drug accessory of choice. I eventually learned why the cop asked Mom about the spoon.) But the Porkpie Man was something else, something bordering on supernatural. Or at least a force of visceral nature.

Greg, Tweedle-Dee and Tweedle-Dum rummaged around in the next room over, moving and kicking at would-be hiding places trying to flush me out. I ignored what they were saying, too panicked over the Porkpie Man. I couldn't see him anywhere. Greg and the other two bullies were suddenly the last thing on my mind.

"Shane," Greg said to one of them. "You go upstairs. Chris, you go into that side room. I'll take the kitchen."

"Why split up?" One asked. It sounded like Tweedle-Dum.

"Because idiot… if we don't, he's going to get away and this way he's got nowhere to go. YOU HEAR THAT, COWBOY? YOU'VE GOT NOWHERE TO GO. WHEN WE FIND YOU, YOU'RE FUCKIN' TOAST."

I was shaking, wondering what in the world I was going to do. If I hallucinated the Porkpie Man, then Greg was going to beat me so badly I'd end up in the hospital. Cobwebs clung to my clothing and draped across my neck, making my skin itch. I tried to ignore it. One of them, it looked like Tweedle-Dee—snuck into the room I hid in. Tweedle-Dee's name was Chris. (In the papers later, I'd learn that Chris and Shane were brothers, and their last name was Laferriere.)

Crouching as low as I could, I tensed, hoping Chris would walk past me. I could hear the others shuffling across the house above and near the kitchen, shouting threats. Chris kicked over a chair on the other side of the room and screamed, trying to flush me out again. As he searched for movement, I saw some. A figure materialized in the shadows behind him.

As much as I hated Chris and the others, I wanted to scream a warning. The Porkpie Man came out from the recess of a door, a dirty cloth in his hand. I rose, but the Porkpie Man looked at me and waved a sausage finger and put it to his lips again as if to shush me. Then, with a beefy arm inside his black woolen pea coat, he constricted Chris's neck and held the cloth to the boy's mouth.

Chris panicked and tried to elbow the Porkpie Man, who cracked the kid's arm out of its socket. The boy screamed through the cloth, but the force of the Porkpie Man's massive hand pressing against his mouth muffled the cry. Chris' eyes rolled back into his head, and he slumped over, his arm dangling at an odd angle. The cloth, when pulled away, was wet with snot, spit, and tears. A chemical odor I'd never smelled before rose from the soiled rag. Chloroform?

The Porkpie Man again produced the spoon. He winked at me, then pushed the silverware into Chris's left eye socket. It made a sickening metal on bone crunch as the Porkpie Man cracked through the plating behind Chris' eye and severed the nerves. Chris spasmed, but otherwise stayed silent as the Porkpie Man performed his grisly work. The Porkpie Man produced a jar from somewhere within his pea coat before lifting his spoon into the air to examine Chris' severed eye. With a whistle, Porkpie Man dropped the orb into the jar with a plop, where it settled atop other severed eyes. As the Porkpie Man went to work on eyeball number two, he whistled *London Bridge Is Falling Down*.

I bent over the old wooden floor and puked. My throat and eyes were burning. When I looked up, the Porkpie Man was nowhere to be seen, but Chris' body was lying on the floor. I needed to get out of there. I crawled over toward him, as the door to the main room was the only way inside. The smell hit me at once, and I almost laughed despite everything. The boy smelled like a popsicle kid, though one that had gone to rot, and the red was not cherry but something else.

As I crawled over his body, bloody black holes stared back at me from where his eyes once were, his eyelids open as eyes are sometimes in death. I felt my stomach drop out from under me and I'll never quite forget that dead, eyeless stare. In some ways, it still feels like I'm falling and staring into that face and that I've just never moved on.

That day, though, I had to move on. I finished crawling over the body, (Poor Tweedle Dee) and on shaky arms and quivering knees, made my way as quietly as I could toward the front door. My whole body shook like Jell-O, and I'm pretty sure I was sobbing. With some effort, I found my feet and moved toward the door.

"HEY," I heard Greg's voice cry out. I stopped and looked up on the balcony from the ledge where I had fallen over.

When did he get up there? Didn't matter. "Get out of here," I said. "He's going to kill you!"

"I'm going to kill YOU, motherfu…"

A massive, fingerless-gloved hand wrapped around Greg's mouth, cutting his voice off. I still remember the look in Greg's eyes to this day, and I suspect I'll take it to the grave with me. Fear, sorrow, and surprise. As Greg lost consciousness, the Porkpie Man laid the boy on the wood floor of the landing and produced the gleaming silver spoon and jar full of eyes—which looked fuller than when I first saw it. If I was correct, it meant he found Shane. Poor Tweedle Dum. I was next if I didn't get out of there.

The telltale crunch sounded as the Porkpie man set to work, again whistling London Bridge Is Falling Down. I bolted from that house, and it would be the last time I ever set foot in there.

When I arrived back home, I marched straight inside. Bonnie was asleep, drunk, her head resting on the table as eighties rock blared from a radio with a blown-out speaker. My younger brother crawled around on the floor by himself, covered in dirt. I picked him up, brought him into our room, shut the door, and blocked it with a dresser.

The aftermath was a media fiasco. Lewiston became the center of a national manhunt after they found the three boys dead and eyeless, in the old house in the park. They never found the killer. I watched teary-eyed news conferences featuring the boys' parents, but I never came forward. The Porkpie Man was still out there. Sometimes, I swear I can hear him whistling.

I've finally written it down, but now I believe I will never share this with my therapist. Judy thinks I am crazy enough already. And as hot as she is, she is also expensive. I am not sure how much money and time I would want to spend trying to get over Koutaliaphobia. It is a real thing. Look it up. It is the deathly fear of spoons.

COFFEE & MILK

WEST LOS ANGELES, CA

I f one is prone to be intolerant of lactose, they may fear the name of this unique little coffee shop. This is one of the many which exist in an office building in Los Angeles and caters to the professional women and men who navigate a different type of horror every day, corporate structure.

Besides the overly cheery baristas, the interior comprises spotless white furniture which should be impossible at a place which exists to serve dark liquid beverages. It makes sense that the interior is so pristine since the customers in line are all greeted by name, and all appear to be as free from life's problems as the furniture is of espresso drippings.

The upbeat nature of the shop makes it almost feel as though it exists in a different time, one commonly referred to as simpler. People often categorize history that way precisely because it is just that—the past. It has been experienced; its outcome already certain. Any threats or chaos which surely existed back then have since been resolved.

The music they play at a distractingly loud volume is from the 1950s. The very music which existed when a cultural change in films began, when the known became the unknown and sci-fi films surged, especially alien invasion films...

SHIRTS & SKINS

PAUL CARRO

G rowing up, classmates picked Freddie Weaver last for everything. Whether dodgeball, football, basketball, or even square dancing during that two-week long exercise in humility in gym class when he was fourteen. All other students paired off quickly until only Freddie and four-eyed Sally remained. Even then, Sally did not choose him. Coach Brannigan yelled, "hold hands, geeks!" Those words forced their partnership into existence. The entire class laughed, which flushed his face crimson for the rest of the class. Freddie found it difficult to hide his embarrassment, given that both his frame and complexion were delicate as porcelain.

Being picked last bothered Freddy terribly. Even unathletic bookworms got picked before him, no matter the sport or activity. Heck, they would choose him last for a booger picking team, and he was good at that. During the miserable picking process, at least one person would chant, "Freddie, Freddie, never ready."

While the constant bullying could have set him on a warped path, making him a Columbine kid waiting to happen, something eventually changed his lot in life. Freddie found a girlfriend.

The relationship left Freddie no time for thoughts of revenge, no time for despair. He lived in a romantic haze where all the problems of the world disappeared the day that he first kissed two-eyed Sally. She had matured in all the right places since their square- dancing days and ditched the frames for color treated contacts. Freddie now spent all his free time willingly drowning in her baby blue pools.

Falling for her coincided with his newfound appreciation of sports. Not taking part but watching from the sidelines as a fan. The jocks even lightened up on Freddie after realizing he was getting a little tail. Sports were suddenly enjoyable thanks to his status as a guy with a female on his arm.

There was something special about those fall nights under the arc lights of a football field on bleachers with air so crisp. Freddie and Sally enjoyed watching their declarations of love take the form of floating mist in the chilly fall air, a physical manifestation of the greatest relationship ever known.

Everything was special at sixteen, even simple things like feeding one another nachos buried under a cheese that most likely glowed in the dark. Freddie speculated if ever there was a power outage during a game, the nacho cheese could guide them all to safety. Chernobyl cheese, he called it, and Sally would laugh. Sally always laughed, and from the day he kissed her, so did he.

What he enjoyed most about those nights was how it felt to reach around her body and bury his hands into the pouch of her Tether Falls High sweatshirt. It kept them both warm—sweaty, even—despite the chill. Freddie frequently sniffed the magical scent of her hair, the smell of which would follow him home and into his dreams.

Every time the team scored, drawing the crowd to their feet, Freddie and Sally used the opportunity to hug. Freddie would often believe *they are cheering for us, everyone is cheering for us*. That was love at sixteen.

Age eighteen changed everything. Youth and innocence were like Bonnie and Clyde. Even if their death were to be long and slow, they would do it together. Nights on the bleachers for the young couple eventually became nights under the bleachers. Once they secured a dark corner under the bleachers (and after adjusting to the smell of feet and farts) Freddie would explore areas normally hidden by Sally's bra.

When Freddie fondled her breasts, it was as if he were more an outsider than a participant. The mechanics of it all fascinated him, despite his uncontrollable excitement. During his explorations she would eventually shake and mention she "felt weird down there." After a halftime break for hot chocolate, they would return to making out for a time. Then during the fourth quarter when the roars of the crowd usually grew loudest, Sally would explore Freddie's lower half. He usually exploded immediately, much to his embarrassment and immense pleasure. The sights and sounds of something so alien fascinated Sally. That is what she called it. Alien. If she only knew.

Eventually the couple gave up their season seats altogether to spend further time burying innocence inside Dimples. Dimples was Freddie's first car, his mother's old one. A freak hailstorm lobbing ice the size of grapefruit pinged and dented every other inch of the Ford along with many other vehicles in town. Insurance companies declared the affected vehicles a total loss even though they ran fine. His mother received a new car while he inherited hers, naming it Dimples. The front and back driver side windows remained covered in plastic sheeting and masking tape, awaiting windows that were a fast-food job away.

Whenever anyone remarked on the plastic and tape combo, Freddie would joke that, "At least Dimples is terrorist ready!" He did not joke about things like terrorists anymore, nobody did. Eighteen was looking like nothing but a bitch in high heels.

Eighteen.

That specific age became a topic of conversation for the entire world. An age that should have been about friends, about fun, about recklessness grew into a national debate topic. There were discussions about lowering the drinking age to eighteen. Talk about a lot of stuff related to those "lucky enough" to turn eighteen. Having already reached that age, Freddie wondered whether such changes would come in his lifetime.

There were relationship changes that accompanied the milestone age as well. Freddie grew increasingly angry at Sally, insisting they should be fucking. Freddie said things like fuck and shit a lot lately. Everybody did. Freddie angrily thought, *I already managed three fingers up there, so what was the holdup?*

Sally always provided a one-word answer. God. Sex before marriage was a sin. People were talking about God a lot lately too, enough so that churches began operating on 7-11 hours. Hell, one church even installed a drive through confessional! Despite everything going on, Freddy had a milk through nose moment when he heard about that. *Hey, Father. How about super-sizing my salvation while you're at it?* Freddie thought, laughing at the absurdity of it all.

The God thing was a growing barrier between citizens of the same land. There were more talking heads than one could shake a stick at talking about red states and blue states on cable channels. Freddie understood better than the chuckleheads on TV that soon there would be no such thing as blue states anymore. Soon there would be only red. Red and dripping.

Freddie's house was modest. A prefab one step away from a trailer home but in a pleasant neighborhood. His bedroom leaned testosterone heavy. The original walls lost somewhere under rock and rap posters, along with several pinups of barely clad women. Many a night Freddie lay in bed staring at the women on his wall while wishing Sally were in his bed. The same circumstances that changed the entire world for those eighteen and older finally got her to lie beside him.

When Sally joined him in bed, the whole thing disappointed him. Despite spooning, he felt a barrier. Dogs could smell fear. Hers was so great it reached even his nose through her perfume, leaving him to consider himself more dog than man. While wishing for nothing more than fornicating to his heart's desire, Sally trembled in fear rather than pleasure.

The scantily clad women in the wall posters beckoned to him, offering that which felt so unattainable. With renewed vigor, Freddie refocused on the real woman, inching a hand forward, creeping toward the promised land of flesh under covers and clothes. It bothered him how she remained clothed. He was mere inches away from success or a slapping when his mother barged in. Neither welcome nor unwelcome given current circumstances.

"It is almost time," Freddie's mother informed them, looking at the teens with sorrow. "You two can do stuff, you know. It's okay, your father and I don't mind."

"No kidding, I've heard you two through the walls every day lately," Freddie said in an honesty that reflected the times they lived in.

His Mother smiled momentarily before turning a stern look on her child, which was what he was. Age eighteen or not. Freddie recognized a look on her mother's face, a thought dancing behind the woman's eyes. He had the same one. How could a single second in a single minute in a single hour in a three hundred and sixty-fifth day on an eighteenth year change a boy to a man?

"Freddie, I'm still your mother," she said before leaving the room.

The teen could not argue. No matter what happened in the coming days, his mom's statement was accurate. He wished she were his mother under different circumstances. Freddie's mind and guts churned with emotions stirring for weeks. He wondered whether it was time to share some of those feelings with the woman in his arms. After consideration, he decided talking would impede progress toward finally scoring a piece of ass. Freddie went for the gold.

"We just got parental approval and we're almost out of time. What do you say, beautiful?" Freddie stated more than asked.

Thrusting his overactive pelvis in her direction. But as he positioned himself tighter into their spoon, angling for rear entry, the scent of her hair brought him to a different place. One where holding was not so bad.

"I'm sorry, I can't give it to you. I'm afraid of the blood," Sally whimpered.

For the first time, Freddie realized maybe he too was afraid. As he held her, he abandoned his efforts to get it on. Suddenly, all he wanted was to comfort her. Maybe that was what eighteen was about. Perhaps he was growing up.

Freddie pulled her tight and allowed her to do what she had been doing all morning—weeping. Freddie never saw so many tears and snot come from one person before. Then as her body shook just so from another uncontrollable crying jag, his body stirred again, dissolving his resolve. Before he could follow through with the idea that he needed to take charge of ending their collective virginity, the talking heads on the TV at the end of his bed gave way to a signal from the emergency broadcast system. The crawl on the screen assured them (and the world) that this was not a test.

And just like that, Sally stopped weeping. Freddie knew in that moment that he would never live long enough to understand women. Anyway, he did not have the time to figure her out or get laid. It was time for him and his entire family to head into town.

It was game time.

· · • • •• • • • ·

Once they arrived in town for the start of the game, butterflies attacked Freddie's stomach. His guts churned with worry about his elevated position in the contest. Freddie was overwhelmed to find himself a team captain after so many years of being picked last.

A thousand thoughts ran through his mind as he considered who to pick first. Recent reality television shows jumped to his frontal lobe. Such shows always relied on strategy and alliances. Should he pick those he liked, or would it be better to split the pot and leave some he cared about on the other side of the line of scrimmage?

The pressure of what he needed to do creeped in, causing his pulse to race and his palms to sweat. Freddie worried he might faint. His father eyed him with a look bordering on pride or fear. Whichever, it strengthened his resolve enough to bring him back to the thought which sustained him in recent days.

For the first time, Freddie was a team captain!

No matter the circumstances, he finally achieved that which he never did. No matter how things turned out, win or lose—if there was such a thing—Freddie would finally pick a team. There was no robbing him of that. This was his moment.

Fate had a sense of humor, he supposed. How else to explain the choice of opposing team captain? Mitch Solomon, the biggest bully in the neighborhood who tortured Freddie for years with dropped shorts in gym class, two-a-day beatings, and much name calling (which somehow hurt worse than attacks resulting in bruises). As a star athlete in high school, Freddie and Sally cheered for Mitch despite their history. Freddie missed those days, cheering for his enemy.

How they chose team captains of the first annual neighborhood game (for those eighteen and over) remained a mystery. Was it a cosmic coin toss or something bigger? It did not much matter in the end. With great responsibility came great power. The stakes were high. The team captain held the fate of many in their hands. At least one team captain would not return the following season. Winning was everything in this game.

An earthbound coin flip determined who would go first. Freddie correctly called tails. Richard Reynolds, owner of Reynold's Hardware, served as the master of ceremonies. The portly man, shaped like the bags of concrete sold in his stores, announced it was time to pick. Failure to do so meant forfeiting the game. The consequences of which would be severe.

Freddie outlined a strategy prior to the game, but in real time, he doubted his plan. Scanning the crowd, he located Sally, who looked mighty pretty since she stopped crying. She was, however, staring blankly into space. In that moment Freddie wondered what the weather was like on her planet and smiled at the joke. Mr. Reynold's urged him on with a clearing of throat.

Eyeing all the contestants (the group of people spread further than he could see) left him feeling dizzy. He spotted his parents smiling at him, counting on him to do the right thing. Then Lindsey Logan suddenly caught his eye.

The woman graduated two years ahead of him but was about ten years ahead in experience and popularity. Lindsey was a former cheerleading captain with a body that forcefully yanked puberty out of any late blooming freshmen in the years she pom-pommed. The school featured Lindsey on every third page of the yearbook. The popular coed had her pick of high school boys until sophomore year when she moved up to college men.

Staring at her was a major faux pas. Freddie understood that, but the leering was nothing compared to the lurid thoughts running through his mind. He could almost feel Sally's gaze smacking him on the back of the head. But when Mr. Reynolds announced it was time to pick or forfeit.

"Lindsey Logan," Freddie blurted.

Lindsey reacted with nearly as much shock as the crowd. To her credit, she recovered quickly, sashaying forward in a manner suggesting, *of course I got picked first, I always am.* Freddie hoped for an acknowledgement from her, a sign it pleased her to end up on his team, but she gave him nothing. Instead, she moved behind him where he could not even steal sideways glances. He smelled her though, all strawberries and jasmine. He settled for that. This was the closest he ever stood near her, and he fought to hide his excitement from the crowd.

Once the psychological dust settled, Freddie noticed Sally, who appeared different. Her normally sparkling eyes faded to emptiness. The direct result of his first decision as team captain. Freddie placed a word to the look on her face. Betrayal.

As for Freddie's Mother and Father, their faces flushed red with embarrassment (so that is where he got it from) and disappointment. Freddie wanted to yell how he was under pressure, that it was difficult being a team captain. Then Mitch proved him wrong.

"Mom", Mitch said.

The crowd clapped and hooted their approval at the pick. Mitch's Mom joined her son's side with a hug and a kiss. The woman did not hide behind the man like Lindsey did. The coup de grâce came as a smug look from Mitch.

Damn, while Mitch went for strategy, I went for tits, Freddie thought. There was a lot at stake in the neighborhood game. Some would talk about it for as close to forever as there was anymore. Freddie sniffed the air and realized that Lindsey was not such an awful choice at all. Heck, if they won today, she might be incredibly grateful.

Freddie chose his own mother next. She greeted him with a kiss. The choice drew minimal applause from the crowd. The lackadaisical response related to his bungling the first pick. Freddie knew he should have picked his mother first.

Mitch's next move changed the nature of the game and Freddie's life forever. Mitch picked Sally! The crowd roared in disapproval, but Freddy did not hear them. He was too busy lunging at Mitch. Both moms placed themselves between their sons.

Freddie's mother said, "What are you planning? Violence? It's just a game, sweetie, just a game."

The two captains retook their positions, aware of the ticking clock. They would resolve all animosity on the playing field. Sally shuffled in shock toward her team, never glancing at Freddie, only staring at her own feet. The spark in her eye extinguished for eternity.

Freddie did not wish to be captain anymore, did not want the responsibility. The rules were clear that he could step away anytime. There was a literal line drawn that he could step across. Painted with spray paint, (hey in blood red color everybody!) it stretched for about a half mile.

To cross it meant giving up, which would ensure he would never play again. Worse, another captain would take his place instantly. No, Freddie was finally a captain, and he planned to see it through. A new strategy formed in his mind, one designed around the new circumstances. He planned revenge.

Freddie chose his father next and received the applause he expected. Mitch then chose his own father, which played right into Freddie's hands. Freddie chose Scott Foster next. Scott was Mitch's best friend and stand-in bully. If ever Mitch missed school because of illness or being too stoned or hungover, Scott was there to fill in with fists and attitude cocked and ready. Scott's signature move was hitting bruises that had yet to heal from Mitch's previous assaults.

Scott and Mitch locked eyes with a sorrow as apparent as Freddy felt when Sally joined the opposing team.

Freddy looked to Sally, who still stared at her shoes. Freddie felt a pang of guilt over having chosen Mitch's best friend. But the guilt dissipated under a string of invectives from Scott that could have filled a thesaurus with variations of the "F word."

When Scott ran out of colorful language, he stood defiantly. "No way am I joining your team geek, I will not be on a losing team when the stakes are so high."

Scott took a single step towards Mitch. It was his last. Scott froze, the veins in his neck pulsing as he struggled to move. Then he moved, but not of his own volition. His right arm extended straight out as if someone pulled it. The man was now a puppet controlled under invisible strings, and the entire neighborhood had front row seats for the show. (Even those too far from the action could see it all in their heads.)

Scott could only control his voice and eyes. Both pleaded with Mitch. "Help me buddy!"

"I'm sorry…" Mitch answered.

Scott's right hand originally balled into a fist (because why wouldn't it be?) shook itself open. Suddenly, his right index finger shot straight up and back with a horrific snap. Scott screamed in agony. His middle finger raised next, far enough for bone to pierce skin. The horrific debacle looked as though an invisible loan shark was collecting payment. Scott's remaining fingers and thumbs on the right arm followed suit, snapping back toward his forearm until breaking loudly.

Scott's screaming settled into a whimper when his left arm extended itself involuntary. "No, please, no more," he screamed.

Scott squinted, eyeing the fresh fingers he believed were about to break, but something else happened. His left forearm snapped at an unnatural angle, breaking his arm at the elbow, exposing bone, muscle, and far too much blood. Scott's screams went high pitched until nothing escaped his lips any longer as he went white with shock. There were rules to the game and Scott had broken them. His punishment had only just begun.

··•••••••··

Weeks earlier, rules of the game made themselves mysteriously known to the world. The whole thing relayed as if a flash drive downloaded information into every individual over eighteen across the globe. News anchors, politicians, celebrities, and even tribal leaders in the most remote places shared the communication they received as confirmation.

The rules were quite simple, every community would pick teams. Only one team would be victorious. The purveyors of the information explained everyone eighteen and older would take part. Failure to do so meant forfeit.

Freddie remembered how scared he was when a bully of a Fox News host cried on live TV. The anchor informed viewers that while unaware of how the information came to him, but he was certain the reporting was accurate. This was not fake news. The game was on.

What followed cemented the stakes in the minds of an entire world. The anchor made it clear something inappropriate for younger viewers was about to air. Viewers received the same instructions in their minds. They also understood devices were unnecessary, the video would stream in eligible players' mind's eyes. Families rushed children younger than eighteen away from the screens or out of the room.

Grainy footage appeared on the TV, but the image cleared up in citizen's minds. The broadcast showed two lines of anxious citizens in what on-screen lettering identified as a small town in Russia. Hundreds of people stood opposite one another. Many wept, with some reaching toward their counterparts in the opposite line. It appeared not all family members or loved ones ended up on the same team.

Freddie flipped through the channels, drawing protests from his parents, but every single station aired the same footage. He finally settled on CNN. The female anchor announced the start of the game. The team on the right twitched and their eyes went wide. Each lost control of their bodies as appendages spun in various directions, at horrific and unusual angles. One man's head thrust back until it slapped his shoulder blades. The man dropped immediately.

The visual input was too great, the sight so horrific that most averted their gaze, yet the images played on with clarity internally. Freddie shook his head, but the image failed to even blur. There was no pause button. The grotesque circus of agony continued as the losers dropped one after another in horrific fashion.

Rib cages freed themselves from victims, springing wildly into the open. Fingernails popped off, only to float down like snowflakes. Blood splashed so high it looked like rain despite the sunny day. From there, much worse things happened to the losing team. In the end, only one line stood, though the looks on their faces suggested winning was not everything.

Once the footage ended, the anchor returned to the air, pale from puking. Someone in Freddie's living room did the same, but Freddie was not sure who. The sick regurgitation only served as background noise. Freddie had since refocused on the screen.

"Game day for the balance of the globe is now set," the anchor announced. "No corner of the earth shall be exempt. Only those under eighteen are ineligible to play, though they will eventually. The game is hereby declared an annual event. Just as we news anchors understand this information, we believe our audience is internally aware where to report on game day and who the team captains will be."

The woman was correct. Freddie turned to his parents. "I'm a team captain."

"We know," they replied.

The "World Games" as the press dubbed it changed the world itself. There was some initial rioting after the footage that day, but people soon lost interest in violence. The general citizenry wandered around dazed as if zombies. Within days of the announcement, as the gravity of it all set, the country set a milestone. For the first time in modern U.S. history, the entire country went a full week without a single murder.

Suicides were another story. Many people refused to take part in the games by ending their existence. Before one could even pull a trigger, the most horrific manipulations of flesh occurred to those individuals. With each attempt, the community at large received an announcement in their heads that someone forfeited. Each thwarted effort played out in citizen's minds.

One scene played out in Freddie's head as though he were standing nearby as a witness. An individual leapt off a bridge. Mid-leap, the man's body twisted at the waist until the individual could see his own back. The person was dead before hitting the water. People soon stopped attempts to take their own lives.

Citizens abandoned jobs en masse. While some businesses remained open, there was no rhyme or reason to the hours. A single employee opened the nearby supermarket by himself but did not charge anyone for anything. TV stations fell mostly into repeats or static.

The voices relayed instructions for citizens to shelter in place until after game day. The first flight after the global announcement resulted in forfeit for all passengers and crew. Unimaginable gore filled the cabin in the skies shortly after takeoff. All expired in horrendous fashion before the plane crashed a short distance from the runway and exploded. Fire crews never responded. They let the thing burn as a warning. They grounded all flights after that. Other countries followed suit.

Faith became a growth industry, rivaling the dot.com boom of years past. Preachers talked fire and brimstone with a righteous fury while pews filled with salvation seekers. Freddie's own priest regularly spoke about the day of reckoning at hand.

'No shit, Sherlock,' Freddie thought.

Of course, with saints came sinners. Strangers engaged in sex on the streets. Cops did nothing other than occasionally join in. One pair of local anchors even did it live on the news desk. Yeah, everyone was getting end-of-the-world tail except for Freddie. Imagine that, facing what they were facing, and somehow Sally still feared losing her virginity.

"It would hurt too much," she said. The funny thing was Freddie loved her for it as much as it frustrated him.

· · • • • • • • • ·

Finally, Freddie picked his last teammate, a homeless guy who reeked of alcohol. Though many people did. The teams lined up opposite one another, stretching on as if forever. The Game Makers (whomever they were) controlled all aspects of the game other than who lined up against whom. Everyone chose who they would see for the last time.

Sally stood before Freddie, trembling. She took his hands and then they kissed. His chest heaved over the guilt of their circumstances. He wished to lose, unwilling to be the sole-surviving half of the ill-fated couple. More than that, he wanted Sally to live. She deserved life more than he. The world revealed its character in recent weeks, and Freddie found it lacking in grace, something Sally had in spades. With her in the world, perhaps others would find theirs too.

For a moment, Freddie forgot where he was, losing himself in Sally. A part of him felt if a person loved someone enough, everything would be alright. Maybe that conquered all. Then it happened.

A pain shot through his gut like a hot knife. The sharp stab surely confirming his presence on the losing team.

Though when blood splattered across his face with no accompanying pain, he realized it was not his own.

Sally never screamed, never even had the chance. Freddie never saw her the same again. Like most things in life, TV failed to do justice to reality. What happened on that crisp autumn morning, where warm blood spread clouds of steam into the main street, was far worse than all the images from that small Russian town combined.

The person he loved more than anyone turned inside out, starting at her head. Sally had not screamed, only emitted a surprised grunt before becoming 'not Sally.' Her body made no sense after the gameplay. The stab he felt in his gut was only that of one of her ribs poking him.

Freddie refused to watch the rest of the opposing team lose the game. He did not need to, as the sounds and screams were more than enough. Visuals would have overloaded his system. In the game's aftermath, some people informed Freddie how Sally was probably the luckiest of the group. Freddie took much comfort in that.

The voice or voices in their heads congratulated the winners and announced they would have the honor of competing again the following year along with some new contestants. Many too young now would finally be eighteen by then. Then, just like that, the voices (Aliens? Demons?) vanished. Well, the authoritative voices vanished, the sounds of screams still echoed in most survivors' heads.

········

Part of Freddie's strategy paid off in the end. Lindsey was indeed grateful for winning. As a result, Freddie lost his virginity to her the night of the big game. Freddie enjoyed it but figured not as much as Lindsey, who showed her pleasure by screaming at the top of her lungs the whole time. As a matter of fact, an hour after they finished, Lindsey still screamed.

Things changed after that day. There was zero unemployment as people who wanted to work could work, though most chose not to. The government legalized drugs both recreational and pharmaceutical. Happy hours at most bars included Zoloft and Xanax.

The game tested religious faiths. Many came up lacking. Far too many religious leaders took their flocks down Machiavellian paths, bringing into the light things they had long done secretly behind closed doors.

But there were some religious leaders who held firm to their beliefs and demanded the same of their patrons. Many revered those dwindling groups. Faith became scarcer than gold and people deemed those who maintained faith rich in ways the rest of the world could only dream of. Freddie figured if Sally were still around, she would lead a church herself. He tried not to miss her. What was the point?

Freddie continued dating Lindsey, who did not scream as much anymore but also did not really talk either. He figured that was okay, as he had a lot to say. Freddie was quick to brag about his days as a team captain and how he won the big game. Lindsey would twitch during his tales of glory, but likely because he told the story so well. It pleased him she never seemed to get sick of hearing about it. Well, sometimes she vomited, but that was likely bad food, nothing to do with his glory days.

As the next game day neared, Freddie felt a pang of jealousy that he would not be team leader again. But digging down deep into what remained of him, he decided he did not mind being only a contestant. It occurred to him that in the days when people bullied him, humiliated him and without fail picked him last? Well, truthfully, those were the good old days.

STARBUCKS

FOREST AVENUE - PORTLAND, MAINE

W hen I was writing this story, it was an idea I had while in my grad school program. Again, like one of the other stories I had in this collection, I didn't know it would eventually become part of a horror anthology and I actually started writing it back then but didn't finish it until recently in the above mentioned coffee shop. Back then, I was flooded with ideas for stories, most of them being horror, but I completed some of them before this one and eventually moved on until the coffee shop helped me flesh out the idea for the anthology. It finally has a home.

Portland is my life because I was born in that city. I was away for a while as I grew up in Lewiston, Maine… but then I returned as an adult and made it my home for almost a decade. I have so many great memories of the city and my time there during my late 20s and into my late 30s, but there are times also that I regret. While partying and drinking, sometimes you forget propriety and tact and some people I knew in my life unintentionally caused problems that didn't need to be there. I am also very interested in the paranormal and this story reflects both things in different ways. Treat others as you wish to be treated is a motto I live by.

This location was a store I worked in for a few years. It's very busy and isn't set up very well for drive-thru but manages just fine (it used to be an old Taco Bell). The café is on the smaller side but is very cozy, and the people are all friendly and that goes for customers and employees alike. I've had many an impromptu conversation in that café as I wrote this story and others, or as I sketched in my drawing pad. It's on the outskirts of Portland proper, but it's where the remnants of the real Portlanders are living these days.

ANKOU

JOSEPH CARRO

"Babe? Are we dead yet?"
"Not yet, Baby."
"Then when?"
"Soon, Baby, soon."
--Overheard at coffee shop

"I'm really, *really* hungry, you guys."

Micaelah and Mike weren't exactly listening to me at full capacity, because they were being disgustingly cute, playfully shoving one another while walking behind me on the cold streets of Portland, Maine. Devan, my boyfriend (basically my boyfriend, anyway—although we didn't label it) stared at me from my left, his dark eyes searching and expecting.

"Babe," I turned and said to him, "I'm gonna' die." He shrugged and looked at the other two, then back at me, implying it was their fault.

I sighed in exasperation and threw up my hands. *At least I tried.* We'd been walking around aimlessly in the Old Port for at least an hour and the bars would close soon. The food places even sooner than that. We'd probably have to resort to visiting the Burger King drive thru on Forest Avenue except I hated getting fast food (*a girl's gotta' watch her figure, amirite?*) and it seemed like that's all I'd eaten lately. Tonight, a rare night away from work at the hotel, it was nice to be outside with friends despite the cold. It was easy for work to take over your life, and I hated when I allowed it to happen. The hotel didn't own me, it's just where I spent most of my time.

Micaelah had been my friend for a few years now. We met in college (sharing a dorm at the University of Southern Maine). She was in the middle of a bout of laughter, her eyes closed, budding tears glistening in the streetlight, face raised skyward. Her brown hair hung down to her shoulders. She could barely stand up. She looked so *happy*.

Mike, her husband, hugged her around the waist as much to support himself as to share in her warmth and mirth. His slight frame rocked with hers, his features scrunched up into a smile, and his long hair culminated in a "man-bun" at the top of his head. I hadn't known Mike for as long as I'd known Micaelah, but the three of us had shared *a lot* over the past few years (including one another). It wasn't something Devan knew about yet; it also wasn't something that he needed to know at all. Ignorance was bliss. Devan sensed it, I thought, but so far hadn't figured it out. He just knew something was off about how we three acted when together.

I'd dated Devan for about eight months. He'd left behind a relationship just like I had. We both worked at a boutique hotel in Portland called The Arms. He was a line cook, and I was a restaurant night manager and we'd both cheated on our significant others but had otherwise remained with each other since. Sometimes, he annoyed the shit out of me, but other times he seemed pretty chill. Tonight was a mixture.

Micaelah and Mike had been bantering back and forth for the past fifteen minutes, both beyond the threshold of buzzing. I hadn't been able to break through that barrier all night. *Bonus annoyance points for me, I guess.* I followed their conversation here and there but ignored most of it as the rumbling in my stomach persisted and grew louder. I'd scratch someone's eyes out soon if we didn't find some damned french fries.

"You guys," I said, frustrated beyond belief. "What do you want to eat? Mike? Micaelah? Babe?" Babe was what I called Devan. He called me Baby.

Mike and Micaelah suddenly seemed to realize we were there. Mike lifted his heavy-lidded eyes, which were glossed over with laugh-tears. I stopped and ran a hand through my hair in a fidgety manner while resting the other against my hip, fingers drumming, waiting for the lovebirds to process what I'd said. Devan lowered his face and stayed silent.

"What?" Mike asked in a monotone voice. "Oh, food? I dunno... maybe grab a burger at Five Guys? I don't care."

"Ooh, only if they have chicken nuggies," Micaelah said, grabbing the front of Mike's coat and almost dragging him down into the snow with her.

"Baby," Devan said. "It's probably the only thing open unless we get some BK on the way home." I knew by the way he emphasized the word home, he wanted to leave.

"Yeah, you pick, Ash," said Micaelah, swaying and smiling in my direction.

Micaelah nuzzled her head into Mike's chest like a creature burrowing into the dirt to hibernate. I forced myself to look once I realized I'd been staring too long. Devan kicked a rock across the road. The noise reverberated up and down Wharf Street where I spent many nights in college drinking life away at Oasis or Amigo's.

I pulled away from Devan's grasp. "Five Guys it is. Keep up or lose out." I walked ahead, hearing the others follow.

I walked across the rain-slicked cobblestones that made up a good chunk of the walkways in the Old Port; remnants of a time gone by of horse-drawn carriages and canes and heeled shoes clacking against the ground, boisterous voices echoing across the wharf, buildings lit by candlelight before the first whisperings of electricity. Mike, Micaelah, and Devan stumbled along behind me, laughing at things, at each other, at me and my hunger.

"Wow, Ash," I heard Micaelah say. "You're so hangry. And fast. You should be in a marathon."

More laughing. I rolled my eyes. Drunks were never as fun to be around unless one was drunk themselves. I wished I were. Were that the case, we'd all be clambering around like newborn foals, clinging to each other while drowning out the world's sounds with laughter. Devan would never get drunk unless we were by ourselves at home, though. He didn't trust other guys, which meant he didn't trust me.

We rounded a corner, cobblestones giving way to the paved road and sidewalks of Congress Street. A few scattered cars rolled by, one of which was full of guys yelling something piggish out the window at me or at Micaelah or at both of us. I ignored it. Devan didn't, as usual. He shouted, calling them pieces of shit. I shook my head.

"I hate motherfuckers who do that shit," said Mike. "Think they can say whatever the hell they want to. Disrespectful motherfuckers."

"You tell 'em, babe," Micaelah said.

Devan stayed silent, and I knew he was boiling on the inside. Anytime another man talked to me or even looked at me, he'd get upset and rage on about it for hours. A couple of my friends had told me Devan seemed manipulative and controlling, but I just shrugged it off. *He was just protective.*

We reached Five Guys which stayed open until 2am on weekends. *Thank Christ.* I loved their fries, but when you're drunk, anything greasy tastes like some house-elves prepared it in the kitchens at Hogwarts. I was about to try them sober. Upon entering, a bored cashier looked me up and down as I strolled up to the counter.

"Hey, y'all," he said. He had a nose ring through his septum and scruff all over his face. He looked like someone I would have found attractive back in high school, when I was a scene kid. "What can I get for you tonight, beautiful?" His smile made me want to smile, but I kept it in check and fumbled around in my purse to hide my face.

Devan was immediately next to me. "We're gonna' have two burgers and a large order of fries. A large Sprite and a large Coke."

"Yeah, what he said."

The cashier went back to looking bored as he punched in the order on the screen, his ability to flirt hampered by Devan's presence.

"TWO PATTIES," the cashier shouted back to the cooks, as he finished ringing through Devan's debit card.

Devan nodded his head toward a table with four chairs. I walked over with him and took my coat off, placing it around the back of my chair. We sat and stared at one another as we listened to Micaelah and Mike labor their way through their own orders. Once we picked up the food, we all ate in relative silence before speaking. The hungry want in my stomach finally subsided enough for me to focus on something else. I dabbed the corners of my mouth with a napkin, my roiling stomach satisfied and content. Devan held my hand under the table, his hands clammy. He kept moving his thumbs around in circles.

"How's your food?" I asked of everyone after a while. Mike had bits of lettuce and mayo in the nether regions of his beard.

"Yo, this shit is bomb," he said, muffling his voice with another bite. "Excellent choice, Ash. Excellent choice."

"She's got good taste," Micaelah said, giving me a look and then Mike, who smiled. I felt Devan tap his foot.

"How was yours, Babe?" I asked, looking up at him. His dark hair spilled out from under a grey beanie, and I could make out portions of his neck tattoo poking out from above the neckline on his shirt. The tattoo was of a naked woman riding a horse. He had another tattoo of Johnny Cash giving the finger on his chest.

"It was good," he said.

Devan was self-conscious about his teeth, so he didn't like to talk much or smile in public. He was a former drug addict and lost his top teeth to drug abuse... something I didn't mind. Looks weren't everything. He had a lot to offer, aside from his talent as a chef and a musician. He knew a lot about music, and his band was getting more famous by the day. They'd blow up soon, I was sure of it.

"Word," said Mike, going in for a high five from Devan. "They're fries are the best. Local potatoes. Hand cut. Saw that on a sign out front."

Devan only looked at Mike, ignoring his high five.

"Yo, bro... you're just gonna' leave me hangin?"

"Yeah," Devan said.

Awkward. Awkward, awkward, awkward. I never knew what to talk to the two of them about, or even how to converse with Mike in a normal and familiar way with Devan around. I knew Devan would complain to me about the two of them later. For me, my threesome with Micaelah and Mike wasn't about anything other than physicality and it made me feel good to be the center of attention in such a powerful couple dynamic.

"I'll be right back," Devan said, getting up from the table. "Gotta' use the bathroom before we head home."

"Okay, babe," I said, watching him walk through the restaurant and disappear around a corner.

"Ash," Micaelah said, reaching out to grab my forearm. "Thank you so much. This was a fun night. Perfect way to end it; with a good burger."

"Yeah, Ash," Mike said, tousling my hair. "Hope it wasn't too weird for you. Devan seems kind of tense. He should smoke a J."

He looked into my eyes, trying to be honest and meaningful. It was hard to take him seriously with the bits of food on his chin and the glazed, dull look in his own eyes.

"No, it wasn't weird," I said. "He's just kind of an introvert."

"Weird for someone who's in a band," Micaelah said. "I don't get it."

"Me neither," Mike said, turning to look at Micaelah, who started laughing. "What?" he asked.

"Mike, baby, you've got some, um, food in your beard," Micaelah said.

He laughed and felt it. "Saving it for later."

"Nasty," Micaelah said. "After November I'm going to start a petition for you to shave that thing off your chin."

He shook his head before she'd finished speaking the words.

"No, no... not a chance."

"If you know what's good for you."

They were cute and weren't completely drunk any longer. Watching them interact reinforced in my mind what drew me to their relationship and why I'd let them talk me into a threesome several times. Once since I'd been with Devan. That dropped my stomach with guilt until remembering Devan had lied to me about his wife not being pregnant when he cheated on her with me. We all had ghosts in our closet.

"It's my face, baby," Mike said. He stroked his beard and smiled, looking back over at me. I smiled back.

"Maybe I'll grow my own beard then," Micaelah said, taunting.

"Yo, that'd be lit. We could rub beards."

"Totally," she said, tousling his beard and then his hair.

There was an uncomfortable silence and then they forgot I was there again.

"You guys all done with your stuff?" I asked, gathering the trays and napkins, piling them on top of one another so they'd be easy to carry.

"Oh, yeah. Can't eat another fry," Mike said.

As I moved toward the trashcan, Devan came out of the bathroom, rubbing at his nose. I hoped he hadn't done coke. He'd promised he'd quit. But his coworkers in the kitchen at The Arms partied 24/7 and somehow fit work into their busy cocaine schedules.

"Baby," he said, coming toward me. "I'll get it."

"No, really, it's fine. I can take it up there."

Ignoring me, he grabbed the trays and trash out of my hands and walked over toward the waste bins. I held up my hands in exasperation. Mike and Micaelah gave a weak grin.

So awkward.

"So, Mike and I were thinking if maybe you guys wanted, you could crash at our place since it's closer?"

"Yeah?" I replied. *Great. Here we go.*

I looked over at Devan and I knew before turning that he'd already be staring, steel-gazed into a firm *no*. And he was.

"I don't think so," I said. "Devan has to be in at six tomorrow."

"Okay," Mike said, throwing on his coat. "I lost my buzz. Let's skip out of here." He seemed to be half-correct. His eyelids no longer drooped as much, and he seemed to focus on the two of us individually.

"Okay, baby," Micaelah said, putting on her own coat.

Devan found my coat and handed it to me, and I slipped it on while the others walked outside into the chill air. The cashier winked at me before I left. This time, I didn't feel like smiling back.

We all exited the warmth of the store and it seemed as if it had somehow become colder and windier during our time eating burgers in the heated restaurant. The wind seemed eager to steal my breath with every gust, an invisible thief.

Having parked next to one another, we walked back down to Wharf Street and its cobblestones. The moon was out and shining full force, with a small halo of light surrounding its orb. Someone, sometime, told me it meant there was going to be a storm. It sure smelled like snow was in the air. Water shimmered in the distance and every once in a while we heard an air horn blast from somewhere in the dark, from up toward Munjoy Hill. My feet had been aching without my realizing it. I was finally feeling it. Blisters formed around my heels. I stumbled ahead of the trio, listening to bits of conversation.

"Hey, slow down Usain," said Micaelah. Mike laughed. Devan was silent, as he had been since the car full of guys had driven by earlier.

"Mr. Bolt," Mike said, still laughing, "Can we get your autograph?"

I turned around, walking backward, hands in my coat pockets to protect them from the wind. My hair pushed out from underneath my wool hat and blew past my ears, framing my face in blonde streaks and temporarily muffling the breeze and making me blind.

"Sorry, but I'm freezing," I said, spitting out strands of my hair. There was definitely a hint of annoyance there, which I realized had been building after Devan had denied another potential encounter with Mike and Micaelah, though it shouldn't have surprised me in the least. "Nothing against any of you slow asses, but I'm tired and freezing. I want to go home."

"Baby," Devan said, taking his hands out of his pockets and rushing forward. "Look out!"

"Omigosh," Micaelah said, mouth open in shock.

"What are you guys…" I turned while pushing my hair out of my eyes, my response cut off as the world went crazy.

My brain failed to register fast enough for me to stop, or get out of the way as I collided with—what? A person? Upon contact, a series of images and sensations, created by the chaos of the moment, flashed through my mind. They burned like photographs into my thoughts and would remain with me forever.

A wall of darkness, black against even the dark of the sky, in the shape of a man. A voice like two soap stones grinding together to form a single word. "Ankou". A cart. The sweet and sickening smell of decay. Cold like I've never felt before or since. Slate-grey eyes somehow even colder than that. Hard features set into leathery, ash-colored skin. Flowing cloth, tattered hems. Long, stringy black hair trickling down over a long white neck that looked like marble. I stumble. Pain throbs in my head, the front of my skull, like hammers. I feel the breath go out of me. Muffled yelling and screaming invades my ears. I'm being cradled. Ears ringing. The taste of copper in my mouth, the taste of fear. I piss myself, feeling the temporary warmth spread to my back and legs… which soon chills with the wind.

"… I said get away from her, motherfucker!"

"What's… happ…" I began, unable to finish the words, unable to move my mouth the way I wanted to at that precise moment. I was somewhere between conscious and unconscious. Had someone roofied me? Maybe the cashier? He winked at me before I left, after all. "… *ening.*" *What's happening*? *Why couldn't I say it out loud*? *What was an Ankou*? Whatever it was, it hurt to think the word.

"Baby, call the police," Micaelah said, cradling me. "He just keeps staring at us. Why won't he move? Why won't he talk?"

My eyes slid open. I saw a man, maybe six or seven feet tall, which was hard to tell because of his hat. It's a wide-brimmed one like Hugh Jackman wore in *Van Helsing*. This guy was no Hugh Jackman, that's for sure. He sported a long black duster. The cloth rustled like a bunch of dead leaves, a sound which grew louder as I met his gaze. I found I could not stare too long because my eyelids felt like there were thousands of tiny spiders crawling underneath them. My eyes water. I close them and scream. Micaelah joins in.

When I opened them again, Devan charged the dark figure, hurling himself, fists flying until he connected with Van Helsing's chin. With a sickening snap, Devan's hand broke. He dropped hard, shaking, and convulsing on the cobblestones, his hand forgotten and limp. Threat extinguished, Van Helsing took one last look through his soulless eyes, then dragged his cart down Wharf Street before disappearing around a corner toward the water.

It took several minutes before we got ourselves together. The wooden wheels continued to echo on the cobblestones as the creepy stranger moved away from us. As soon as the mysterious man disappeared around the corner, I felt better again. Micaelah helped me up as the disoriented haze finally lifted. Was the mysterious homeless man (Ankou?) ever actually there in the first place? Or only a crazy fever dream?

"Thanks, Micaelah," I said, my legs shaking, embarrassed to discover I had peed my pants. A huge wet spot covered my jeans. I abandoned thoughts of modesty to rush to Devan. Once out of my fugue, I realized I must've been in shock, as Devan had already been lying unconscious for minutes.

"Somebody, call the police!" I shouted. "Help!"

· · • •• • • • ··

It took about twenty minutes for the paramedics to arrive. They loaded Devan onto a stretcher and into the back of the ambulance. Though alive, his bowels had released into his jeans. His hand, broken by punching the mysterious stranger, appeared infected and gangrenous. They would eventually amputate it to save the rest of his arm, but that wasn't until much later.

Mike and Micaelah returned home while I waited with Devan in the ICU of the Maine Medical Center. The waiting area was small but there was a sunlit hallway just short of it that looked out into the garden area. It was empty but looked peaceful and gave me a little comfort. Micaelah texted me multiple times, but I never answered. I didn't want to talk to anyone.

· · • •• • • • ··

Days later, Devan's condition worsened. His mother, Judy, a constant presence, barred me from seeing him after my initial visit. He died a few days later, and from what I understood, his entire body had broken down and rotted from the inside. I felt like I was rotting from the inside, too, throwing up frequently, and I couldn't sleep. Reporters hounded me outside of work for the inside scoop, wanting to know if we'd contracted a disease or illness. I did my best to evade them.

It shocked me to learn Mike ended up in the hospital a day later. His eyesight vanished when his eyes dried to husks overnight in his sleep. I spent the day crying when I found out. Micaelah wouldn't return my texts or calls and after a while, I gave up. If she wanted to, she'd get back to me.

· · · ● ● · ● ● · · ·

Two days after hearing about Mike, I was opening the hotel restaurant dining room during an early shift and grew nauseous and light-headed. Was I pregnant? It was the last thought on my mind before I slipped into unconsciousness. It felt like I was tumbling down a massive, bottomless hole. When I woke, I found myself strapped to a gurney at the hospital. Cold oxygen blew into my nostrils via a breathing apparatus. I had an IV in my arm, which made my legs tingle.

A nurse hovered nearby, checking the fluid bags attached.

"Oh, you're awake," said the nurse. She was stocky with blonde hair, but had a pretty face.

"What happened?" I asked.

"We're trying to figure that out ourselves," she said. "Are you comfortable? Can we get you some pillows?"

"I'm fine," I said. "Can you call my friend Micaelah?"

"Of course, honey," she said.

The nurse called Micaelah's number, but it turned out she was already in the hospital. I eventually spoke to her mother, Anne, who informed me Micaelah was dying. I asked about Mike and learned he passed. That day, my teeth began falling out. I would have taken it harder, but it was the least of my worries. I struggled just to breathe. Each breath was like taking air in through a straw-sized hole with a wet paper towel covering the other end.

The hospital staff soon only entered my room with hazmat suits. I only learned that through touch and when I asked them what they were wearing. My eyes no longer opened. All I wanted to do was sleep, and that's what I did. Soon, Micaelah, Mike, and Devan were all forgotten. I relived some memories of my mother and father, which seemed so long ago.

· · • • • • • • · ·

I'm tired and wish to sleep, waking as little as possible. My chest hurts when I wake, so I don't want to be awake anymore. I've had glimpses of Devan, hitched to the wooden cart of that mysterious man who looked like Van Helsing. Devan, Mike, Micaelah, all hitched to the wooden cart while the mysterious figure sits at the forefront. When I look more closely, I see my friends hitched in a gruesome manner. Large iron hooks gouged into their backs and tight harnesses bind their heads and waists. Their palms and knees are bloody, and a dark red trail leads off into nowhere. There appears to be a spot open for me.

"Why are you doing this?" I say to the figure, who stares at me. That is when I realize I am somewhere else. For back in the hospital, I cannot see.

He answers in the soap-stoned voice. "I am the Ankou, and your souls are mine to collect. You have earned your places carrying my wagon."

I feel a sharp pain in my chest. Images flash back and forth between the hospital realm and this one. Are any places real? Am I? I glimpse doctors and nurses trying to jumpstart my heart with a defibrillator, but I sink further and further into the world of the Ankou as my physical body dies.

After a surge of pain, I find myself naked like the rest of them, strapped to the front of the wagon. I look over at Devan. There are tears in his eyes. I feel the hooks tighten and a barbed whip lashes out at our wounded, exposed flesh. We unwillingly crawl forward on bloody hands and knees into the void.

UNURBAN COFFEE SHOP

SANTA MONICA, CA

U nurban Coffee Shop is a cultural oasis in a slick studio town. Art of varying levels adorn every open space of the shop. Old school paper fliers are strewn about or hung haphazardly in spots where artwork does not adorn the walls.

The bathroom is New York city studio apartment small, and the chairs are a mish mosh of different styles and generations, which could also describe the clientele. A mix of ages flows through the doors. Writers write, singers sing in a rear lounge space. Occasionally a comedy night may break out.

From time to time, one might encounter a studio exec type gabbing on his phone, unaware of the vibe of the place, unaware of the creative energy he is sucking from the room. Most folks are aware, however, and friendly with one another.

The offerings are vegan, a plus for the type of neighborhood. This shop is a waystation for those crossing the border from West Los Angeles to Santa Monica. From hippy-light to full-blown hippy territory.

Like its name, the place is unique. It does truly stand out as a place worth visiting for more than just its fine coffee. It is an experience where anything can happen.

More than anything though, the place is what one might call—Strange.

STRANGE

PAUL CARRO

Okay ladies, this article you are reading is not your normal self-help or spruce up your love life fare. This one is a little different, a little more real world than your normal reading habits might provide. Brace yourself for a real horror story, no fairy tale endings or beginnings, just the hardcore truth here. That truth is all men like strange. I know you do not wish to hear it. I bet a lot of you are saying, "not my man!" If you are one of those spouting such a denial, all I can say is, wise up! What part of ALL men do you not understand?

Forgive me. A little harsh in the delivery, but I needed to get your attention. You really need to listen because all that advice you are getting from Oprah, The View, and other feminine gurus is wishful thinking. This document is the ultimate self-help article but to benefit you must first admit men have a problem, ergo you have a problem. I am not putting the onus on you. In fact, I am cutting you all some slack by noting how it is all mostly on the dude. I would be remiss not to mention that some of you hasten men's straying eyes more than others, though.

So why offer this advice? Why am I authoring this article in a tone and language that is far less glossy than the model on the cover? Maybe because I do not own an airbrush. Ha! Sorry, there is not much in this article that lends itself to humor so I feel the need to fit it in where I can.

The real reason for my styling is because despite being a writer with only rejection slips under my belt, I finally found an editor with the balls to take a chance on me. You are holding a quality piece of merchandise in your hands. I urge you to read everything this editor does.

Okay, that is the technical answer to why I am offering sage advice. But what prompted me to consider writing such an article? I have stood in one too many checkout lanes in supermarkets. You surely have seen the headlines, maybe even read the articles: 'Ten Ways to Keep Your Man,' 'Positions Guaranteed to Drive Him Wild,' 'How to Leave Him Begging for More.' You get the idea. After noticing such articles for years, I needed to put in my two cents—per word, that is. Sorry, my last joke. I promise.

The truth is one can only delay the inevitable for so long. Men will seek strange no matter how well or how often you massage their—well, let us call them egos. I must give thanks to the magazines that peddle sexually adventurous advice, however. At minimum they provide women twelve different moves a year to keep men entertained. The editors of those magazines obviously understand that which I do about men. Therefore, they publish in a cycle reminding women to keep things fresh as possible every thirty days. Sadly, those magazines could go weekly (and some probably are) and we men would still find our eyes wandering for at least a full day or two before the newest issue arrived.

"I know I'll get to try a new magazine inspired position from the love of my life tomorrow night, but wow, I wonder what that barista at Starbuck's could do under the sheets," is something a man might say despite your weekly reading habits.

I am certain you are familiar with the adage: 'Opinions are like assholes. Everyone has one and they all stink.' Substitute the word men for 'opinions,' and the statement remains accurate. That is where I come in. I have an informed opinion on this subject. I am honest enough to admit I am the word listed above. Yes, I am a—man. Fine, I am the second word as well.

Who am I to offer advice? Why should you listen to someone like me instead of a Kardashian? Maybe because a Kardashian never thought of sleeping with your sister like I did. Maybe because a Kardashian did not fantasize about sleeping with a bridesmaid at your best friend's wedding. Perhaps because my best buddy at work, Toni, is not a guy at all but a woman who might be a Los Angeles five but a Michigan ten.

You should listen to me because a Kardashian pushes ideals. That clan could make their followers get crazy over pirates on romance novel covers if they considered it trendy. You know the swoon worthy type. But men? We are the real pirates. We strategize how to steal both forms of your booty. Only one of us is real, and I know it is not the anointed family.

Now the funny thing is, men really try to fight it. We desire to be the loyal, faithful man any woman could be proud of. We understand women talk and what they talk about. Our ideal is to treat you so well you might claim us as your best in bed. Or (more importantly) your biggest. Collectively, we understand that the happier you are with us, the better you will endow us in your stories.

So, given that knowledge, one could assume men would run from strange in exchange for standing out with our BAE. One might assume, but they would be wrong, as wrong as the day couples exchange vows. Unfortunately, the whole moth to a flame thing exists in the un-fairer sex (I admit it, we are not fair). However, unlike the moth, men do not flutter all over the place, they dive right in.

The thrust of my article is not how to avoid your man chasing strange but how to recognize it. A warning if you will. The more information you have, the better your chances at stopping things before he crosses a line. At worst, you can document the event to use as ammunition in divorce proceedings. (See? I am a helpful guy.) Then there are those of you who are a little more forgiving, with higher tolerances for strange chasing than others. I am not here to judge. Like I said, this ain't no fairy tale.

What follows is an example of what to watch for. It contains intimate details of just such an occurrence. Why? Because it happened to me. Or more accurately, it happened to my wife. The man always gets the benefits of strange while subjecting the women to the repercussions.

Despite all I have shared so far, there is a caveat. If a man placed a ring on that finger of yours, you did something right. There was a brief time in my relationship where I walked around like a grinning fool, feeling fortunate to have found someone as beautiful as my wife. My wife is blonde as blondes are wont to be. The way the sun would catch her hair, and twinkle off her violet eyes, literally caused me to catch my breath. At the start, seeing her for the first thousand times was like seeing her that first time.

Every workday I kissed that beauty in the doorway, lingering, calling her names, declaring my love before heading out to work. Once at work, I continued declaring my love to any coworkers who would listen. The number willing to accommodate my blustering eventually shrank. Many took my gushing as a mockery of their own stale relationships. They grew annoyed with me for being blinded by love while I grew angry at them for being cynical about the same.

Ah, what a difference a year makes. A fire can only burn so long whether it be a candle, a structural fire, or that tire fire in Pennsylvania. That last one is a poor example I suppose. That tire fire has been burning forever.

Another piece of advice in this article: if anyone around you appears cynical about love, understand the correct term is experience. If you are still reading, I assume you already labelled me a cynic. Along with a variety of four-letter words. But I wear the label like a badge of honor. In the end, cynics are usually correct in hindsight.

I am not writing this advice piece from the position of a relationship guru. I am not a relationship doctor here to provide sweet slogans designed to sugarcoat marital problems. Instead, I write as a man of experience. I am an individual who (like many of you currently) believed love could last forever. But alas, reality showed its ugly mug. Trust me when I say reality wields a tremendously large blade and does not miss much when it cleaves.

So how did I go from the loving walking on air husband to the everyman seeking strange? Allow me to relate it in ways that you may understand. Every day I come home and throw my dress shirts in the hamper. When my wife does laundry, she finds one arm turned inside out on EVERY SINGLE shirt. She clarified that the whole shirt turned inside out would be tolerable, but only one sleeve on EVERY SINGLE shirt somehow riled her sensibilities.

Occasionally her eye twitches when she speaks about it. I could go on about the other "little" things I do that set her off, except I figure you already have a list of such incidents in your own life. Your issues are more personalized than mine so what is the point of me sharing more? You get the idea.

Those things that drive you crazy, that seem never ending no matter how many times you talk about them? That, my dear reader, is what we call a two-way street. Do not get me started on the makeup crap lying around everywhere. By the way, the courting stage when the only face we ever saw was a made up one designed to entice? When we finally see the tools of your transformation taking up every free inch of the bathroom, it feels like someone pulled back the curtain in Oz. Quite disappointing.

We may not bring the issue up as often as you do your grievances with us, but believe me when I say women drive us crazy as well. Men deal with things differently, whether an extra drink, more time at work, or trips to the golf course.

I recently took up running (which is a warning sign by the way ladies). If your man suddenly wants to spruce his goose with a workout routine after living on the couch for so long then he is likely sprucing for someone new, not the woman around whom he has been a slob lo these many years.

At the very least (as in my case) he wants out—of the house, that is. The wife complaining about my lack of structure in both life and body took a toll. I could not stand the griping any longer, so decided running was a great way to prove I could get my body back. Though mostly it was just to get away from her constant yapping about my shortcomings.

The very first day running, I learned an amazing number of women walk their dogs in Los Angeles. I noticed at least a dozen. Each dog was obnoxiously friendly, as if trained to sniff out potential mates for their female masters. I can attest that it was not only dogs wagging their tails that day.

Now I know, I know, you want to call me misogynistic then go ahead. I would only argue that sometimes truth is not misogynistic therefore neither am I. I can only express my truth. There is a reason I am being so forthcoming and hardened in my words. You will understand in time, so for now let me continue to tell my tale. Label me all you want, knock yourself out, but I am going somewhere with this.

Occasionally I spotted a woman in my West Los Angeles neighborhood walking her dog in mussed up hair or a dowdy wardrobe. I learned to take those individuals for happily involved with someone as they paid no attention to me or any other neighborhood men. They were likely in their own love-struck phase with a lover. Or I simply did not float their boat, or possibly they played for another team. All of that is fine, refreshing even.

There was more to experience out in the great old world than simply dog walkers. I encountered female joggers who wore tops designed to move with them as they bounced around the neighborhood. With dog walkers, one could stop and chat, but the permanent motion of joggers allowed only smiles and head nods. Over time, the minimal interactions grew a comfortable familiarity with an end goal of eventually running together. (With the possibility of more. So much more.)

By the time I took up running, my desire for strange was strong, but the wedding band on my hand kept me in check. Still, strange remained the key word. If I got too familiar with any of the women on my route, they eventually became 'un-strange' so to speak. Familiarity bred boredom. That is what you are up against, ladies. I had not even made physical contact, but talking to them too often dulled my desires.

If someone new came along, however, then it was all stations go all over again. At least to start.

One day I encountered a woman who was clearly too young for me. She was a student from the college listed on her shirt—UCLA. She was brunette, in amazing shape with a midriff that showed off a belly button piercing that matched the one in her upper lip. Her tattoos were what I would consider tasteful. We passed each other twice in opposing circular routes. Each time we shared smiles and nods.

On the third go around, she stopped to talk, running in place. She asked me the threesome question. No, not that kind. If that is where your mind went, then maybe you too, dear reader, are also seeking strange. No, she asked: name, occupation, and residence. I must have passed whatever mental tests she ran because she announced a desire to visit my home. Fate sometimes gives things a push. A car swerved around the corner, almost hitting the two of us. In our initial exuberance, we had stopped mid street.

The near miss forced her to leap into me as we both narrowly averted the disaster. After the car passed with horn blaring, she gazed at me. We shared a nervous laugh before she announced she was eager to take a tumble of a different sort. While desirous to experience strange, the car had knocked at least a little sense into me. I remembered how my wife was at the same home the young thing wished me to take her to.

I suggested her place instead. She suggested her boyfriend would not appreciate my presence. Oh, one more thing, ladies. Not only must you worry about guys, but the upcoming generation of females. They are of a take no prisoners mindset regarding instant gratification.

My UCLA buddy smiled and suggested we rendezvous some other time before running on her way. A block away, she looked over her shoulder and winked. Vixen. I get it; you dislike the way I talk about her, objectifying her? She started it. Our intentions were mutual, despite us both being spoken for. See how this works?

So, there it is, ladies. The cheating did not happen but would have if my wife had not been home. I would have partaken of strange. Even though I felt a rush of excitement as I ran, I also experienced guilt. I understood how close I came to a transgression. Maybe there is some hope in the male species after all. The guilt, however, did not keep me from dreaming of Ms. UCLA that night. I never saw her again after that day. Soon, it would no longer matter to me. Things were about to change.

Two weeks after my near infidelity, I dug deep and recommitted to my relationship. I used the energy born of my runs to return home and tear up the house with my wife. While uncertain what came over me, she enjoyed it, as did I. My wife is beautiful and sexy, hence the reason I put a ring on it. She makes me laugh and to be honest I consider her my best friend. You know there is a 'but' coming though, right? And I do not mean my wife's butt as cute and firm as it is.

After a few months of freshly renewed wedded bliss, I considered myself cured of the need for strange. Remember the article I dreamed up one day while in that checkout line? I considered whether I ever needed to write it. I even adapted to the general hotness of the regulars around the neighborhood, categorizing them as nothing more than running buddies now and forever.

Until THE woman in the window.

Now one might think of West Los Angeles as a big city to those who never traveled to it, but the area comprises many quiet tree-lined streets blended with rows of apartment complexes. My jogs took me past many such complexes.

One day I arrived along a row of apartments far removed from the omnipresent traffic of the area. The street was west of the 405, which gave it a nice quiet feeling far removed from the hustle and bustle of normal city life. The roar of the freeway in the distance could easily be mistaken for the crashing waves of the beaches in nearby Santa Monica.

Many apartments comprised a dozen units or fewer, unlike cattle call housing units found in more dense areas of the city. Well-tended trees, yards, and flora lined a long stretch, making it one of my favorite routes. Because I passed by so often, it was odd that I never noticed her before. Maybe the correct word was strange.

I could only see the woman from breasts to head. The woman sat in a chair at a desk just inside a window on a second floor. She was striking. A lovely woman with hair flowing over her shoulders so far that I could not spot where the locks ended from my position in the street. The woman's nationality eluded me. Asian, I surmised.

She was reading or writing in a book of considerable size which lay open on the desk before her. It reminded me of encyclopedia volumes from the days before the internet. She appeared studious, immersed in the book's subject, which is why it surprised me so when she noticed my stare.

I watched her from the far side of the street even as my run brought me nearer to her window. I could not take my eyes off the beauty as I drew closer. There was something about her that seemed so innocent. Despite appearing as bookish as a librarian, there was an exotic look to her, one which screamed sexuality. I was trying to wrap my brain around the dichotomy born of a single glance when she met my gaze and smiled.

The smile was brief (bashful?). A quick flash of teeth and sparkling brown eyes before she turned shyly away. Her long locks dropped over part of her face. Rather than hide her beauty, it merely highlighted it. Before I could return the smile, I stumbled over an invisible obstacle.

Pulling myself together, red faced at my clumsiness, I turned back, only to discover her smile remained in place. Apparently, she was a fan of my folly. In my embarrassment, I ran off, not looking back.

Within an hour, I knew I was in trouble. I had never run so far before. Somehow, I ran all the way to Venice Beach. Though locals consider West LA beach adjacent (realtors take advantage as do landlords) the distance was beyond what I knew my limits to be. Worse, my mind raced with thoughts of the woman the entire way. This was abnormal.

Having not consumed any water along the way, I retreated to the nearest beachside snack bar, where I purchased an overpriced bottle and drank my fill. The distance caught up to me in the form of painful leg cramps. I considered calling my wife for a lift because the walk back to my place would take hours. Any more running was out of the question for the day.

My mind was in a fog as I tried to shake off how beautiful the woman was. It was ridiculous that someone could be that beautiful. I mean, she was too young for me, right? Or was it too old? I could not determine her age, no matter how much I thought about it. No bother, she looked amazing for any age.

And then I noticed I was in real trouble because two cute tourists were heading in my direction on the Venice Boardwalk. They were stunning, wearing barely there bikinis in 'notice me' neon colors. They grinned widely while asking me (in heavy German accents) where to have fun in the area.

Their grins subsided as I coldly guided them to the nearest hot spots, culminating in my wish that they enjoy their stay in America. As they shrugged and moved on, I internally kicked myself, wondering what was wrong with me. I had encountered the 'strange' gold standard—female tourists, no links to the city, traveling in a pair, no less. Yet I not only failed to make a move, but it never occurred to me. The entire time I only wondered whether the woman in the window would still be there when I returned.

It took an hour and a half walking to get back to the familiar environs of West LA. I could have arrived home much sooner by utilizing a major street like Olympic Boulevard (my original plan) but I stuck to back roads ensuring I would pass the woman in the window's apartment once again. (I had no reason to expect her to be in the same spot though.)

Take note ladies, this is when I tried—and I mean really tried—to change my course of action. All I had to do was use Olympic Boulevard. Do not pass Go, do not look at the woman in the window. Yet somehow my feet drew me back to where I first spotted her.

When I reached her apartment, I stationed myself across the street and looked up, surprised to find her in the same place. I assumed she would have abandoned the book for dinner, a nap, or some TV maybe. It felt strange that she could sit for that long.

The book remained open. She used a finger on the pages as if reading in braille. Were her breasts bigger than before? Like many guys, I am a breast man. If I did not know better, a part of me considered whether she somehow determined the preference from my initial gaze-a-thon earlier and adjusted her look. Impossible.

She smiled, and my legs went weak. I understood it was from the too long run. Never would I feel such a thing merely from the presence of a woman. Yet I did. See what strange can do, ladies? This is what you are up against. I knew I was up against something I could no longer fight.

Somewhere in the back of my mind lived the thought of my wife waiting for me. The sight of this woman stirred me enough to guarantee my wife a great time when I returned home. Except the idea of applying such raw energy to the familiar felt a waste. There was newness right before me.

The woman pushed her hair back over her ear and traced a hand toward cleavage. She smiled again at me before returning to the book. I understood if I did not leave immediately, I would make a choice that would change my relationship forever.

The answer was obvious. Put one foot in front of the other and return home. Instead, I crossed the street. I looked up, closer now, hoping she might see me as clearly as I could see her. Did not want buyer's remorse on either end if we were going to do this. From below the open window, her scent caught the breeze. Floral, elusive, unique. Strange.

Excitement rushed through me. This was the moment readers where I gave in. I knew right then there was nothing I wanted more on the earth than to enter the woman above, to be inside her. Nothing else mattered. I was awestruck by her beauty.

Without a word spoken, I pointed at myself, then at the doorway. She licked her lips slightly. The sight of her tongue drove me wild. I wanted to taste it, to taste her. She did not nod, did not signal her intention other than offering the sweetest sound I ever heard in my life. She buzzed me in.

Where her buzzer was, I could not be sure, but clearly it was near her desk. (Likely the push of a button from a cellphone.) I rushed to the door before either of us could change our minds.

Despite my eagerness and hunger, I stumbled upon entering the hallway. It appeared so dark after hours of sun. I took a moment to adjust to the light. A small hallway bisected the apartment complex, with three rooms on either side of a narrow hall. A stairway ran straight up just past the entrance, which would lead to her floor. What I found odd, (strange?) about the complex was a preponderance of books. Shelves lined the entire length of the hall, filled with volumes of books, mostly thick, some thin. Many appeared so old I would think they were book versions of antiques. I believe rare is the term.

The smell of the pages threatened to overwhelm me until her scent danced down the stairs. I could not place the fragrance, but it filled me with a rush of warmth and a need to sniff it from the source.

I climbed the stairs, noticing how books even lined the stairwell walls, filling shelves tilted at weird angles but straight enough to hold. Quick glimpses of the volumes revealed names, which meant nothing to me. With every step, my heart beat faster. This was the moment. I was about to abandon everything involved in my current love life. I never wanted a woman more, and all I had done so far was watch her through a window.

Her scent grew heavier as I neared. No longer could I smell the mustiness of the tomes on the walls, nor did I care why they were there. Nothing mattered anymore except finding her. Who cared what line of work prompted her collection? The scent of the woman swirled around me, and I felt almost drunk as I ascended. I stopped midway and realized I was growing erect.

My teenage year had long passed, yet I continued growing hard. See what "strange" can do ladies? Apparently, it also serves as a time machine. When was the last time your man involuntarily grew erect at just the thought of you?

The smell overwhelmed me as I crested the top stair and stepped gingerly onto the second floor, fearful of waking myself or the woman of my dreams. A hallway opened before me, filled with more books. Based on how she overlooked the street, she would be in the first room.

An obstacle stood in the way. The door was closed. Was there a buzzer to be had here, too? She wanted me to enter, correct? If I opened that door and read her signals wrong, she would be within her right to call the police or defend herself. But she knew I was here. She had to. I felt my pulse quicken, felt it lining up with hers. Through the door, I could almost sense her excitement. It was palpable.

I touched the door and had to stop myself. I almost lost control. I grew so excited I thought I was about to pre-mature myself. Her scent was too much. One of the first things I planned to ask was what the scent was. But after I ravaged her, after going HAM on her.

I lost all sense of modicum. The woman brought out an animalistic side I was unaware of. I threw the door open, which revealed a study with a desk sitting under the window. Candles, spread throughout the room, flickered with delight. I froze in the doorway. What I saw eluded my ability to comprehend.

The woman technically sat at the desk, but there was no chair to be found. Her torso from chest up appeared as I knew it to be from the window. But just below her tits, (the area I could not see from the street) her body comprised a gelatinous blob. Massive, wide, spreading across the room almost as far as the door.

Her lower body could have emerged from an enormous Jell-O mold. It jiggled the same as the desert. Its shimmering proved hypnotic. The color was a soft sparkly pink, reminiscent of the banana seat of so many girl's bikes in the neighborhood where I grew up.

The woman in the window maintained her posture and continued reading her book, never looking back even as her scent drew me inexplicably closer. Her presence terrified me. This was no woman. The thing was worse than any nightmares from my youth. Running away was in order, despite my exhaustion.

Inexplicably, I stepped closer. With every inch closer to the odor, I grew more turgid, harder than I thought possible at my age. It was then I disrobed. A shoe first, then a sock. Soon I flailed wildly, needing to be nude, needing to be with her.

It was wrong. The massive gel continued to shudder, to quake and even ooze toward my feet. I found myself naked, erect, drawn to her in ways I could not understand. The need to experience her superseded any other thoughts, even my earlier fear. I stepped forward and reached out. As I touched the very edge of her pink mass, I instantly orgasmed. It was involuntary and shook my body. I closed my eyes in an ecstasy I never could have imagined. When the waves of pleasure subsided, my erection remained and felt ready for round two. My legs, however, had enough.

Whether the pleasure robbed me of the inability to stand, or the running, I stumbled, falling into her pink. She caught me gently with her blob glistening with the softness of silk. I lay atop her body mass and soon felt an embrace, a hug from her wetness, as if a thousand people were caressing me. I sensed thousands of voices entering my mind as I slid into her body.

Slipping into her slickness was easy. I may have orgasmed again. I lost all sense of where pleasure began and ended. The scent kept me floating in my head, somewhere far away, somewhere wonderful. The woman at the window opened herself to receive me and swallowed me whole. I floated in a vastness where I could still see the room, but through the eyes of thousands before me.

I am uncertain how long I remained inside her, or how long she wanted me there. I never technically authored the article mentioned here. She penned it for me (or for you). It was in my mind, the plans to write such a self-help guide. The idea came to me when I saw a woman's magazine while shopping. It occurred to me women might need a real world kick in the ass. This is likely not being read in a checkout line. The words most likely appear in a different kind of book.

The article that I planned to write? The one you are reading, and the nice publisher I spoke of? I still do not know her name, but I am one with her, and she penned my stories for me. All the ones I planned to write (along with a lifetime of memories). Even now I see through the woman in the window's eyes as she smiles at a beautiful young woman walking along the street down below.

Carrying an armful of groceries, the young woman stops suddenly confused, perhaps excited. She stops to look at the woman in the window despite being burdened with a heavy load. I can see (sense?) the pedestrian's nipples harden through her top. The woman turns, shakes her head, then departs, but I am certain she will return. That coed will eventually climb the same stairs I did. Just in time too, because I can tell the woman in the window is all but done writing my lifetime of thoughts, ideas, and stories.

Then again, if you are reading this, you are too close, as the saying goes. Maybe you are her next volume. Maybe you climbed those stairs and opened a book along the way. The one with my name on the spine. No matter how you discovered these words, my story is nearing its end.

The woman in the window is ready for some strange.

ALFRED'S

WEST HOLLYWOOD, CA

Alfred's in West Hollywood near famed Melrose Avenue is what I would consider a speakeasy. While there is traditional outdoor seating nestled on a great street for people watching, given how the neighboring shops are those of high-end designer clothing.

Just past the green oasis of outdoor seating, one steps into a cramped indoor seating area where all heads turn when anyone enters. People watching from the interior as well. A lot of beautiful people flow through the doors of this shop, so not all people watching is celebrity related, it is also a primal, lizard part of the brain people watching.

Once one passes the gauntlet of swiped right couples, and incognito screenwriters on laptops, to get to the coffee, one must enter the speakeasy by travelling down a flight of stairs leading underground.

We shall call the size of the actual coffee shop "quaint." Intimate might be more appropriate because it is easy to invade someone else's personal space in such tight quarters. The staff is exceptional and too bright for the vampiric underground style lighting.

They talk coffee with a knowledge bordering on PHD level. These baristas are not yeomen (and women) they are connoisseurs. Sounds great, right? It is but also feels too good to be true.

In the bowels of this basement people sit too close, whisper despite the loud music blaring overhead, attempting to keep secrets in a space designed to hold none. What other reason might people hook up in such an intimate space for if not to keep witnesses around during transactions of one sort or another.

Could it be actors and actresses meet producers in an environment designed to create visibility leading to buzz about upcoming projects? Maybe they hope to rope in the trades or blind items with rumors designed to grow until becoming reality.

Perhaps the reverse is the case. Keep witnesses around to stave off a casting couch situation. Given the locale it is easy to imagine many scenarios. Surely influencers would snap pictures in a place like this, maybe holding one of the shop's famous mustache cups over their face.

Influencers. Thousands of followers, but how many actual friends? It is an interesting thought. When an influencer kills their site and stops broadcasting, does anyone inquire about their health or do they fade away with time as if they never existed at all. Or do they live on forever? This story, inspired by this coffee shop, explores those questions all while celebrating a great cup of coffee.

KOPI DARAH

PAUL CARRO

Destiny made her displeasure known to all, up to and including the local guides who failed to understand the nature of her complaint. The young woman of exquisite beauty gestured to the private jet parked on a makeshift asphalt runway. The narrow layer of blacktop cut through a forest so lush it was only a matter of time before nature reclaimed the land used for the man-made strip. In the distance, a large native bird crossed the asphalt on foot before taking off. The feathered animal launched into the azure skies with wings flapping more leisurely than Destiny flapped her arms in protest.

"First, why didn't we fly here? Why did we drive for two hours when there is a perfectly good jet parked here?" The oldest of the five men waiting for her on the beach raised a finger as if to answer before she cut him off. "I want pictures of me in that Gulf Airstream, or I'm not going anywhere."

The man lowered hand and head, exasperated at the woman's unreasonable demands. His maturity and attire stood apart from the others, suggesting he oversaw the assembled group. The salt and pepper of his beard hinted at his age, while the pilot's cap confirmed his occupation. After arriving at the rendezvous point, the porters (who drove the trio to the beach from the mainland) introduced the man as Mr. Martin. A different plane sat moored offshore. That plane was less sexy than its runway cousin, amphibian style, sporting touches of duct tape in choice spots.

A jeep sat parked so close to the water it threatened to wash away under the slightest of waves. The porters hustled bags from the vehicle, splitting them between the floatplane and a small skiff tethered to the leg of the aircraft. Two other men, roughly Destiny's age (low to mid-twenties) watched the drama play out. Destiny finally took a breath, which gave the man his opening.

"Please, that belongs to our benefactor. We may use it for a celebratory flight home in the chance our business together comes to fruition. My crew drove you from the mainland airport. That is how we reach the islands. You can take all the pictures you want inside the seaplane," Martin said.

A baggage handler whistled to signal departure. The porters' dark, leathery skin suggested too much time in the sun. Both were of an indeterminate age in solid shape, lean, muscled, and thin. They wore linen short sleeve shirts over waterproof hiking pants with wraps on their heads. The first, a bandana tied at the rear, while the next, the mustached one of the two, sported a flowing garment tied in an elaborate bow along its front. Both men smiled coffee-stained teeth over the woman's antics. The pilot waved off the leering men, emphasizing the delicate nature of negotiations.

Martin gestured toward the seaplane, trying to suggest grandeur. Destiny shook her head, removed her Gucci sunglasses, and squinted in the sun. Or tried to because of the Botox. She dabbed the back of her hand on her forehead under the oppressive heat. Climate appropriate clothing remained packed in her bag—another indignity, she felt, being allowed only one suitcase for the trip. She showed them by packing a thirty-nine-inch hard-side, the largest on the market.

Despite all the posturing, the heat made Destiny eager to end the standoff. With her items in transport, the Hermes scarf around her neck was the best item to wick away moisture from her brow. Unwilling to give in to such blasphemy, she continued using the rear of her hand. Destiny wanted nothing more than to retrieve her belongings, though she would not let on to the others.

"What will it be? I'm an influencer. I can't influence squat if they see me on that joke of a plane. I need to show first class. I require pictures from the nicer jet. I refuse to go anywhere until I get them," Destiny said.

The other two influencers stepped away from the skiff and looked impatiently back at the drama unfolding on the white sand. DJ, a fitness buff, dressed on brand wearing an open linen shirt over a muscle tee designed to showcase his physique with every flutter of wind. He also sported shorts and sandals to highlight the results of never missing leg day at the gym. He raised his hands in frustration.

"What's the holdup?" DJ yelled from alongside the boat.

Zach appeared more mellow about the situation. Zach fell into the hipster category down to a nineteen-twenties baseball player beard. While liberally tatted and pierced in several creative places, he kept more of his skin covered than the others, despite the tropical surrounding. His clothes leaned into baggy, designed to camouflage a soft shape born of the junk food snack regimen of a full-time gamer. The two men played off one another while Destiny stood firm in the distance. Meanwhile, the sun baked them all.

"Seriously? What's her deal?" DJ asked.

"Have you seen her media presence? She's her own interstellar event, that one. Birthed by the collision of the High and Maintenance Galaxies. The celestial coupling resulted in a vapid black hole. She'll suck you in if you're not careful," Zach said.

"Is that true? You'll suck me in if I'm not careful? Because I've never been careful," DJ hollered.

Destiny was not above raising two tropical birds, one on each hand.

DJ laughed and yelled anew. "I wish to get a run in before it gets dark. Today?"

"Will it be today?" Destiny asked their guide.

Martin acceded, leading her toward the private jet. The other two influencers took seats in the skiff and the porters pushed off. Zach gestured from one airplane to the other.

"Somehow she finds herself in both planes while we partake of neither. What do you think, guys?" Zach turned to the guides, who settled into positions on the boat. "You think the pilot is smashing her inside there?"

The two workers eyed each one another before shrugging shoulders in unison. Zach pumped an arm slowly in the universal sex gesture. The porters smiled and nodded.

"Congratulations. I believe you invited them to a threesome with yourself," DJ said, leaning back in his seat.

Zach's face went red. He faced the workers who still grinned, one repeating the sexual innuendo gesture. Zach waved his hands.

"No, not me. The woman! Just go. Endale!"

The porters appeared confused but set off toward a nearby island, the first of several dotting a pristine crystal-clear ocean. DJ laughed as he dropped a hat over his head and settled in for a nap.

"They know I meant her, right?" Zach asked.

"Hey, don't be so uptight. Make some new friends. What happens in the Archipelagos stays in the Archipelagos."

Zach leaned back on the wooden seat alongside his travel companion. The boat cleared the beach, heading out to sea, their guides doing all the work while the two men rested.

"You ever have the coffee?"

"Kopi Luwak? Yeah, worth every penny though I had a sugar Momma paying, so not sure if she felt the same. Hundred bucks a cup," DJ replied.

"And this stuff is better?"

"That's what they say."

"We get in on this, that's amazing, could be huge for us."

"You know, since we do not have internet here and can't post anything, it leaves a situation where, believe it or not, we don't have to communicate every second of the day."

"Is that a hint?"

"More like a request."

Zach leaned back, closing his eyes. The boat rocked gently over the water. The world drifted into serenity and calm, as gentle as the waves. While in repose he declared, "I miss my video games."

· · · ● · ● · · · ·

"One more, please."

Destiny dropped into a seat on the side of the jet overlooking the beach. The compact window provided flattering selfie lighting along with a stunning view of sand so white it could have been spray painted. Destiny snapped away with practiced ease.

In her exuberance, she leaped up for a pose and bumped a bar cart toppling a Baccarat tumbler. A steady hand shot out, catching the glass before it hit the ground. A man stepped forward with the rescued barware intact. Destiny noted the crisp white lines of his sleeves cinched closed by Dior cufflinks. He wore a custom-made chambray linen suit with oxblood slip-on designer shoes.

The mystery man placed the object back as if the tumble never happened. The individual stood over six-feet, gym fit thin, with crystal blue eyes that would camouflage against the water outside. Despite an air of authority, he displayed a tranquil smile.

"Ah, my young Destiny."

He took her hand. Destiny flushed from more than the heat of the island. The man had presence. She regularly met with startup investors, old and new money folks. The latter she found mostly sloppy frat boys graced with a sudden inheritance. She deemed old money classier. It was her intention to become a new money figure with the prestige of old, to be self-aware of her elevated lot in life.

The stranger in front of her appeared privileged in ways she could not fully articulate. Handsome, confident, and intriguing, check. Yet there was more, something deeper. Besides the designer accoutrements, she sensed the man carried a heaviness about him, the burden of having seen certain things. A bad boy equation that flummoxed her too often. She hoped to learn more about him.

"You have me at a disadvantage," Destiny said.

"That would appear so. Call me Harrison. I am the benefactor of your little group today. Welcome to the Patalas Archipelago."

"We're sorry to invade your privacy, she was insistent on pictures..." Martin began.

Harrison waved the man off, then released Destiny's hand and refreshed his smile. She blushed, becoming cognizant of how long the pair held hands. He studied her as if encountering an invasive species.

"An interesting business model, media influencers, yes?"

"We hustle." She groaned in her mind over the immature retort.

"We are on a schedule. Tight. There is one thing I insist upon before we depart, however."

"What's that?"

"You take some of your cherished selfies in the cockpit."

"For reals?" Destiny bounced in excitement.

Harrison nodded to Martin before departing the plane. The pilot led the young woman into the forward.

· · • • • • • • · ·

DJ and Zach waited on the pristine beach of a scenic island. From such a distance, the mainland appeared different. It looked like a massive jungle where even the runway they knew to exist vanished into a blur of trees and vines. Both men had backpacks at the ready, prepped for a hike inland. DJ ran sprints on the beach while Zach played Candy Crush, decrying how it was one of the few games he could manage on his phone without an internet connection. The seaplane bounced in for a landing and turned about to shore. The porters rushed to greet the plane's passengers.

Harrison emerged first, helping Destiny exit the vehicle. DJ ceased his exercise and joined his trip companion. Both noted the older stranger.

"Pegged her for hooking up with you. Possibly some competition?" Zach asked.

"Grandpa? Good shape for his age, but I think I can take him in a charm off."

The groups converged on the sand. Harrison introduced himself and shook hands with the pair, showing great enthusiasm at meeting them.

"Welcome to my island, gentlemen. I'm impressed with your work. I have followed both of you for some time.

Let's make our way to camp, and I will fill you in on our itinerary for the day," Harrison said.

Everyone headed off, the porters leading the charge. Zach turned to DJ as they marched through the tropical forest. "I don't know, I'd say he's charming."

"So is the devil."

"What does that mean?"

"It means it's all in the packaging. And I've got it." DJ gestured to his crotch.

"Gross, all kinds of gross."

DJ laughed as they moved deeper into the lush surroundings, following a path well worn, often traveled. One porter used a machete with which he chopped the occasional overgrowth. Soon they broke through into a clearing.

"No way!" Destiny chirped.

Half a dozen pods dangled from trees circling the encampment. Martin explained they were the sleeping quarters everyone would use that night. The crew reacted in awe at the unique design, another sign they were not in the states any longer. A wooden communal dining table centered the open space, the furniture surrounded by tree stumps carved into post-modern variations of stools.

A barbecue pit constructed from half an oil drum raised atop crossed legs made of branches sat next to the dining area. Past the drum, a large metal grate rested over a hole in the ground, a second grilling area.

Destiny leaned back and took a selfie with the pods in view behind her. She turned to take another, capturing Harrison in the frame. He grabbed her hand and pulled the shot clear. She scrunched her face over the aggressive move.

"No pictures. The money I make, people look for reasons to connect me with women of ill repute," Harrison said.

"You think I'm yachting?"

Zach leaned into DJ. "What's 'yachting'?"

"Rich people prostitution," he whispered. Zach's eyes went wide, intrigued.

"If that was my intention, I would not have invited your friends along." Harrison gestured to the other two.

Destiny pulled her arm free. "They are not my friends. I don't have any."

"Over fifty thousand followers and no friends. Sad, that. I hope to be one."

"Well, you're off to a shaky start."

"I meant no disrespect, but my rule regarding being seen with others stands. With excellent reason. I have need of your services and hope you all are interested in money because there is much at stake." Harrison opened the conversation to all.

"We have a meal to prep, a feast for our esteemed guests. Please enjoy the island while we begin. Only one rule. Stay on the beaches or paths. If you encounter any caves, do not enter under any circumstances," Martin said.

"Why?" DJ asked.

"Critters," the mustached porter hissed.

The other worker delivered a rucksack to Destiny, who looked at it as if it were an alien object. "What's this?"

Harrison sidled up to her. "If you want to pretend to be upper class, you must learn to behave with a modicum of banality. Do not flaunt," he touched her scarf, "outside of proper functions. Travel wisely. We distilled your things down. I suggest you change. I will watch over you for safety."

Destiny took the bag. The host gestured the way. Destiny trudged through an overgrowth. Upon reaching a moderate clearing, Harrison turned his back as she started undressing.

"If you really follow my socials, then you've seen plenty of me, I suppose," she said.

"Is that an invitation to turn around?"

"It is."

He did. Destiny stood before him, wearing only a bra and panties. He approached, looming over her petite height.

"Show me." She offered him the bag.

He handed off a pair of linen khaki shorts. She inspected them before putting them on languorously for his benefit. She leaned on him, gripping his biceps while changing, hoping he noticed her interest.

"These clothes aren't mine," she said.

"When I say we distilled your things down, I meant we packed for you, a decision made after noticing your garish oversized luggage. The contents of our pack will serve you well."

Next, he offered a sleeveless white ribbed tee. She turned back, allowing him unfettered access to her breasts. When he did not partake, she pulled the top over her head. Finally, he handed off a button down Indian Madras shirt. She slipped it on without fastening the buttons, tying it off at the waist. The open front displayed the abundance under her first layer.

Once dressed, he offered a pair of lace free Sperry slip-ons. Destiny kicked off her designer variant (with a hidden wedge to add some height) and slipped on the perfectly size replacements. She noted how the man never once faltered in her presence, used no tired lines to impress her. His confidence intrigued her even more. She leaned into him.

"I want to learn about old money from you."

"You will. I promise to teach you what it takes to be rich, of that I am certain. It is why I have invited you here."

He searched her eyes. She stared back, nodded subtly that the invite was open. He moved his face close, lips so near, a stumble from either would cause a kiss. The man surprised her by speaking instead of acting.

"Please do not misunderstand my intentions. I never meant to imply that you are one who 'yachts' as you call it. And even if you do, it is of no concern to me. While we are on my island, I conduct business only. Transactions unrelated to the type you alluded to. I assure you my interest in your presence equals that of the two accompanying you. Take that as you choose."

They walked back to the camp.

· · • • • • • · · ·

"Pretty sure he's gay," Destiny said.

"He sure knows how to dress a woman." Zach said while hiking behind Destiny, staring at her assets.

"Right?"

"What I'm hearing is someone got shot down," DJ said.

"What about you? Has he hit on you?" Destiny asked DJ.

The fitness buff stopped and turned on her. "I look at you and my brain defaults to primal. You are objectively hot, just this side of stunning." She leaned into a smile and his compliment. "Then you open your mouth and all I see is…"

"What?"

"Never mind. I have seen some badass in you. How about we cling to that, huh? How about we bring that out more?"

DJ walked away. Zach chimed in from behind. "I still think you're hot when you open your mouth."

Destiny rolled her eyes and sighed. Pickup lines even in the jungle. The group marched until encountering a lagoon. An oasis within an oasis.

Zach spread his arms, taking it in. "This is amazing. I won't even say how long since I've been out in nature."

"Some people own islands like this, can you imagine?" Destiny said as she pouted for a few selfies, fluffing her hair in between takes.

DJ looked at it differently, concern crossing his face. "Why us? There are much bigger influencers."

"Cross section of America, baby," Zach said.

"Exactly my point. We're not even remotely global here. Why us?"

"OMG. A cave!" Destiny yelled. "And I have quite the global reach, thank you. I'm huge in Yemen."

Across the basin, a waterfall poured in a thin sheen. Visible behind the thin falls was an opening in the rock face. A cave. Destiny circled until she stood near the flow. The men followed. She handed Zach her camera.

"Take my picture."

Destiny routinely took selfies, so having an actual photographer in such an exotic setting excited her. These types of images could lift her sites to the next level, might get advertisers to notice. She stepped under the waterfall to strike several poses while fully aware of how the water drenched her front. Zach lifted his head from behind the phone to encourage her antics. Once she felt she had enough body shots, she gestured him closer and flirted with the camera while squeegeeing her hair.

Once partially dried, she retrieved her cellphone from him and covered it as she ran through the waterfall. She stepped far enough into the cave entrance so that water no longer splashed. Then she viewed the pics so far. Occasionally, a shot drew a yip of excitement from her. She tapped the favorites bookmark on the pics she knew would get the most likes when posted. She yelled through the water.

"These are great! Thank you. I am going to take some selfies in here."

"You heard them. Stay out of the caves," Zach yelled, trying to be heard over the waterfall.

"Are you kidding? How cool would it be to get pics in here?"

She left her new photographer behind and snapped away. She started near the entrance, where sunlight trickled and served as a natural filter. The light against shadowed stone would create magnificent pictures. She took several, then peered into the tenebrous cavern. She snapped a pic toward the dark and checked the image. Her flash lit a sea of darkness but revealed nothing to be frightened of.

Followers loved when she changed up her routine. The tropical island alone would give her followers a sense of adventure missing in their own work cubicle lives. But a cave? That was next level. Destiny would conquer their fears of darkness for them. She planned to brag about her daring forays into a rainforest halfway across the globe. What better way than to take shots in the great unknown?

She waded into the pitch black, using her cell to light the way. Shadows enveloped her every step, and the air dipped noticeably cooler. Destiny failed to identify a cause of worry behind the warnings of her hosts. Surely, nothing could live in such an environment. She continued until the last remnants of light vanished at her back. Once immersed in blackness, she started snapping.

The environment made previewing the shots useless. There was nothing but dark. All she could do was trigger a fast burst, timed with the flash and hope to cull a few delightful images. Filters would do the rest. The process involved playing a numbers game. Shoot fifty, keep five. Uncertain which part of the cavern offered the ideal backdrop, she rotated while clicking the shutter button.

Red eye would be unavoidable as the flash burst so quickly it was as if she danced under a strobe light. While circling in the herky-jerky motions of the 'strobe light' she noticed a movement near her feet. She stopped spinning and aimed her cell phone screen at the approximate spot. Nothing.

Something fluttered nearby. The cavern amplified the most subtle sounds to consequential echoes. A slight whoosh of air flowed past her ankles. Destiny redirected the light of her cellphone but found nothing. Until. Something tapped on her shoulder! A shadowy image of something long and thick slithered alongside her.

Destiny scrambled back and bounced into a rock face. Before she even found her footing, she stumbled into a run. The light at the end of the tunnel beckoned. She dashed for it, launching herself into DJ's waiting arms.

"What? I heard you scream. What is it?"

"OMG! Huge freaking snake. It stood as tall as me!"

"Snakes don't stand," Zach said.

"This one did. Or hung from the cave roof. Who knows, but it touched my shoulder!" She shivered and brushed herself off, trying to shed the memory like a snake sheds skin.

"So maybe we stay out of the caves?" DJ asked.

She nodded as they escorted her back to the camp.

The aroma hit them long before they arrived. Zach's stomach grumbled audibly. He mentioned he had not eaten since they were on the skiff. Smoke rose above the trees, guiding their way.

They stepped into the clearing to find both fire pits in use. The porters cooked a feast of native fish, lobster, and various other offerings. Plates fashioned from palm leaves lined the table. An overflowing fruit bowl served as a centerpiece. The proximity to the grills and their succulent odors drew a gurgle from DJ's stomach, rivalling Zach's.

"This is unreal," Destiny whispered, a peek into a future lifestyle.

"It smells amazing. Maybe a cheat day is in order," DJ said.

Harrison occupied the head of the table with Martin seated adjacent. The two hosts broke off a conversation about websites and social media marketing once their guests arrived. A coffee filtration system occupied a spot on the table near the hosts. An elaborate series of hoses, knobs, and test tubes made up the device. The hardware looked as though it could round out the lab of a mad scientist. Everyone sat, Destiny nearest the front.

Martin rose without a word, snapping his fingers. A worker retrieved a kettle from the pit while Martin tapped a finger against various intersecting points on the device. After checking the connections, the man poured boiling water into a funnel atop the contraption, running the liquid in a slow circular motion. The water exited the funnel black, gushing through tubes until damming at a point above a staged decanter where it slowed to a drip.

Harrison spoke while Martin continued the brewing process. "Each of you are influencers of different stripes. One sells dreams of unachievable fitness, another stunted adulthood, and the last sexuality. Together, you represent a wide cross section of followers in the demographics we seek. There are drawbacks. None of your brands are evergreen. Age will eventually diminish your collective followings unless any of you learn to pivot. I hear there is a macrame influencer that the blue hairs appreciate."

"Unachievable? I expect to stay fit forever. If one follows my fitness plan, they too can be. I sell a lifestyle," DJ protested.

"You are subject to lottery ticket DNA. The science behind your dietary plan is not sustainable long term. Both your parents were athletic. I am aware your mother passed. Condolences. As for your father, you have not spoken to him in five years, nor anyone else from your family. Had you kept in touch often enough to see his before and after, you would better understand what your own future holds. I've done my homework. I know what he looks like. Time has not been kind."

DJ stood up, angry. "What the hell?"

"Please, sit down. You are on an island. Where are you going to go? Can you fly the plane?"

Destiny pulled him down. Harrison turned to her.

"I have seen you nude."

Despite his anger, DJ shot her a look as if asking when that happened. Zach stopped his round of Candy Crush, suddenly interested in the conversation. Destiny blushed and avoided looking at her traveling companions, though she matched Harrison's gaze, refusing to back down. He continued.

"While lovely now, the years can nudge those who live off their appearance to dabble in plastic surgery. The addictive nature of which eventually transforms women of even spectacular DNA into an unrecognizable state. Highly paid flesh doctors will nip and tuck your youth into submission, one procedure after another. Conversely, if you do not undergo the knife, time will abscond with those looks."

"Harsh," Zack said.

"Accurate. As for yourself, your brand is the closest to evergreen. There is the slightest chance your unwillingness to grow up to be a proper man might continue to play as rebellious. The question then becomes how long before age steals your reflexes? Will younger gamers catch up to the pinball wizard?"

"Hey, that sounds like you insulted me. And what's pinball?"

The tension in the air suggested if one walked, all would follow. Harrison remained calm, stoic as he gestured all to relax.

"I have studied each of you. No families, all estranged or expired. No friends to speak of, despite having followers of staggering numbers. Lives half-lived."

"Hey, I've got tons of women in my life. I post them all over my pages. You would know that if you did the research that you claim," DJ protested.

"Beards. You are closeted. You never ask the names of your male lovers and seldom reconnect with them twice. Easier to convince yourself of your orientation if you do not develop feelings for anyone, I suppose. You encountered a gentleman in a fifth street bar two months ago. The one with a tattoo of the ace of spades on his loins? He works for me, my ace in the hole, so to speak."

"All the staring at my ass since we arrived was only a front?" Destiny asked him.

DJ ignored her, too busy pleading to the host. "Is this a shakedown? If you say anything, it will ruin my brand."

"My research shows the revelation would increase your following by a large percentage. Even simply listing yourself as *they*/*them* would grow your audience. In the end, that is your choice. It does not concern me. And no, this is not a shakedown. This is about opportunity."

Everyone fell silent as Martin set up three cups on a thatched fabric tray. He then detached the carafe and poured while Harrison continued.

"The Asian palm civet. Paradoxurus Hermaphroditus. A rat like creature that eats coffee cherries, half-digests them, then defecates. The result is the Kopi Luwok blend, typically sold for fifty to a hundred dollars per serving. Imagine an upgraded offering, even better, more delicate, rarer still. The wealthy would flock to its unique flavor profile without question. But we need volume to make the fortune the rarest of coffees deserves. That is where you all come in."

Martin placed the half-filled cups in front of the guests. "Drink."

Destiny sniffed and shared a curious look with the server who nodded to suggest, 'yes, it is that good.' She sipped, then closed her eyes. An involuntary moan of pleasure escaped her lips. Harrison laughed at the reaction. A second sip found her looking at the cup as if she had never seen one before.

"I forgive all the horrible things you said if you let me be a part of this. No way, this is just coffee. Never have I experienced anything remotely close to this." She sipped again.

The other two reacted similarly. Zach drank his in one enormous glug, wiped his mouth on a sleeve and slammed the cup down.

The video gamer struggled to relay his thoughts. "No fricking way! I love chocolate and oranges blended, which this is like except not really. My aunt does a nutmeg thing. Is there nutmeg? No, not that. Why do I want to say it tastes like flowers? How would I know what those taste like?"

The other two finished their serving as Harrison continued. "The civets are voracious eaters with sharp teeth that will chew down anything in their path. As with the youth of any species, their digestive systems work efficiently, too much so. Imagine an older animal, one that digests more slowly."

Martin made a second round with the flask. Each guest extending empty cups as if begging for more gruel in a Dicken's novel. The group speculated over flavor profiles. Each shouted out various ideas on ingredients. None of which could ever come together to form a cohesive whole, at least not in a combination approximating the delicate balance of the charcoal liquid in their hands. They abandoned their quest for an answer by declaring it Umami. That they all agreed upon. They reached out for more.

Martin held the decanter hostage while he took over the conversation. "Genetic engineering was the start. As with all things, it is never that simple. The older creatures proved to be more demanding, harder to control, more finicky than their young."

"Enough. I can tell they are uninterested in the specifics. What I wish to know is whether each of you would pay two hundred a serving?" All three nodded. "So too will the world when people like you nudge them into action."

"I would so totally sponsor this," Destiny said, gesturing for another round.

Martin left her hanging. "More later. Now, we feast on our new partnerships. This island offers the finest seafood in the province, our guides are phenomenal chefs."

"I feel warm all over. This, it's…" Destiny began before finding all male eyes on her. "The taste is overwhelming. The smell alone affected me. I'm having trouble explaining how good this was."

"I'd drop a game controller for this, for sure."

DJ set his cup down. "So why not a Kardashian, why not bring out the big guns? Who the hell are we compared to them? You're asking the Amish to sell Teslas."

"Wise question. Answers after we dine." The polished man spread his arms wide, and the porters moved in with food.

Unlike the drink, the meal appeared endless, beginning with a tray of elegantly plated sushi served atop empty seashells as plates. A stew followed, light on broth, heavy on fish. Then more seafood, impossibly fresh and elegantly prepared. The group dug in.

The three marveled at the abundance and fell into a camaraderie of shared experience, whispering conspiratorially about their wonderful fortune. Soon enough, the visitors abandoned chatter to feast. Harrison and Martin used their time to study a map while conversing about weather relating to their scheduled departure the next day.

Once the trio finished gorging, they rose to examine the brewing machine. Harrison looked over their shoulders.

"The process for our special brew has unique—needs. You asked earlier why you. The three of you all match up in ways that others do not. Most influencers focus on a bevy of products to push. Too many choices for consumers and nothing stands out. My intention is for you to continue to sell yourselves, your own personal brand, but beyond that, only a single product. Mine."

"If we sign up," Zach said.

Harrison smiled at the foolish response. "If you do, yes. We are not much longer for light. If you wish for more time on the beach, might I suggest now? I have a flight plan to attend to."

The three retired to the shore, laying on the salt white sand to allow the meal to digest. The entire time they talked about their futures possibly being set, lives changed by a financial tsunami surely on its way. When the sun faded into dusk, they made their way back.

Upon returning to the encampment, tiki torches greeted them, lighting the path. Candles flickered in each of three pod tents above. The hosts stood at the ready with a carafe already full.

"A last cup for the evening?" Martin asked.

The black liquid glistened under the flickering of the staggered torches, beckoning them closer. The two men thundered past Destiny, grabbed cups, and held them out in anticipation. Martin poured.

As Destiny drew closer, Harrison intercepted, pulling her aside, out of earshot of the others. She gasped in surprise and excitement until the man spoke.

"Nancy Walker, just a sad girl from the wrong side of the tracks. Still financially struggling because everything you earn gets pumped into your plastic surgeries. I spoke earlier about surgery in your future to facilitate your ruse with the other guests. But the future I mentioned is already here. You are an individual of the non-biodegradable variety. Nose, chin, tits. What is next? Do you own any of your original parts? I am not talking just biology. How about friendships? You cut all those from your life also, as cleanly as any plastic surgeon. You slept with all your friends' boyfriends. For what reason? To prove that you are pretty? To show you are not the awkward little girl from Kansas?"

Destiny tried half-heartedly to pull away. She wished for him to stop, but also needed to understand how he knew so much. "Who are you?"

"One who will change the course of your life more than you realize. A man of old money. Tomorrow I meet with my suppliers over a tense negotiation. You wanted to know what old money will do? At the least, it avoids temptations wrapped in packages like you. It ignores the internet other than as a tool to advertise product. Old money cares not for how many times someone clicks a 'like' button. Old money does anything necessary, Ms. Walker."

"Destiny."

"I suppose you are right."

He released her, and she staggered to the table, shaken. A few sips into the brew, and her discomfort faded. She held in her hands her future. Her fortunes would soon change. Fine, she had ruined some of her besties' relationships, but only to prove how disloyal their boyfriends were. She never slept with the guys more than necessary to break up her friends' relationships. If Destiny could have achieved such results with a single slip up, she would have. It was not her fault her friends were so forgiving of those they loved, forcing her to carry some affairs on for weeks and months until the women could no longer ignore the signs or the video footage she eventually 'accidentally' texted each.

Destiny planned to show her island host. She had it in her to make the man bend his rules regarding business and pleasure. She only needed some Kopi money to pay for a few more surgeries until becoming someone the world could not ignore. Dreams of her future warmed her almost as much as the silky brew gliding down her throat.

Harrison coughed to draw their attention. "I take my leave now. This will be your only night here. I must fly to the next island to negotiate my fresh supply of beans. I thank you all in advance for your commitment to our product."

With a tip to a non-existent cap, he faded into the jungle. The group finished their cups. The Porters accompanied everyone to the nearby pods as Martin explained the setup.

"We keep them off ground because of critters."

"Like snakes in the caves?" Destiny asked.

"Something like that, yes. We have placed your bags inside the tents."

Each positioned themselves below their individual pods, then slipped into body straps with carabiners. They hooked onto the dangling ropes. Martin pulled a line, lifting Destiny slowly into the tree while the porters did the same for the men. Martin grunted and explained as he lifted her.

"These are open top, that is how you gain entry. They do not close. No worries, there is no rain forecast. The balance of the fabric is Kevlar, so no danger of ripping through no matter your weight."

Destiny reached the branch which held her pod and used it to lower herself inside before unstrapping. Per instructions, she attached the carabiner to a loop along the interior near the opening for the return descent the next morning. She rolled out the provided sleeping bag and settled in, weary from the interminable day though still buzzing with excitement and caffeine. What appeared as candlelight outside proved to be a small battery powered lamp low on charge. She turned it off.

She pulled out her cell. The darkness offered perfect viewing for her to check the photos. She grimaced as an unflattering pic filled her screen.

"How long have I been at this, and I still can't remember to keep my eyes open? Oh, cute!"

Destiny forgave herself with the next pic. She scrolled through, hitting the favorite button on the keepers while deleting all bad ones. One caused her to yip in glee, perfect lighting and showing her ass off in just the right way.

"Damn, wish I had internet to post some of these," she said.

Something rustled above, followed by a gentle tug at the pod. She shone her cell at the opening. Nothing. She chalked it up to unfamiliar surroundings and continued to flip through. When she came upon a few pictures of Zach and DJ, she laughed at their goofy abandon. Then she reached the images from the lagoon.

She grinned at the ones outside in the waterfall. Flipping through, she found herself somewhat surprised by the daring nature of the poses. Zach framed the shots perfectly, and they highlighted her breasts. What he liked, so would her followers. Appreciative of the bounty of images, Destiny yelled thank you to Zach.

Destiny laughed when Zach replied, "you're welcome," despite him not knowing the reason for the thanks.

"Wonder if the nips will get me banned on certain platforms. Find out soon. Ooh, the cave!"

Even with the flash, most of the pics were too dark to do anything with. Red eye was plentiful and disconcerting. She zipped through them when something caught her attention. Was it the snake? Destiny sat up and squinted for a better look before enlarging it with a swipe.

She examined the image. Or tried to. The tree housing her rustled harder. Instinctively, Destiny aimed her light overhead again. Nothing. She returned to her phone.

Impossible.

The object behind her in the pic was tubular like a reptile with a girth that tapered down as it neared the end. It appeared a tip, not a head. The 'snake' rose to shoulder height as she proclaimed to the others earlier. The proof was in her hands.

The tree shook again. She ignored it, too focused on identifying what it was she was looking at. A closer examination revealed patches of hair along its length. It appeared to be a tail! Destiny scrolled through the next few until reaching one showing—*oh God*! Her set of red eyes were not the only ones in the shot! A second set of eyes appeared over her shoulder, too large to be those of a snake.

Enlarging the picture further, she gasped. An abhorrent creature filled the screen. The cave dweller inhabited features of a rat. No, more like a mole. She knew the foul vermin well from living in Kansas. Harrison was correct, Destiny (not her actual name) was a country girl, always poor, always an afterthought to the hayseed men in her life. Her time living in squalor taught her everything about rodents, the human and animal kind.

The thing in the picture was both!

It had the facial features of a mole, including its signature beady eyes which she assumed were black, though the flash made them appear milky white. The center of its furry face jutted into a pointed snout, which tapered to a dotted nose sprouting whiskers like an old man's ear hair.

The creature appeared bipedal, standing on twin rat feet with extended claws while the upper limbs dangled a short distance from its body. T-Rex style arms. The arms, small compared to the balance of the beast, curled up as much as out, the hands pulled tight as if palsied, ending in sharp daggers of fingernails curling in indiscriminate directions.

Gnarled ridges of ears covered either side of the monstrous head. The pinkish hue of the aural cavities segued into a matted black fur, blending the rigid structures into the folds of the creature's skull. As it stood, the monster, the thing that could not be, rose above Destiny by almost two feet.

The tree shook again. While worried about the tree's unnatural motion, she remained in bed. The image of the grotesque anthropomorphic being on her phone rooted her in place with fear. It took all her will to swipe through additional pics, fearful of what they might reveal.

With each new photo, a scream built in her throat. The images revealed the creature's claws extending, its jaw opening wide. Jagged teeth lined the gaping maw like soldiers standing in crooked formations. Before Destiny could scream, someone else did. The cry was guttural and raw. Feminine. (Zach?)

The tree shook harder, the branches dancing above the open top of the pod. Then it happened. A flood of large rodents poured from above into the tent. She raised her arms, finally screaming. Destiny felt a rough tug followed by a warm wetness pouring down both limbs. The searing agony struck as pointed teeth made quick work of several digits. Yanking one arm toward her face, she discovered three fingers were missing. Blood gushed down her forearm, leaking from the first wound into a second, that of a gaping hole near her wrist where something had bitten away a chunk of flesh.

Destiny danced a lonely dance with shock and, for a moment, witnessed beauty as tufts of white fluttered through the air. She wondered if it was snowing. Then fresh pain brought her back, causing her to realize the whiteness was nothing more than down gnashed free from the sleeping bag. Dozens swarmed, all larger than New York city rats. She absorbed the collective weight of swarm massed atop her.

Twin excruciating bites changed the nature of the horrific experience as the invaders made off with her eyes, biting them clean from her face. (*No more red eye*, Destiny thought, and for some insane reason she fought a burst of laughter.) With her sight gone, the sound of gnawing carnage filled her ears.

DJ screamed all too briefly in the distance. Upon opening her mouth to scream anew, a massive creature bit off her tongue. Soon, the thrashing of her body became involuntary, the motion supplied by the actions of the feasting rodents. A bite and an audible snap of something inside caused her left arm to fall limp, useless. A fresh pain rose above all else when one chewed through her Achilles. The agony of the wound mercifully subsided when a group of vermin removed the same leg at the knee.

Destiny experienced the warmth of their fur as they burrowed into her ribcage to feast, though even that soon bled into a frigid coldness. To the end, she felt the phantom pain of her hand still gripping her phone, her life. No more selfies, no more posting. Eventually, she felt nothing at all.

Martin and the Porters drank slowly from their cups of Kopi Darah. The porter's toasted their employer for another successful job. The sheer number of civets flooding like black lava through branches into the pods never ceased to amaze Martin. It reminded him of the coffee running through the tubes into the carafe.

Destiny proved to be the best fighter as her tent continued to rock long after the other two had stilled. Martin returned the toast.

"It seems our guests understood Kopi means coffee. I am not so certain they know Darah means blood. To prosperity."

Harrison worked well into the night inside the jet. He had much work to do that evening and then more to do in the morning. He filled the same glass the lovely woman had toppled. Scotch. Black-market sources already supplied him with their guest's passwords up to and including their phone codes.

He planned to update the influencers' posts himself for now but would eventually hand off those duties to a lackey, where posts would follow for years. Harrison asked the guests if they knew how to freeze a life in time. They did not, but he did. Like vampires, these three brought to the island would never age online. For that, they should be grateful, Harrison thought. The most recent group would be one of many who would hawk his product once he sourced enough beans. That was the reason for tomorrow's trip.

The plane came equipped with internet hotspot capability. It remained turned off in the presence of living guests to ensure no one inadvertently posted any identifying location markers. Harrison would scrub all pictures of such things, including any images of himself, before handing the files off to his staff. The remaining images would feed the influencer accounts for quite some time. Before forgetting, he changed DJ's designation to *they/them*. The likes poured in immediately.

His phone dinged with a text relaying mission accomplished. That meant the porters had cut down the pods and buried the guests alongside previous visitors. There was never much organic material left to deal with. Mostly bones, the ones not carried away as prizes or chew toys. After that, they would hang new pods for the next round of guests destined to arrive soon.

Martin would have already collected the phones from the tents and those would prove a trove of pictures old and new to post over the years. Harrison worked diligently to gather all the media images from the influencers' various hard drives, which he accessed remotely. The sheer volume of unused photos and videos never ceased to stun the notoriously camera-shy man.

In his experience, Harrison found them a vain bunch. He secured all their data and updated their social pages. The scandalous 'Only Fans' page Destiny ran would be the first that he would shutter. He had ethics despite having available a shocking number of nudes the woman kept at the ready.

Once the sun rose, Harrison boarded the seaplane and flew to the next island. He landed the plane and waded onto the shore. Minimal sand greeted him, an almost absent beach that merged directly into a lush tropical forest. He followed a narrow path inland until arriving at a cave where he whistled a strange high-pitched sound.

The tap, tap of claws on stone sounded from within before three six-foot palm civet rodents identical to the one Destiny encountered appeared. Mole men, Harrison called them when around his human employees. The mole men's nostrils flared, sniffing the scent of their visitor.

"Per our agreement, we have fed your young. More food for them is on the way as we speak. Now get to work, yes?"

The tallest of the three whistled. Dozens more emerged from the cave, all heading toward distant coffee fields where they would feast on the cherries. Harrison would leave the dirty job of collecting the digested product to his crew. His sole focus would be to secure contracts with suppliers to collect the fruits of all the labor.

"That, my dear Destiny, is old money at play," the magnate said before turning away where a life of luxury awaited.

JAHO COFFEE ROASTER & WINE BAR

SALEM, MASSACHUSETTS

I have been a yearly visitor to Salem, MA every October for the past decade except for 2021. In October, Salem transforms into Halloween Town, with thousands of people walking down Essex Street in costume or out of costume, gawking and/or taking part in Halloween antics. Religious fanatics scream on bullhorns that people will burn in Hell for all eternity. Salem is a mixture of people who both hate and love Halloween. It's a very special place.

While sitting there having a latte in my Star-Lord Cosplay, taking a break from wandering the streets and posing for photos with strangers. I got the idea for a pseudo-religious pervert. One who the reader would immediately detest. I thought of all the Salem tropes and the ideas people have of it and just sort of have fun with my twist.

JAHO is a nicely located coffee and wine bar with AMAZING baked goods smack dab in the middle of Salem. Not too far from Essex Street where all the action happens, and not too far from the non-mainstream attractions like the wharf or the *House of the Seven Gables* (Yes, I've visited it and yes it's the one that inspired the story by Nathaniel Hawthorne). The interior of JAHO is welcoming and always full of a mixture of tourists and locals.

SALEM

JOSEPH CARRO

I stared at Jennifer's breasts as she sopped up my spilled coffee with a dirty rag. She strained, making small grunts of effort, leaving thin brown streaks on the white marble top of the counter. She apologized to me for her clumsiness. Her mouth moved, her wet lips parted and full, her tongue working along with the syllables as if in slow motion. Her eyes were blue and bright, her hair dyed an almost neon red. Freckles dotted the bridge of her nose. My own eyes aimed low, staring *unwillingly* into the sinful crest of her cleavage, into the soft and inviting flesh on display.

There I lost myself with a greedy, deprived hunger. I envisioned angrily stripping her clothing off while making her apologize to me. Then visions of her bending me over her knee and striking my ass with the leather belt she wore. The rapid-fire visions were too much in too short a time for my already overloaded brain *under attack* every second of the day by images of women's bodies. An unwanted erection burst free of my boxer shorts and rode up my outer thigh until it pressed hard against the inside of my khakis, creating a small but noticeable bulge in the fabric.

Jennifer was too busy cleaning the coffee she'd spilled to notice my lingering stare, my slack jaw, and my awkward stance. I buckled myself at the knees and bent my torso forward to hide what pulsated under my clothing.

I hobbled to my favorite pleather covered corner chair next to a rack containing day-old newspapers. Sometimes I liked to do the crossword puzzle in USA Today, but not in the New York Times. I shambled the last couple of steps and let out a slight moan as the fabric caressed me unexpectedly. The moan was louder than I intended. My face flushed with anger and embarrassment as my thin voice echoed throughout the café.

"Are you okay?" Jennifer asked, peeking out from behind the cash register, a mix of curiosity and pity marking her features. She twisted a ragged white cloth with her delicate fingers and tiny hands into a big red bucket full of hot sanitizer. I pictured her bent over that same counter, breasts free and swinging as I pounded her from behind, both of us moaning the Lord's name in vain.

I rocked my head to rid myself of the unwanted vision.

"Oh my god!" she said. "Do you need me to call an ambulance? You're not having a heart attack, are you?" She was already running a cup underneath the faucet, filling it with cold filtered water, no doubt for me. Water cascaded over her knuckles and wrists. Her display of kindness made the shame even more palpable, which made it even more exciting and, therefore, *sinful* and *disgusting*.

"No," I almost shouted. "Just... just a cramp. Darned things." I gave a half smile and then shuffled to the chair. I sat down awkwardly, just about breaking my penis as the shifting fabric of my pants pressed down at an awkward angle, straining it without mercy. She brought me the cup of water, placing one of her thin, soft hands on my left shoulder. My heart almost beat out of my chest as I side-eyed her touch. I took the water with a trembling hand and drank the liquid, a little of it dribbling from the corners of my mouth. *What a bitch.*

"I said, are you okay?" she repeated, looking more anxious.

I nodded, water still running down my neck and soaking into the collar of my undershirt. She walked away, shooting worried glances back in my direction, before finally returning to her post behind the counter.

"You just let me know if you need anything," she said, a condescending smile spreading across her face.

"You're too kind," I replied, my voice cracking, causing me to wince with further embarrassment. I lifted the cup of water to toast her, a stupid gesture meant to be much smoother than it was. The cup flew from my hand and onto the floor. Luckily, it was already almost empty. "Oh, darn," I said. She had already gone out back into the café's stockroom, so didn't notice my idiotic mistake. I slapped my head and pulled my hair in frustration. I crouched down on the floor like an animal and wiped up the water with my coat sleeves, hoping nobody would come in and notice the indignities she'd made me suffer.

"Stupid, stupid, stupid," I chanted.

Once I composed myself and finally settled into my chair, I tried to ignore Jennifer for once. I set about my work of locating her address and personal information via

Google. *It was time.* She'd tortured me for weeks now. After agreeing to the terms and conditions required to use the café's Internet, I brought up the Google search bar and, with shaky fingers, typed in the name JENNIFER LEEDS.

Nothing happened for a moment. The screen turned white. I panicked, thinking something compromised my laptop, but finally the search results popped out and onto the display and I let out my breath.

The screen read: JENNIFER LEEDS E-MAIL AND ADDRESS courtesy PrivateSleuth.com. 1 Result Nearby.

I clicked the link and entered the information for my credit card. When it processed, the website showed me there was only one result in Salem, Massachusetts. *It had to be her.* With each passing second, I grew more and more excited. The thought of watching her from outside her own home exhilarated me. Maybe I'd see her undressing or sunbathing topless in her backyard. Of course, the thought also shamed me. Typing with one hand, I reached down the front of my pants with the other pinched my scrotum. I stifled a yell, but almost knocked over my laptop. I looked around, expecting to find gawkers, but there was no one there but me.

It was all for the best. People were nosy, and on occasionally in other cities, I needed to move to another café because someone had been curious about what I'd been doing on my computer and peeked. So sensitive, those people. Sometimes, I played pornography (silently) watching the gyrations of the performers, watching them stick disgusting body parts inside one another, all for the *almighty dollar.* I felt bile rise in my throat as I thought about a penis penetrating a vagina and needed to shake it off. I slammed my laptop shut, the noise startling Jennifer. The move also pinched the skin of my left hand between the laptop's monitor and keyboard, eliciting a small groan of pain. I tried to avoid her judgmental gaze as I stood and angrily stuffed my laptop into my backpack.

"I hope the rest of your day goes well!" She said, leaning over the counter.

"I have an… appointment I forgot about," I huffed, throwing my backpack strap over my right shoulder, and shuffled outside. The door to the coffee shop momentarily stymied me. It moved in a different direction than I'd expected, pushing when the sign showed pull. I bumped into the door and heard her giggle behind me before I escaped. She had me so flustered, the bitch.

***.

The walk home was tedious. I couldn't stop thinking about Jennifer, but I knew there were precautions I'd have to take if I were to snoop around her residence. She lived near Essex Street, one of the busiest streets in downtown Salem in the fall. First, I'd have to wait for it to get dark. Second, I'd have to dress in dark clothing. Third was equipment check. I didn't want to worry about camera batteries dying at an inopportune moment. In matters such as these, one couldn't be too prepared.

When I arrived home, I padded up the fire escape to the upstairs portion of the house, which was built in the 1800s. It had belonged to a relative of Nathaniel Hawthorne. I rented the top half of the house with another man named Chris, and the owner lived on the bottom level by himself. Neither was home. A red lightbulb glared at me as I ascended the steps and opened the door. I made my way from the common kitchen area to my room in the rear, which shared a wall with Chris. I gathered everything I'd need for the night. The entire ordeal took about an hour. My batteries held an almost full charge from a trip to a nearby cemetery a few days prior. There I ran some test shots with the manual settings of my camera.

I was all set, but I didn't want to leave too early and face rush hour traffic. Though I also couldn't leave too late and chance that she'd be sleeping. Out of view, that is. Sleeping where I could easily see would fall under mission accomplished. I still had to be careful. Salem was a small town and until the evening, traffic bustled as tourists came and went. *Evil morons, the lot of them.* They would all rot in Hell for their fixation on witchcraft and devilry. It was only the beginning of October, and the masses already clogged the streets. By the end of October, it grew intolerable. Despite the crowds, in my spare time, I sometimes stood by the Barbara Eden statue shouting into a megaphone at all the gathered sinners.

I bided my time, watching the minutes pass by on my phone's digital display. I was feverish and shaky in anticipation. To make the minutes go by faster, and to punish myself ahead of time for my efforts, I took my roommate's dish sponge and scrubbed the head of my penis until the skin was pink and stung from the air. By then, it was almost time to leave. I put the dish sponge back, walked back into my room at the end of the hall, and gathered my things.

When I stepped outside, the warmth immediately left my body as I sucked in a lung full of chilly autumn air. It was crisp and was one of the few things I liked about living in a New England town (full of sin and impropriety as it was). I let my breath exhale and watched it cloud into the night sky. My heart raced.

I made my way through downtown Salem, past the business sector and into the old neighborhood. As I passed the condominium that used to be the Old Salem Jail, I watched a drunken male in a mobile bar toss an axe at a red ring target on a backing board. He took long draws from a bottle of beer. I shook my head. I never had much rapport with other males; they all disgusted me. They spent their time simping over young women, elevating them on unattainable pedestals when women really wished to subjugate the male sex. I saw through their feminine subterfuge. It's what saved me from being chained to a woman and living a life of duty bound to her like a slave. *I was a free man.*

Forgetting the ignorant simp behind me, I stalked up the hill, past the old jail, the Salem Mall, and found Jennifer's two-story home nestled among the oldest buildings in Salem Village. From Google, I discovered her home once belonged to a judge during the Salem Witch Trials. Hiding in the shadows across the street next to a Dunkin' Donuts, I saw a light on in the window of the bottom floor of her building, which was good news because that meant she was home. I waited a long time until the street emptied before dropping to my belly and crawling along the cold grass to the side of her house.

Whenever a car passed, I pressed against the ground and held my breath, making myself small and hiding myself in the dark with my hoodie. I tried to look as if I belonged among the shadows. *Stupid bitch,* I thought, frowning at the lengths she was putting me through. She knew what she was doing to draw me out and here I was crawling on my belly like a snake. Pathetic. She invited me. She should have left a key, maybe a hot meal.

Once the coast cleared, I rose to my feet and looked through the lit window into a living room. An orange cat relaxed on the back of an expensive-looking couch, and a red light emanated from a hallway to another portion of first floor. No sign of the girl. Tapestries hung on the wall of a tapestry filled room. She had a strange sense of interior decorating, but women often did. I'd once seen an Instagram influencer hang wicker baskets to a wall. Somehow, that was *fashionable*. Women often wasted their time and what talent they had with pointless exercises such as that.

I crouched, carefully picking my way among the weeds and bushes in the backyard. There was an iron fence, no doubt placed there to protect the backyard from gawkers such as me. I seethed with anger at the slight. With my gloved hands, I pulled myself as quietly as I could over the wrought iron and slid over onto the other side, impressing even myself with my stealth.

There was another lit window on the second floor. The light projected through the panes and onto a back porch area, complete with stairs leading up to it. I painstakingly climbed each step silently, trying to walk on eggshells without breakage. I ascended until arriving at the illuminated window, where I could hardly believe my eyes. Jennifer, the demure girl from the café, was nude and bathed in candlelight.

Her breasts were supple with pointing toward the ceiling. She faced a black mirror. My heart raced within my chest, but I could barely feel it as my eyes scoured her pale, milky skin. Her arms were outstretched, and she danced to music I couldn't hear. She was like a marble statue crafted by one of the great artists. With trembling hands, I lifted my camera, transfixed and silent as she moved and gyrated. Shockingly, after a few moments of my breathless lust, she turned her head and looked straight at me through the window.

I lowered my camera slightly once she realized I was there. I sucked in my breath, but she continued her dance, her mouth forming a wicked grin. My lips dried out, so I licked them absentmindedly. She turned and allowed me to capture all her lusty curves on screen. (Posing?) My thoughts wandered to all the times sweet Jennifer placed her hands on me or looked my way in the cafe. I trembled and tried to hold my filming hand still. I gazed into the LCD screen to ensure I was getting it all.

Looking up from the screen, I found her staring at me, her face and breasts pressed against the glass. Only it was not the face of the Jennifer I knew. Her skin had turned a shade of a dark purple, like someone asphyxiated. Her eyes blazed like two red embers in a dying fire surrounded by forest night. She smiled with a mouthful of sharp teeth, too many to fit in the face of the petite woman I knew. Her grin grew wider, too big for her body and head.

I gasped and fell off the porch. Everything went black when I hit ground, but I could still see those pinpoints of red ember reaching out to me from the ether.

· · · ●·●· · · ·

I woke to extreme pain. Uncertain how long I'd been out, I grasped my head, which bled around my eyebrow. Trying to clear my vision, I lifted myself up slightly until my lower back spasmed. I let out a groan of pain and dropped back down. *I needed to move.* Fighting the cramps, I sat up, using my scuffed and bruised arms, and tried to stand. My right ankle felt twisted, so I favored my strong foot to bring upright myself. Hobbling to a support beam for the porch, I leaned against it to get my bearings.

"Stupid, stupid, stupid," I said. My camera remained around my neck, the lens cap busted, but otherwise fine.

Light footsteps sounded on the porch above me. I did not wish to see those ember eyes again, so spurred on by terror, I ran forward and climbed the fence. It took great effort. I succeeded only because of pure adrenaline. And fear. Fear of whatever unholy thing Jennifer had become.

I landed in a heap on the other side of the fence and scrambled to my feet, crying out as the toes on my injured foot curled up inside my shoe. I shuffled out of the darkness, onto the sidewalk. The street was empty at this time of night. My foot and back fought for attention, each trying to prove it cramp harder. The battle for pain dominance forced me to stop and stifle cries several times. My eyes watered with every step. The entire way home, I feared Jennifer followed.

· · • • • • • · ·

Upon arriving home, I hopped on one foot as quietly as I could up the fire escape. My roommates were both home and likely asleep. I locked the door behind me and peered out through the slats in the window shade to see if someone followed me. All clear. I stripped down in my room, filled a bowl with ice and water, wrapped my ankle in a small towel, and placed my foot in the bowl. I popped my AirPods into my ears and listened to Bach while drifting off to sleep.

About three in the morning, I woke with a start, groggy and still aching. My AirPods had fallen out of my ears as I slept. Scooping them up, I put them in my pocket and yawned. I'd tipped over the bowl of water in my sleep, leaving the floor and bedding soaked with melted ice. The pain in my ankle remained but died down some. Perhaps I hadn't sprained it. That would be lucky. I rose, slipped on sweatpants and a tee, then reached for my camera. The dirt covered plastic casing showed some nicks and scratches but appeared otherwise intact. *That was a close one.* I pressed the power button, relieved when it powered on.

The LCD screen flared to life, and I saw Jennifer's window as I'd seen it in person, but instead of an alluring and naked dancing Jennifer, I saw only the purple face and ember eyes version staring back at me from the screen. My heart jumped. I'd have to rewind to get to the good stuff. I did, but the image stayed the same. My eyes narrowed as I tried to understand what I saw. While scrolling through the footage in reverse, the image of Jennifer waved at me. I felt dizzy.

Then she appeared as if she were coming out of the screen. *Impossible*! A miniature nude and purple Jennifer Leeds wrapped her hands around the edges of the viewfinder with fingers as real as my waking nightmare. The screen dissolved, transforming into a miniature image of her window. She pulled herself up out of the camera and stabbed my thumb with a bone knife. I howled in pain and fright. A scream erupted from my gullet, filled with pure existential horror.

I threw my camera, smashing it against the wall. Tiny Jennifer was nowhere to be seen. I made for the kitchen on my hands and knees, leaving a small trail of blood dripping from my injured thumb. I huffed in fear, my eyes wide, mouth gaping. When I reached the kitchen doorway, I spotted my roommate Chris inside. He rubbed his eyes as I struggled to my feet.

"Hey, man," he said. "What's with the noise? You okay? It's three in the morning. I gotta' work. What's the problem?"

"She's here," I said. "The bitch from the coffee shop is here. She's punishing me All for doing what comes naturally!"

"Watch your language, Dude. Don't call women that. What woman? What coffee shop?" he asked, peering into my room. He noticed my wrapped foot. "You need an ambulance or something?"

"No, what I need for you is to understand that she's here!"

"Hey, listen," he began.

I lost focus on his words because the moment he began speaking (in an exasperated tone) tiny Jennifer appeared on his shoulder. She placed a hand on her lips, shushing me into secrecy. She gestured to her knife, then Chris' head, and nodded, grinning from ear to ear.

"She's on you," I shouted, cutting him off. "She's on you!"

I reached out to shove her off his shoulder, but Chris was a former Marine. When I tried to grasp her tiny body with my right hand, he grabbed my wrist and put me in an arm bar. I shouted in pain.

"You're fucking crazy, buddy!" he yelled in anger. "I'm tired of your creepy, crazy ass. I'm talking to Jeff and either you're out, or I'm out."

"She's going to hurt you," I said. "Let me go, she's an evil bitch!"

The downstairs light turned on. No doubt Jeff waking up to see what was happening. *Good.* He'd see how crazy Chris was when I was just trying to *help* him.

"Who's an evil bitch? Bro, you are the creepiest motherfucker alive, you know that? You think I don't hear you talking to yourself and whacking off all the time? Give it a rest, God damn. I feel gross just touching you! I'm going to keep holding you until Jeff gets up here, and then…"

Chris suddenly screamed, unable to complete his thought. He released me so he could attempt to pull Jennifer out of his left ear. Her legs dangled from his ear canal. He grabbed at them to no avail. Blood drained out around her tiny body and Chris frothed at the mouth, writhing in pain, slamming himself into the fridge, then the kitchen table, knocking over chairs and salt and pepper shakers. Jeff appeared at the top of the stairs with a golf club.

"Guys, guys, guys," Jeff said, looking alarmed and confused in his pajamas. "What the fuck is going on up here?"

"You wouldn't understand," I said. "Chris wouldn't listen to me, and you won't either. Sinners, the both of you."

I moved toward the kitchen door, but Jeff moved in front of me, barring my exit. He raised his golf club as if to strike me with it. I raised my arms in defense, though he stopped short of clubbing me.

"I don't want to hit you, Tom," Jeff said, "but if you don't back the fuck up and let me figure this out, I'm going to knock your head off. What'd you do to Chris?"

Chris continued screaming and writhing on the floor. Then, with a jerk, he went silent, falling mercifully unconscious. His head rested in a small pool of blood.

"Jennifer is inside his ear," I said, knowing full well Jeff would think I was a lunatic. I backed against the sink, hopping on one foot.

"Jennifer?" Jeff asked dismissively, suggesting I'd brained Chris. Jeff crouched down by the body and took out his iPhone. "I'm calling the police." He dialed. "Yes, I have a murder. Please come quickly. One of my tenants with another tenant. They're renting rooms from me. No, he's not breathing. There's lots of blood. Yes, I'll stay on the line. I have a golf club; I don't own guns. No, he's unarmed. Sure, let me just…"

As Jeff talked with the dispatcher, Chris's body seized. A melon-sized bubble formed in his stomach. Jeff didn't notice Chris' abdomen swelling or his back arching into the air. I stared in disbelief while Jeff did the golf club shaking boogie, keeping me backed up against the sink. Chris did his own voluntary dance on the floor.

Chris' body arched with his (almost pregnant looking) stomach serving as the highest point. A woman's leg burst from the small of Chris' back, its bare foot and painted nails slapping the linoleum floor. The leg took over for Chris, who no longer supported his own body. Instead, it dangled in midair, suspended by a woman's leg. A second leg followed. The twin slaps finally drew Jeff's attention. He turned around. In confusion, he dropped his club, which clattered to the floor.

"Chris?" he said, confused, unable to fathom Chris' body being suspended in midair by two shapely feminine legs.

I picked up the golf club, hands shaking in fear. A woman's torso erupted from Chris' distended belly, yawning as if she were waking at noon after a long night out. She wore Chris' body fluids and stomach organs. She slid the mess (that being Chris' body) down her legs as if removing a Sunday dress after church. Jennifer stood there now full size. Jeff dropped his iPhone and ran screaming for the stairs.

Jennifer winked at me as if she just served me a Frappuccino on the house. Then she ran after Jeff. Her bare feet left Chris' blood trailing behind in red, streaky footprints. She screeched in the tone of a dinosaur. The horrific sound caused me to piss myself.

I grabbed Jeff's iPhone. "Hello?" I spoke while moving for the door. I pulled on it and it wouldn't open despite the actual door not being in the "locked" position. My eyes welled with tears. Jeff screamed in terror from downstairs.

"Yes, this is the police," a woman's voice said from the other end. "What can I help you with today?"

"There's a crazy woman killing my roommates," I said. "I know it sounds nuts, but she really is. I'm telling you."

"Can you leave the room you're in?"

"I mean, normally I can, but she's somehow locked the door. She's downstairs killing Jeff, I think. She already killed Chris. I don't want to die. I think she's a witch!"

"You're trapped? What if you jumped out a window?"

"It's kind of high. I already sprained my ankle today."

"Thomas? How did you sprain your ankle?"

"It was an accident," I said, out of breath. Jeff wailed on the other side of the door for me to let him in and to call the police. Feminine laughter sounded on the other side followed by a feminine scream from Jeff. The door jostled. Then, silence.

"Oh, poor baby," the woman dispatcher said on the other end. "An accident you say?"

"Yeah, I fell."

"Thomas. Were you perhaps injured while looking at a naked girl half your age?"

My mouth went dry. "What?"

"This is the part where I would help you, send backup and all that, but I am merely a woman. I do not even know how to do my job. Just a bitch, really?"

"What is this? I need help!"

"You did not need any help to sneak onto someone else's property, did you now? How was her body, Thomas? Was it worth the peek? Were her tits nice enough for you to jack off to, even without your video?"

"How did..."

"You're a pervert, Thomas. A fucking pervert. And guess what?"

"What?"

The signal dropped, and the line went dead. Then, silence.

"What?" I asked.

There was a knock at the kitchen window. My heart jumped, but I knew who it was before even looking. Jennifer Leeds floated outside the second-floor window, her face and hair still covered in blood but no longer nude. She now wore a tee reading SALEM 1692, WHOOPS, MISSED ONE.

Her eyes became dying embers that were previously burned into my thoughts, and I felt myself rising. She beckoned me closer with a finger and I walked forward, despite my sprain. Each step sent pain shooting through my ankle, but I couldn't stop.

"Stop, please!" I shouted. "I'm sorry! I didn't know!"

I neared the window as Jennifer motioned with her hands. The glass burst, shredding my chest and face with tiny shards. I wanted to scream, wanted to pass out, but the embers of Jennifer's eyes held me in place, forcing me to stand on the sprained ankle. She floated backward from the window, beckoning.

"No, please," I said. "I'm afraid of heights."

I took a step forward, stepping on shards of glass with my bare feet. I screamed as the debris shredded and punctured my feet. Jennifer beckoned, and I found my leg lifting out the window. She planned to make me jump. Sirens screamed in the distance. She held out her hand, revealing the bone knife she'd used to kill Jeff. Something compelled me to take the knife in my hand, even as I supported my body using my left leg and left arm. It was a long way down.

"You don't have to do this," I said. "Please, God."

"Oh, I must do this, Thomas, because you're a predator and now you know how it is to be prey. You will continue to be prey in prison for the rest of your life."

"Prison?"

She laughed and beckoned to me once more. I had a brief sensation of falling, but everything went black.

· · • • • • • • • · ·

I remembered little after that, but police claimed I'd murdered Chris and Jeff before attempting suicide by leaping out a window. I'd broken both of my legs during the failed attempt.

When a tired-looking detective sought confession from me by sharing photos of my dead roommates, I admitted to the whole thing, taking the blame for the murders committed by Jennifer. The detective seemed surprised at my cooperation. Occasionally, he followed my gaze to a corner in the ceiling but saw nothing. She did not want him to. Jennifer Leeds floated in a corner near the ceiling, smiling the entire interrogation. Nobody saw her but me. *Fucking witch.*

BOARDHOUSE COFFEE

WEST LOS ANGELES, CA

I n a strip mall alongside a Chinese restaurant and car rental business, this unique little shop with great food for a "coffee shop" has a vibrant Californian feel. A surfboard dangles from the ceiling alongside two overhead fans, which work overtime in the summer months. Small comfortable tables surround a glass coffee table flanked by soft chairs and a couch which centers the dining area.

The clientele is a mix of nearby UCLA and SMC students alongside Westside locals and tourists either picking up their car rental or dropping it off and fearfully awaiting the inspection of the returned vehicle, hoping a few questionable driving choices did not create dings large enough to be noticed.

Anchored on one wall of Boardhouse coffee is the front of an old-style surfer van, a VW bug. One cannot help but look at the slim metal bumper and think that driving in Los Angeles once upon a time was pure pleasure, a getaway every day one took to the roads even if the destination was simply to one's job.

But what happens when a vehicle breaks down? There are places in LA which are still remote, where traffic does not flow like the 405. Remote corners and hidden roads galore in portions of the city. There are also long stretches where cellphone service vanishes.

How does one get help if they breakdown in such a spot? It leaves the commuter at the mercy of the kindness of strangers passing by or residents in nearby homes if any exist. There is potential danger in connecting with someone in such an area. Intentions can be hard to decipher. Hopefully, a person steps up with the best of intentions, a desire to help. Kindness in the face of adversity.

Yes, there are places in Los Angeles where roads are still open and where kindness still exists. However, kindness has a twin named evil. Bad things sometimes happen to good people and more frequently bad things happen around good people...

CUL-DE-SAC

PAUL CARRO

If I am honest with myself, I must admit I have a problem. I live on a cul-de-sac for no good reason other than the home was cheap, as am I. Every day I exit my front doors, twin glass sliders, lock them behind me and walk a long dirt road to where it connects with the Pacific Coast Highway. It has often been said people on PCH drive as if they are on PCP. I would not know really, I do not even know what PCP is, am unaware if people inject it or snort it. All I know is they drive crazy fast on PCH. Perhaps they drive more like they are on bath salts. Those I have heard of. Both kinds. I am fond of the non 'face eating' variety.

The morning walk is long. Given the slog, I minimized the weight in my briefcase, removed any scraps of paper, no need for extra pens, and even abandoned physical books for digital. I do not believe a vast library parked in the cloud makes my cellphone any heavier, but I have yet to do the research.

I have lived in the cul-de-sac for two years. Two years since heartbreak, two years since betrayal, two years of minimal contact with the opposite sex, turned off at the thought of being made love to while lied to. If I were in therapy, I am certain I would spend my dollars and time working through trust issues. I am not in therapy.

I should be.

Perhaps I could end the despising women stage of my life. Sorry, let me rephrase that. I love women. I hate Rebecca. Rebecca May Anderson to be precise. She said 'I do' when I kneeled with the ring. Before we made it to the altar, she too kneeled before my (former) best man Mason. That was Colorado. I live in Los Angeles now. I love women other than Rebecca May Anderson.

I left that problem in Colorado along with my past life. No, my current problem, the one I am fully aware of when honest with myself, relates to an oddity. Every time I approach my cul-de-sac, I cannot help but think of its actual definition: a blind pouch or cavity closed at one end, specifically referencing the rectouterine pouch, part of the peritoneal cavity between the rectum and uterus.

I studied medicine. Rebecca May Anderson is now a doctor as is my (former) best friend, Mason. I am not. I sell solar panels. How California is that? My problem is that if I cannot let go of the medical definition of the dead-end street I live on, then how can I ever move past the heartbreak which brought me here?

Mine is the solo home on the road with no name. (A signpost stands erect at the entrance to my street but absent a top, the road likely named something clever enough for teens to have absconded with it.) I use a P.O. Box for my mail. Food delivery I have worked out with some local restaurants. They have figured out how to find me.

At least I have no neighbors to disparage me for having chosen the location poorly, disparaging me for being unable to swing the cost of a home on the straightaway portion of the street. My lot in life and home ownership left me positioned where headlights might routinely circle and sweep through any front facing windows.

My outlier locale in pricey Malibu hints my home was likely once upon a time a drug den for the affluent surrounding me. Looking up from my front yard, I see nothing but trees as I am surrounded by forest. But once I emerge onto PCH, I can spot many homes large enough to swallow mine whole. Several have guest quarters larger than my entire house. Many estates harbor swimming pools and tennis courts. Rumor has it a monastery sits atop the hill. I hope it does as I enjoy the thought of people who eschew material things owning the peak of the toniest of mountainous enclaves. I intended, at some point, to visit their spiritual abode, but since I have not done so in two years, I understand I never will, as sure as I will never marry Rebecca May Anderson.

The elegant homes which surround my scrub brush of a road are ones I could have owned had I stayed on my path to becoming a doctor. I made choices that changed my circumstances. Now I wake at seven every day to walk from the pouch end of the cul-de-sac to a bus stop. It is nothing short of miraculous that vehicular carnage has not ensued at the stop where traffic must navigate past the big blue bus when it stops to pick up two Latina nannies and me every day along a perilous bend in the highway.

The women are friendly, matronly, always smiling. They often bring me food. Tamales mostly. While I do not speak Spanish, kindness is universal. I have learned enough of the language to be aware they believe I should eat more since they consider me too skinny. I believe there is also a relative they wish to hook me up with. Two years in and that is all I have absorbed. The women are fantastic; I enjoy their company. But though I live in Malibu, I will not learn to surf, and I will not learn Spanish, and I will not visit monasteries, even those in my backyard. I have none of that in me.

I would Google translate with the friendly women if I could, but cell phone service does not kick in until I reach Santa Monica. By then they have already left the bus for mansions to care for children likely confused about who their actual mothers are, the ones they see every day or the ones they do not.

One could say my life was routine, boring perhaps, uneventful, and one would be correct. Complacency appeared to be my lot in life, no adventures left in this hard-hearted soul. There were women at work, customers mostly, who appeared interested in my proximity to Malibu. It is safe to assume they equated my run-down shack with money. No, despite my own needs (mostly physical because mentally I had already adjusted to the thought of a forever single life) I vowed not to allow another woman into my home. I chalk up my general lack of cleanliness to a deep-seated way of ensuring I did not waver, did not cave to accepting an invitation to take someone home if even for one night. That or I was just lazy.

That was why the appearance of the Volkswagen van parked midway down the road on which I lived so surprised me.

One would think my proximity to the ocean just across PCH, azure blue, clear all the way to Catalina Island in the distance, would bring traffic to my street daily if for no other reason than to turn around. Someone seemingly designed PCH to never outlet until one left the state. Forgetting the need to turn about, there was always the lure of free parking in a place where spots for cars were more in demand than the real estate.

But no. Crossing PCH from my location would be a folly. Any brave enough to park and gather up all their things would find their lives at risk of being cut short while crossing. If they survived the eighty miles-an-hour traffic rounding a blind curve, they would arrive at a cliff below which existed a beach of questionable nature. The view was stunning. Make no mistake, I have braved the crossing just to snap a few pics. However, anything resembling a beach existed only during the lowest of tides. The rest of the time it turned into rocky surf splashing against the cliff-side.

My section of Malibu was not a tourist destination. Even if it were, there was the matter of my front gate. Unlike my hillside neighbors, I do not live in a gated community, at least not in the traditional sense. A massive overgrowth of trees fronts my street. The man-planted grouping stretches out along both sides of the street, creating a nature's gate of sorts.

A welcome or a warning, depending on the time of day. By dusk, the trees whose branches embrace one another like lovers in an arc over the street appeared to merge into one clump. They might well have been ancient fingers clasping, ready to pull ever tighter until their trunks merged to close off the road and swallow any who dared pass.

To look at them in the light of day, however, one would find the view lovely. Funny how a subtle change in light could so suddenly morph the comfortable to its opposite. Much like a pile of clothes in a bedroom chair that becomes menacing at three AM.

The lack of useable beach combined with the *is it a street or isn't it* nature of the road's entrance was why I found a van sitting there so surprising. I was halfway to the bus stop when I first noticed it. The late model Volkswagen van, sky blue, surfer van style, sat parked half on the road, half in a ditch, nestled under the shade provided by a copse of trees. After spotting the vehicle, I turned back to notice its unobstructed view of the sliding glass doors to my home. Strange, I had not noticed it earlier.

It occurred to me as I drew closer that it may well have parked prior to today. In my lulled sense of routine, I might have walked past it unaware, lost in one of the many podcasts that flowed through my earbuds every morning.

Unlikely. Paranoid of rattlesnakes (despite never having encountered one) I regularly searched for signs of life. Even birds drew my attention with just a flap of feathers. The van must have just now parked. I was never that oblivious. Except upon closer inspection, my argument fell apart.

Tree buds, sprinkled with yellow pollen, peppered the roof of the van. It had to have sat for some time for nature to have painted so thoroughly across the light blue metal canvas. Meanwhile, nature's detritus covered as much as half of each wheel well with branches, windswept dirt, leaves, and even half a Styrofoam cup. Only time and weather could gather such a mess. Strange. How could I have missed it for so long? Yet I did. How else to explain the condition of the parked vehicle?

I thought my problem was my inability to let go of my medical training past, to move on with my life, to not dwell on the true meaning of things like the word cul-de-sac but it appeared my bigger problem was that I had checked out. How I could be so oblivious to something I passed for multiple days concerned me.

The vehicle had a wide front grill with twin headlights only slightly larger than the VW symbol centered on its face. Its quaint white bumper suggested a time when surviving impact was perhaps only an afterthought. Twin square orange lights rested above the main headlights, though what purpose they served I could not fathom.

Any vehicle this close to my home should have drawn my attention. How aloof had I become since untethering myself from my past? How could I not notice such a classic vehicle? Before I could beat myself up any further, I almost leaped out of my skin when something appeared.

A face.

A woman's face. Light reflecting off the windshield partially blinded me, but enough of the vehicle remained in the shade to allow me a partial glimpse of the interior. The front seat remained empty, which is likely why I failed to notice her right away. There in the middle of the van, dead center of the vehicle, sat an old woman. Her head looked out from behind the front seat. She remained motionless, though stared directly at me.

I froze. Strange the vehicle being there, stranger still the signs it had been there for some time (even now I noticed the half-inflated tires. No way she drove so far in such a condition). Strangest of all was the age of the woman. I am twenty-eight. I would guess her to be more than double my age. Sixties?

There was a healthy air about her that many in California possess. The temperate climate bakes folks into old age slowly. A length of shock white hair cascaded over her shoulders, the length indeterminate, blocked by-what? The front seat? Maybe just the glare from the window, but it was hard to see the woman in her entirety. What I could make out the best was her head. Wrinkles lined her face like the folds of a gas station map. Her eyes were deep green, startlingly clear even from a distance, greener than any I had seen. A model losing a contract to age only to wind up living in a van felt as Californian dreaming as the surfer van before me.

"Hello?"

I regretted saying it as soon as the words left my mouth. I had long since lost my way with women, no matter their age, but I had expected at least a smile of recognition, you know, me being the guy coming out of the nearby house and all. But no, she did not answer, failed to even react. That left me to wonder, did she not hear me given her advanced age? Or was she bothered by my presence? Afraid even?

I stepped closer.

"Are you okay?"

Again, I consider myself slow on the uptake, cannot read a woman's clues well. Once upon a time some called it charming. No charm now, only concern for her, and she did not appear open to offering me reassurance. In my current position, yards away from her, I was closer to invading her personal space than she was of mine, though her clear view into the front of my house gave me pause.

My cell phone buzzed which startled me as there is no signal in the area. It was not a call, but my daily alarm set to remind me of the departure time for the bus. I was about to be late for transportation that arrived only once an hour, so I ran. It likely looked to her as though I were about to attack, though she took it well, remaining seated as I moved closer. I shouted one last thing while passing.

"I hope you're okay. Please don't break into my house while I'm gone!"

I ran off to meet my Spanish nannies, who scolded me for being late. I explained about the blue van and the old woman and how I worried about her situation only to get a "Que?" for my troubles.

· · · ● · ● · · · ·

I did not think about the woman for the rest of the day. Too busy with clean energy, tax rebates, and cold calling. While sympathetic to the greater good of my industry, the banality of it all was mind numbing even on the best of days. After work, an accident on PCH slowed our return home. That being me and the nannies. It was darker than usual by the time we arrived.

Our drop-off point was the same spot as our pickup. The route turned off a canyon road past my place where it looped around to the Palisades, then Santa Monica, before circling back to Malibu. Upon returning home, a Lexus SUV waited to pick up the two women on the same small inlet the bus used. I believed the driver to be the relative the nannies wished me to meet. Nadia was her name, a lovely young woman in her twenties, bespectacled, with luxurious brown flowing hair and an amiable smile. Her eyes twinkled as she greeted the two women who chattily got into the vehicle, even as they pantomimed introductions between me and Nadia. I think Nadia understood I am broken, so she never encouraged the older women. I appreciated that about her. Still, as was her occasional custom, Nadia handed off a tinfoil-wrapped paper plate of tamales.

The one I believed to be Nadia's mother stepped back out of the SUV and walked the plate over to me. I gave Nadia my normal knowing wink and smile like Clark Kent at the end of almost every old Superman serial (which I had been recently watching on YouTube). As I winked, I jerked in sudden fright.

I emerged from the startle quickly, trying to refocus on Nadia's smile except it faded as quickly as a blown candle. Nadia eyed me with concern. (Offended?) The plate in my hands tilted when I startled but I quickly leveled it back out. Nadia rolled up her tinted window with a frown. Then the women drove away.

Nadia existed only as an evening figure. I never glimpsed her in the mornings, since she always dropped the women off prior to my arrival at the stop. I would have to wait until the next evening to see if her smile would ever return or if it vanished forever under my odd behavior. What Nadia would not know, could not know, was that for one beat of my heart, in that short a span, I swear her face changed to that of the woman in the van.

I felt foolish. The woman in the van was likely gone by now. Or was she? How long she parked near my home remained a mystery. I looked toward my road. The massive Sycamores stood like silent sentries in the night. In daylight the sight was stunning, a beauty to Malibu beyond the beaches. At night, the crossed branches appeared formidable, a gauntlet. I walked through the unnerving but familiar passage.

Though I expected the world to brighten upon emerging into the open, the sun had abandoned its post for the day. A gloom settled in. I identified the shape of the van in the distance, looming in shadow. It remained a parked as lazily as an RV at the beach.

There should have been a light on inside the vehicle, but the interior remained dark. Perhaps the woman inside worked from a laptop or was using her phone in dark mode. There was a possibility she might not own any devices. Everyone owned them, even the homeless who filled the alleys and parks of Santa Monica to capacity. Maybe she too was homeless but isolated herself from those in similar circumstances. Perhaps she was hungry. I had food.

If I handed off the tamales, it would require me to lie to the women tomorrow about the meal. What if they inquired about which flavor I most enjoyed? Pork? Beef?

Chicken? Pineapple? I love the pineapple ones. I did not know which I held in my hands without tasting them.

I moved to the front of the van, peering in, but failed to spot the woman. Darkness greeted me. There were no signs of life at all. I pressed my home screen on my phone, aimed it inside the van, but the light proved inadequate. The flashlight function would have helped, but rather than disturb her further, I simply left the tamales.

A small lip of metal jutted from below the wide, bowed windshield. Enough of an edge to grip one end of the plate while the balance would rest against the glass. I decided it was time to return home to cook something less enticing than pineapple tamales. A frozen meal, as per usual.

Upon arriving at my front porch, the chill from earlier returned. The doors were open. More precisely, one side was. Both the glass slider and screen. It would have been easy to turn on the living room lights to announce my presence but given the remote location I questioned whether that was a wise course of action.

The woman was not in the van. I jokingly requested her to not break in earlier, which left her as the most likely culprit. Yet it could be someone more nefarious. Could it be someone in search of the fabled drug dealers of yore? A glint of metal confirmed my TV remained mounted to the wall. Small victories. My bedroom, which contained anything as close to valuables that I owned, was to my left, nestled alongside the bath and laundry rooms.

The right side fed into a tiny dining alcove followed by the kitchen. It was from there I heard a crash. I leaped, instinctively reaching for the exit, ready to run. Yet once clear, I would have no cell service with which to call 911. I needed my landline (seldom used but needed for emergencies like, well, this one) but it was in the kitchen with the intruder. Another crash. I turned on my flashlight app.

I stepped gingerly through the dining area. The sad, tilted table with only three chairs around it (not four) should have shown intruders they were not breaking into the most valuable home on the mountain. Still, what were criminals but professional opportunists? Easy access, no alarm beyond the fake sticker from a security company I am not even sure exists anymore if it ever did. The sticker came with the place.

Rustling sounded ahead. A ransacking in progress, looking for what? I neared the bend in the dining area, the point of no return. Once I turned the corner, there would be no hiding my light or presence. The small kitchen housed a refrigerator right along the entrance, abutted by a gas oven and a storage cabinet. The opposite side offered a kitchen sink, dual tiled countertops and multiple cabinets.

I stepped around the corner. My phone's light illuminated a most horrific sight! The drawer to the storage pantry sat open. Trash from the bin lay strewn along the floor. The disaster was well and good. What hovered over the mess shocked me to my core. Goose pimples rocketed up my arms.

The elderly woman from the truck stood on all fours! Her thin, spindly limbs bent in unnatural directions. She was nude, wrinkled, and frail, though she possessed a tautness to the muscles which allowed her to maintain an animal stance. Her hindquarters (okay, her cul-de-sac) arched high in my direction while her brittle rib strewn torso leaned toward the garbage trail, her white hair splayed over her head, covering most of her face.

She snarled while chewing on a tossed chicken bone, a remnant of a previous night's takeout meal. Her breasts hung down sharply, dry. Her back displayed every bump of vertebrae along a spine arched downward with a wild curve of scoliosis. Shoulder blades rose high off her back, like chicken wings. The twin edges of bone threatened to tear through the paper-thin fabric that was her skin.

The woman turned her head toward me, a bone still in her mouth. A single eye glanced through the mop of hair catching my light. The reflection offered an oversized orb of pure white. I screamed and dropped my phone.

Hissing filled the room. I reached for my phone with no care to whether the screen cracked. I needed the light to escape. My fingers found it, fumbled, brought it back to bear. The dim light glinted off the eye again, revealing a face still in possession of the chicken bone. A face annoyed by my presence. The racoon dropped the chicken wing, hissed at me again, before scooping the food back up. It walked past me nonchalantly with its prize.

I shuddered as the thing brushed my leg, surprised how unconcerned it was over my presence. Switching on the kitchen light, I leaned into the living room and watched the furry burglar lazily take its leave. I slammed the door, locked it, then rushed through my home, turning on every light.

Someone had opened the door unless I left it open that morning. The woman outside was obviously on my mind. How else to explain my vision? I felt silly. She was old. Possibly homeless, no threat. Still, as I sat on the couch to gather myself, before I could even consider attending to the mess in the kitchen, I wondered whether she could see me from her van. Did she watch me even now? With my lights on, she could see into my home, my world. I had never invested in curtains. Why bother? Now I felt exposed, open to scrutiny from a woman living in a van.

I cleaned the kitchen and went to bed without heating a meal. I was no longer hungry. The thought of the woman's face buried in food had sapped me of my appetite, even if it was not real. I slept through the night with no further thoughts of my new neighbor.

··•••••••··

I was late after sleeping too soundly, perhaps working off the adrenaline of the night prior. Glancing at my front door unsettled me. Had someone violated my space? I rushed to my kitchen, reached into the same defiled pantry from the night before, and pulled out my seldom used mop. I returned to the front door, gripped the mop at one end and stomped my foot on the wood handle. It snapped to the desired length. I placed the wooden piece along the track and attempted to slide the glass door open. The obstruction stopped it before even an inch could open. A poor man's security system.

After locking the door from the inside (despite the wooden barrier) I exited through the rear. The back door had a deadbolt, which I locked with my key. I circled my wraparound porch back to the front and discovered a surprise. Sitting at the top step was the empty paper plate with tinfoil loosely reattached. Good for her. She had eaten, and I got to feel like a better human being.

"I'm glad you enjoyed but stay out of my house, please," I yelled from my porch.

I rushed down the road. Once in view of the van, I saw her face in the same spot. There was something off about her which I could not figure out. Perhaps the seat leaned to one side on a broken spring. That would explain her lilt. Her head appeared to float in the confines of a vehicle. I smiled this time, assuming a newfound cordiality given the food offering from the night before. I smiled and waved while she sat there, unmoving.

Oh well, try to do a favor. I had somewhere to be, so raced off. The nannies, perhaps upset at my antics the night before, seemed disinterested in my presence. I said, "gracias for tamales," but it garnered not a single smile from either. They seemed put off by me.

After work I shopped for groceries, enough for a week. On grocery days, I sprang for an Uber to avoid dealing with masses of bags on the bus. While shopping I thought of the woman again, felt silly for thinking she burgled my house. Not one shred of food had gone missing from the fridge, only what the racoon rooted from the garbage bin. I am certain I left the door open, or nearly certain.

The woman was surely nothing more than homeless working her way across the canyons in search of— something. Whatever her pursuit, it required food, so I shopped with her in mind. I purchased an additional bag's worth of mostly fruit, nuts, and non-perishables. Nothing requiring an empty flame. I did not need a spark igniting brush anywhere near my home.

The Uber driver was a young female who appeared at ease until reaching the entrance to my street. The furious rush of cars behind us forced her to enter. Reluctantly, she drove in, searching for signs of a neighborhood before examining me in her rearview. I felt the tension, smiled dorkily to relieve it. She shook her head, harrumphed, and continued driving.

"I'm not a danger," I offered.

"I know. I sized you up, early on. You oversold the smile though, kind of creepy, you might want to work on that," she said.

I smiled, for real. She smiled back in the mirror.

"That's better. Stick with that. No, I am more concerned with how my car might handle this road. I think we're okay."

The van creeped into view when it hit me.

"Hey, do you speak Spanish?"

The woman stopped the car, turned back to face me. Her almond eyes squinted as her pert nose upturned in my direction. She sneered through perfect white teeth.

"Why? Just because I look Latina, I should speak Spanish, is that it?"

"What? No, I just…" I stammered.

"You saw my name on your app, so just because it is Lisa Hernandez, I must speak picture perfect Spanish, is that it?"

"No, listen, I'm sorry, I…"

She laughed. "Just giving you grief. Si, I speak Español. Why?"

I did not respond to her joke, worried I might say something to offend for real. I quickly explained about the woman in the van. Lisa pulled alongside and stepped out. She peered in, pressing her face against the glass. Braver than me. I remained in her backseat with the window rolled down.

"I don't see her. Maybe she's at the beach."

"It's kind of late, isn't it?" I asked.

"Not if she uses it as her bath before retiring for the night," she said.

Good point. I had bought the woman food, but no toiletries, had not considered such needs. Next time. The driver did that which I had asked her to do. She asked in Spanish if anyone was inside and if so, did they need help? Were they okay? There was no answer, so the driver got back in and drove me to my cul-de-sac.

I thanked her and explained my tip would appear tomorrow once my cell was in range. She suggested I carry cash next time but told me she would five star me anyway for looking out for the woman. I offloaded my bags onto the ground while Lisa drove off. I went around the back, let myself in, removed the mop handle and opened the front where I retrieved all but one bag.

The last I carried to the van. Despite the sun setting, I glimpsed the woman's face and almost dropped the bag. How she could have gotten back in the time the Uber departed eluded me. Unnerving how she sat there, so stoic, hard for me to see anything. Why always the same spot? I lifted the bag and approached. Strange how my view did not improve as I got closer. I still could only catch her face and her hair. I was curious about her clothes, wondering how ragged they were, how destitute she was. As usual, the front seat blocked my view. She stared out at me.

I made a show of lifting the bag and setting it down by the driver's side door. As I stood back up, I noticed a handprint on the windshield from inside the vehicle. Was it there initially? It had to be. The woman remained in her seat while I walked home.

·· • • •• • • • ··

The next morning, as I stepped from the shower, I stopped in my tracks. The mirror (fogged over as always after my shower) showed the imprint of a hand. I saw nothing in my daily routine which could have resulted in such an oddity. There was no mistaking it. A handprint was on my mirror, the size of the one on a certain van window.

Before I could investigate it further, the condensation dripped, running into beaded rivulets along the reflective surface until the imprint bled away the shape of a hand and looked more like someone weeping. I wiped it clean, relieved not to find anyone behind me in my reflection.

After exiting my house through the rear, I noticed the strangest thing. The van appeared to be closer. That would be good news, as it would likely mean she got the vehicle in drivable shape. Perhaps my simple act of kindness with the food allowed her to save just enough of her cash to call triple A.

Things were looking up. The other day I had a woman over at my house. Well, an Uber driver creeped out by me. Still, progress. I looked through the front facing glass to examine what visitors would notice when visiting me. It was not good. College was over, I was on course for a professional career, yet as I examined my life from the outside looking in, I might as well live in the van outside.

It was long past the time for me to ask Nadia out. At the least, I owed her an apology for my freakish behavior. The woman was lovely. Hot even. I stepped away from my porch with a spring in my step, determined to liquidate part of my bank account towards the purchase of some real adult furniture, ready to at least attempt an actual adult life. I looked forward to seeing the nannies as I rushed along the road.

The van **was** closer.

I stopped when I reached it. The woman was not in the van. I would have rushed past if she were. But with her nowhere in sight, it allowed me time to inspect the vehicle. It still had deflated tires all around, still showed signs of windblown debris trapped under tire wells. Pollen and cypress leaves remained baked into the roof, too attached for wind removal.

The van could not have moved in its condition. Yet when I looked back to my house, there was no mistaking the shorter distance between the two. There was even a better view of my sad sack living room. A perfect place to watch from, to stalk from. Great, I have attracted an octogenarian stalker. My love life really is looking up.

Turning back, I spotted the woman upright in her seat again. Standing closer than ever before, my brain nudged me in a direction to solve the issue of what appeared "off" about her. Unable to fully grasp an answer, I slinked away, embarrassed at being caught watching.

The bus pulled away as I arrived on PCH. I missed it. I needed a phone to call a ride. But looking back, I shuddered. Something about the woman. I did not wish to face her again so soon. Hugging the shoulder of the busy road, I walked about half a mile to an emergency roadside services phone. The dispatcher was not happy to work out a cab for me, but he did.

There was no pleasant person named Lisa driving this time (and this was not a ride share, it was old school). The driver named Frank argued with his girlfriend over his cell the entire trip. It looked like a one-star kind of day.

An emergency arose early in the day at work requiring travel to a client's house. There were problems between a contractor and the client. I needed to keep both people happy or face losing a substantial commission. While loathe to drive in L.A., renting a car was in order.

After securing a rental, I drove to the client's house. The homeowner was apoplectic over the sheer number of vehicles in her yard. Jorge, the contractor quarreled with the woman. She was elderly, silver-haired, frail. Could have been sisters with my van companion.

"Jacob, I'm so glad you are here. I did not know there would be so many vehicles, such a fuss," said Mrs. Rothbury.

"Listen, Jacob, I was trying to explain to Mrs. **Wrath**bury here," Jorge began.

"Rothbury. You said that on purpose."

"Please, Mrs. Rothbury, he calls me Joe instead of Jacob all the time, he's horrible with names but great with solar systems," I said, lying about the name thing. "I swear to you, this is the best crew for the job. Let us see what we can work out. Yes?"

The woman crossed arms in defiance. There was no moving her. She wanted the vehicles back at street level. We complied, which meant a long slog of carrying materials up to the house. Unnecessary work. I took off my sport coat and joined the grumbling crew. It was hard work carrying all the panels up the driveway, where we staged them on pallets alongside the house.

Jorge partnered with me, which gave allowed time to apologize and offer promises of future work. He was not happy but understood, a hazard of the job, working for people in the most intimate of situations, their homes.

After several trips I was dripping with sweat. The heat radiated off the blacktop at our feet. Jorge walked backward each time while I navigated with the sets of panels packaged in bundles about four feet long each.

When the door to the house opened, I dropped my load. The woman from the van stepped out of the house. She held one of my bags of groceries but was otherwise nude. The woman's skin was deeply wrinkled, tanned hard from years in the California sun.

Jorge cursed and fought to hold up his end. A pair of workers bumped me from behind, causing me to stumble. When I recovered there was no van lady. Only Mrs. Rothbury holding a large silver tray of sandwiches and cans of La Croix.

"All that hard work. You boys must be hungry," she said.

The crew abandoned ship, leaving their packages where they were, and attacked the tray. Jorge waved a finger in a circle around his temple, showing the woman was crazy. That was when it hit me. Mrs. Rothbury was likely senile. What if my neighbor suffered the same condition? Maybe the x-factor of what felt off about the woman related to symptoms of such a malady.

I abandoned the thoughts for a chance at free sandwiches. While eating, I confided in Jorge about the situation. He agreed van lady likely suffered age-related issues. He provided me a non-emergency number to call. I should have thought of that myself, should have done so sooner. But it took the crazy actions of a different older person for the obvious to fall in my lap.

Mid sandwich break, Mrs. Rothbury asked why we were carrying everything so far, suggesting we use the driveway. The crew abandoned their meals and drove onto the property to finish unloading before the woman could change into a different mind.

The confusion bordering on insanity of Mrs. Rothbury prompted me to call for a welfare check on the van lady by the time I left the job site.

· · ● ● · ● ● · · ·

Since I had the rental car, I stocked up on groceries, packing an extra bag filled to the brim with staples for my van friend. I was glad there would be someone to check on her soon. It was dark by the time I arrived home.

Upon returning, I circled into my cul-de-sac when an idea hit me. Rather than stop, I rode through it, heading back the other way. I killed my headlights and used puddles of light from the moon to help me along. I parked my rental, so it faced her van. Retrieving the bag of groceries, I raised it in full view.

"Brought you some more. Stayed away from anything nut related just in case of allergies. Mostly produce, might want to eat it in a timely manner, unless you have a fridge in there, though I don't see how."

Nerves guided my rambling, despite having no reason to be afraid. Perhaps I only reacted to a wind sweeping through with a frigid undercurrent. Fine, I made contact; the rest was up to her.

I set the bag on the top of the vehicle, hoping the height might protect against critters. I suspected the furry bandit who raided my home would have no issues climbing over a bumper.

The bumper.

It too haunted me in the same elusive way the woman's face did. Dots were not connecting on something. I needed a better view to figure out the missing puzzle piece. Lifting the rental key fob, I remotely triggered the high beams. They lit the van's interior. I leaped in fright. There she was, the woman sitting in her normal spot looking out at me, nonplussed by the lights. Her gaze reflected the beams back like an animal's eyes caught on a night scope.

Even fully lit, the view provided me no more insight into what bothered me about her. I quickly extinguished the beams, and she vanished from view. It was time to leave her alone. Poor thing was off, did not know enough to shield herself from the light. I felt awful for subjecting her to it.

"You may get a visit soon! Pay no worry, they only want to check on you!" I shouted, hoping she understood.

I backed up to my house and unloaded my groceries. By the time I came out for the last bag, I noticed the one I left van lady was no longer on her roof. It meant she kept some control of some of her faculties. That was good. Strange I had not heard her door open or close.

I retired early and slept deeply. When I woke, I found myself unable to move. I tried to lift an arm or leg, but it was as if hands held me fast to the bed, pressing me down into the depth of coils at my back. Even screaming was out, my vocal cords as paralyzed as everything else.

My eyes were wide open, glancing around the room, my orbs moving furiously to compensate for the immobility everywhere else. Just beyond my chest I glimpsed a terrifying sight! A tuft of white hair moved in my direction.

I could not feel the advance, still could not feel my body, could only watch as it creeped up my chest. The top of someone's head traveling up my body, following the path of a spine I no longer controlled.

Closer.

Inches at a time. I did not wish to see more, did not want to know that which held me in check, but it approached the edges of my quivering chin. Hair, grey hair, as frazzled as my new reality creeped nearer. Tufts spun in all directions so wildly that some strands likely poked their way into other dimensions.

I shut my eyes to avoid witnessing any more. Pressing them tight to the point of tears, I begged the thing to go away, to vanish like my past. While I could not feel the thing advance further, its timing registered in my mind. Whatever it was, it would be upon me already. I opened my eyes.

She was right in front of me. The van lady's eyes locked with mine. Hers displayed the same milky white reflected in the high beams from earlier. Our lips brushed as close as lovers. She smiled, showing blackened, dried bean teeth.

I yelled while my body finally freed itself from its bedtime prison. I shook every limb, kicking out while screaming in a voice pitching higher than I thought myself capable of. Jolting upright, I ceased my cries to suck in oxygen. Something seemed to keep screaming, but it was not me.

Sirens.

There were sirens outside my home. I blinked to make sure I was in the waking world. I found myself alone. Of course I was. She had never been there. My medical studies covered sleep paralysis, a condition where one's body remains in the protective immobile state even as the mind prematurely awakens. Many experiencing the phenomena suffer images of a witch holding them down. Surely, I suffered the same fate and ascribed my neighbor's face to that of the traditional witch's face. The clock did not display the three AM witching hour. It was almost seven AM.

A tapping on my front doors brought me to my feet. Still in my boxers and tee, I rushed to the living room, surprised to find a female police officer standing outside my doors. I stared at her questioningly.

"You mind?" she asked.

She mimed the act of opening the doors. As I did, I glimpsed others of her kind over her shoulder, gathered by the van. I also noticed my state of undress. She noticed me noticing.

"I'm fine," she said, regarding the underwear. "What's your name?"

"Jacob Forester. Is everything okay?"

"Do you know anything about the van?"

"Yeah, I'm the one who called it in. Thought I dialed 311. Wait, did I accidentally call 911?"

"No. You called the right line. May I ask why you called it in?"

"I worried about the woman," I said before noticing the earlier siren belonged to an ambulance which rode the dirt road carefully, slow. No hurry, despite the sirens. A coroner's van followed behind. I stepped out onto my wraparound; the officer reached for her service weapon at her hip. I raised my hands. "It's my property. I didn't do anything."

"Slow your roll a little in front of me, yes?"

Startled her, check. I nodded, walking down the porch, barefoot, strangely enjoying the feel of nature at my feet. Live in it for so long but forgetting to enjoy it. The officer watched me take in the scene. I turned back to her. The officer was tall, muscled, looked like she could take me out. Having done nothing wrong, I did not fear her, but remained curious why she observed me so closely.

"How do you know it was a woman?" she asked.

"I see her every day," I said. The officer looked at me like I was a Martian. Did I have an officer who planned to give me grief about profiling someone I had only seen from a distance? By all appearances, the person in the van was female. I could be wrong. Listen…" I leaned in to read her badge. She pulled it taught off her uniform, closer to my face.

"Harper."

"Listen, Officer Harper. I know a woman when I see one, I was a med student."

She laughed. I scrunched my nose, tried to figure out what was so funny.

"I take it you failed the program?"

"No. Left, personal issues," I said.

"Might have saved a few lives," she said.

A half dozen other officers danced around the scene, paying us no mind. They were taking a lot of pictures. A cop insulted me for taking time to worry about a woman in the van. I felt a rage rising to the surface.

"Officer, did I do something to tick you off? Last I checked, I live here. Feel free to go insult someone else. I'm going to go back inside. Let me know when you are all done," I said.

I started off, but she grabbed my arm, not violently, but to get my attention. I looked back.

"Clear a path!" An officer from the group yelled, and everyone stepped aside.

Two officers moved away from the side of the van, each holding the side of a blanket. My eyes went wide at the fabric held. It did not take medical school to recognize human bones! The cops bypassed the ambulance and delivered the bounty to the coroner's van.

I suddenly became more aware of what the other officers were doing. They were processing a crime scene, taking pictures, bagging evidence. When one burly officer lifted a small plastic bag from within the van, Harper waved him over. The man refused to let go of the evidence bag even while she pulled the plastic taut in his hands, giving me a good look at the wallet with the driver's license folded out.

The license contained a picture of the old woman. The license was California issued, but an older version than I was familiar with. And yellowed.

"Is this the woman you saw?" Harper asked.

I nodded, unable to speak. She shook her head, and the officer took the evidence away.

"Didn't mean to insult earlier but if you can't tell the difference between the living and the dead, then we were all saved malpractice suits."

"But I saw her," I whispered.

"What year were you born?"

"Nineteen ninety," I said.

"Then you are not a suspect. We have her on file. Went missing on her way to get groceries for her grandkids in nineteen eighty-six. Looks like we finally found her," Harper said.

"That's impossible," I said.

The officer kicked a foot towards the bumper, and it was there I noticed what had thrown me about the vehicle. The registration sticker was larger than normal and the date on it was from nineteen eighty-six!

"Sorry to give you a hard time. You did the right thing. I'm concerned about you though, maybe you're the one who needs a welfare check."

"No, I'm fine. A trick of the light in the van. Surely, that is all I saw," I lied.

She nodded. "We'll tow it today. Be out of your hair soon. Oh, but we will have search teams back for a few days," she said.

"Why?"

"We have the entire skeleton except for one important missing piece, her head."

I nodded and rushed back to my home so she would not see me turn white. Once inside, I went to my restroom, ran the water, and vomited into the sink. That was what bothered me so about the woman in the van. Every time I had seen her, every glimpse of her face, it suddenly became clear what I had never seen. Never did I see her body!

They took the van away later that day. I did not know what to make of what I saw, of what I could not have seen. When darkness fell, I retreated early to the refuge of my covers, hoping to sleep off the impossibility of the day's events.

I woke to a thump. Or thumps. It sounded like fleshy meat slapping against the glass front doors. Like someone drunkenly smacking the windowpanes. I grabbed my cell, noticed it was three AM. I rose to my feet.

Stepping into the living room, my sense of reality crumbled. Both sliding glass doors were covered top to bottom in handprints. They filled almost every inch of space from bottom to top as clear as day. The door lay open, the mop lock defeated. The dowel lay off to the side as if it rolled out of place.

The chill of the night air failed to match that of my blood, which suddenly ran oh so cold. I stepped toward the door, slid it open, and looked down. Sitting there on my porch was the bag of groceries I left for the woman the night before!

I hurriedly filled a suitcase and drove off in my rental car with no concerns over the promised return date of the vehicle. At this point I would return it in another state, at a branch somewhere far away. I drove all night and never returned for the rest of my things. Never even returned to Malibu or California. Wherever I began my new life, I hoped it would be where surfer vans were less prominent. I hoped never to encounter another again, fearful it might contain something I wished to leave behind. Because somewhere out there was a grandmother who, much like me, was trying to find her way home.

STARBUCKS

SACO MAINE

When I got the idea for this story, it never occurred to me it would eventually become part of a horror anthology involving coffee. I began working in the coffee industry in this very store, and sometimes on slow days I'd have time while cleaning to imagine different story ideas while beginning grad school. One day when, looking out the window, I noticed a police cruiser speed down the main drag toward Biddeford. That caught my attention as there were lots of accidents on the road in the summer, but then several other police and rescue vehicles followed suit. I imagined some sort of apocalyptic scenario playing out just down the road while I stood there in relative tranquility and ignorance, cleaning the espresso machines. As you can tell, some of that made it into the story, but everything else is fictitious.

This store sits in my heart because without it, I wouldn't be where I am today. It's on a stretch of highway connecting Saco, Maine (where I used to live) with Biddeford, Maine (where I also used to live) and is a thoroughfare for folks having fun at *Aquaboggan,* *Funtown,* or Old Orchard Beach. They remodeled it a year or two ago, and it has a nice café but is more known for its drive-thru service.

OUTBREAK

JOSEPH CARRO

To steam the perfect milk for a latte every time I make a drink for a customer, I angle the steaming pitcher so the espresso machine's steam wand rests ever so lightly against the inside of the pitcher's rim. The tip of the wand pointed somewhere deep into the middle of the frothing dairy (or non-dairy if one is lactose intolerant). I tilt the pitcher until the milk resembles wet white paint rolling over the wand.

The key to not scorching the milk is to make sure not to produce the rougher-sounding notes of steam that sometimes cascades through the steaming pitcher. To accomplish that, you need to maneuver the pitcher so that the tip of the wand blows steam just under the surface of the milk. The noise should be a constant soft hiss, like a baby snake or the light tearing of paper. When I steam the milk, the process is so quiet it's easy to forget it's happening. I was trained by the best.

I pour the espresso into the mug while the milk still steams, monitoring the consistency and timing to make sure they're not bad shots. The espresso should resemble dripping honey when it drains into the waiting porcelain mug, casting *café au lait*-colored specks against the eggshell white of the ceramic. Nobody pays six bucks to have a latte with dead, bitter shots wafting through the heated milk, at least not on my watch.

Once the shots are finished, I angle the mug and pour in the velvety dairy, then tilt the cup upright at the last second, dragging a stream of milk over the top layer creating one of the many patterns I design with the customer in mind. It's usually a heart. People love the hearts. Sometimes, I do a tree or flower. It really depends on the individual. Once, on top of a hot chocolate, I made a Captain America shield complete with a raspberry syrup red ring. It wasn't the best, but I was proud of it. The customer was jazzed.

With the latte finished, I placed the mug onto the handoff-plane next to the espresso machines, where a half-finished crossword puzzle and the daily horoscope sat on the faux-marble countertop. My horoscope gave me three stars for the day. Typical. It read: "Trust no one. Invest in something that pays dividends and stop acting on impulse." Nonsensical advice, as always, but I enjoy it. The routine of checking the horoscope and the crossword puzzles daily provides a sense of comfort.

I shouted out the name of the beverage. "We have a medium-sized nonfat latte with ristretto shots waiting on the bar."

The customer waiting on the sidelines (or chatting us up if they are a regular) would approach the counter with a smile, grab their beverage and walk away, often to the condiment bar where they could add chocolate, vanilla, or cinnamon flavored powders to their drinks. Then, I repeat the process repeatedly with more customers until quitting time. I can make upwards of fifty orders per half hour on a busy morning shift, sometimes more.

My name is Shane Koons. I'll be your barista today.

"God, it's slow today," I said, looking to my co-workers for solidarity. "Hope it picks up soon."

I wiped some milk off the counter with a rag soaked in sanitizer. After wiping the milk, I continued sliding the rag along the counter just to have something to occupy my mind. The minutes dragged after peak time at midday, and with such a small store, we often finished our cleaning tasks early in the day, at least until more piled up around closing time. I'd been there for nine years already. Regular customers and coworkers alike often referred me to as a *lifer*.

"Oh, it will," said Violette Alves, the store manager. "There's something going on downtown. Accident, I think. It should pick up after they clear it. Richard called to say he was stuck in traffic and would be late."

Richard was a night shift supervisor who came in just after midday to help with the shift changes on Monday through Friday. Violette pressed a series of buttons on the door of the safe and crouched while waiting for it to open. This was part of her everyday routine. She would spend the next ten minutes looking over the figures for the day's sales, or at the schedule to see who'd be in later besides Richard. Manager stuff.

I'd always thought Violette was cute, with her chestnut-colored hair, full lips, and quick wit, but she was my boss, so I never strayed much into flirting territory, at least before I was single. Yet I couldn't ignore the curves on her as she crouched on toned legs. I forced my eyes away and focused on wiping the espresso machine down, taking the wand apart to make sure there was no milk residue blocking the holes where the steam shot out.

I coughed. "An accident? Another tourist, probably," I said, shaking my head in derision. "Je me souviens."

"Yeah, I wouldn't doubt it," she said, chewing on the end of a pen, glancing over some papers, and occasionally looking through the large panel window at the front of the store. "I'm glad I went to the bank when I did, otherwise I'd still be stuck on route one."

"Hello, and welcome to the Latte Lair," Molly Hunter said from behind me to a customer via a headset. I turned and stopped wiping the counter and machinery. My bar was as clean as it was going to get, and I wanted to listen to the order to get a head start on making it.

Molly was a redhead, pretty, but also young, impatient, and naïve. She played on her cell phone while taking the order from the customer. I didn't care if she was on her cell phone if we got the work done, and Violette pretended not to notice, but under the right circumstances Molly could get fired. Molly wouldn't care even if Violette told her to go home right then. It was more work for us to be on her all the time for her phone use than it was to just work around her.

"Uh-huh. Okay, yes, we have that. Sure. Right. A large chai latte with no foam, one hundred and sixty degrees. Nonfat. No water. A bagel with blueberry cream cheese. Toasted. Yes, we do that. No, we can't put the cream cheese on it. Because, sir, we don't have that kind of food license. Uh-huh. Right. I'll have a total for you at the window."

She set her cell phone aside on the counter in front of her and started punching the order into the computer. I was already half-done with making the latte before the ticket even went through. I walked a few steps in Molly's direction with the finished drink in my hand and waited behind her as she took the money from the customer. I handed the drink off to a heavyset man with a Burt-Reynolds mustache behind the wheel of a tan-colored Chevette straight outta' the eighties. He had a song by The Fixx cranked up, probably as loud as it could go. It was *One Thing Leads To Another*. Molly grimaced and rolled her eyes at me so that the man couldn't see.

"Love the car," I said over the music as he grabbed his latte from my hand. I had to stretch out the window, supporting myself with the windowsill under my stomach because he had misjudged the distance. Either that, or he just didn't care if I had to reach out and extend my body so far. It was almost always the latter.

"Thanks," he said. He placed his latte in a cup holder near his dash. "Y'know, ten years ago, nobody would have wanted this car. Now? I have tons of people asking me if I want to sell it. Happens all the time."

Molly handed me his bagel and cream cheese in a small bag. I handed it out the window to him, feeling the warmth through the thin paper and smelling the delicious aroma of baked bread.

"Later, buddy," he said as he drove away. "Keep the change."

I pulled myself back into the window. Molly was already on her smart phone again. It looked like she was playing a Harry Potter mobile game. One time I took one of those Hogwarts House quizzes which said I was a Ravenclaw. I didn't agree because I considered myself a Hufflepuff. I'd have to ask Molly what she thought later.

"I hate that guy," she said. "He always listens to his crappy old music so loud. Like anyone wants to hear that." She closed the drive-thru window and then leaned against the glass, shaking her head.

"I liked the song," I said, walking toward the stockroom to grab some cup and straw re-fills.

"That's because you're old," I could hear her reply as I rounded the corner.

I'm thirty. Molly thinks everyone is old, so it didn't hurt my ego too much. I still felt young. Sometimes.

I entered the stockroom and checked the shelf for sleeves of cups and bags of straws. I grabbed a few and headed toward the break room, which was past the dish sink. As I got closer, I heard Frank Tilson, another employee, doing dishes and singing Billy Joel's, *The Longest Time*. Frank didn't acknowledge me as I walked past, too deep into tasks and his singing.

Poking my head into the break room, I checked the clock hanging on the wall above a mirror. In it, I noticed my reflection and grimaced at how ridiculous I looked in the black apron but thought maybe it took attention away from my tired eyes and messy black hair. Time? 2:23pm. An hour before I was to leave for the day. I sighed and walked back toward the bar, waving to Frank, who still didn't see me. He sang the chorus over the noise of the hose spraying water, his tall frame bobbing up and down with every beat. His head and military-style haircut rocked back with the falsetto.

When I returned to the floor, I stocked cups. Noticing the open safe with Violette crouched down again, adding money she received from the bank into little marked boxes. After a minute or two, she slammed the safe door shut and headed to her office with paperwork. I looked out the window, curious because a bunch of sirens blared as four cop cars screamed past, heading toward downtown. Man, Violette was right. Must be some big accident. I looked over at Molly, who never glance up from her phone despite the ruckus outside.

"Ugh," she said. "My phone is messing up. I can't get a signal. Stupid phone towers."

I laughed and took the last of the straws and stepped out from behind the bar to the condiment counter. As I filled in, a fire truck and two ambulances roared past, lights blazing, sirens screaming, followed by three more cruisers.

"Holy smokes!" I yelled. The streets looked empty, nobody around aside from emergency services. "You seeing this, Molly?"

She shrugged and started making herself a drink at the espresso machine. Her meal break was coming soon. "Like you said," Molly replied, "Probably some French tourist or something."

"I'm telling you," Violette said, returned from the back office. "Nobody knows how to drive anymore. Remember the biker that crashed last summer? That was ugly. Went right under a semi-truck and lost his head."

Within seconds, the tan Chevette sped from the opposite direction of the rescue vehicles, losing control, and flipping over on the road in a pile of screeching metal. It rolled end over end until hitting a newspaper vending machine and a telephone pole across the street where it came to a violent stop. Glass, plastic, and metal exploded onto the road. Leaking fluids strewn over the asphalt. The telephone pole shuddered, and the lights flicker off inside the store. My stomach tightened as I noticed a Latte Lair cup flitting about the ground outside, now empty. I'd just made that drink recently, handing it to the man with the mustache. Now he was probably dead.

Violette, Frank, and even Molly ran to my side. We stood all lined up in the store windows, gawking at the carnage.

"Oh my god," Violette said. "What happened? Who crashed?! Is that one of our customers?!"

"That mustache guy just crashed. He just came flying down the street and crashed," I responded, sounding almost like I didn't believe what I was saying.

There was a pause, and we all stood there, not knowing what we should do. We stared at the wreckage, transfixed.

"Shane, come with me," Violette said, moving toward the front entrance. "Molly, call the police on your cell."

I stood there for a second more until I could get my feet working. My heart thudded in my chest. I wasn't sure I wanted to be a part of Violette's plan. Regardless, I followed my boss to the street, where the odor of burning rubber lingered. Another fire truck blew past, not even stopping for the overturned car despite Violette and me waving our arms to signal them. It headed toward downtown Saco. Probably somewhere near the bridge to Biddeford. A column of smoke rose from somewhere a couple of miles away. (And was that gunfire? Were we under attack? Was this a terrorist thing?)

"Jesus!" Violette said, pointing toward downtown. "That fire truck didn't even stop! What's happening?"

We ran across the street to the Chevette and looked through the shattered windows. It wasn't good. The roof of the car folded inward, and the guy's head looked like hamburger. Blood, bits of brain and skull were everywhere. I could still see his Burt Reynolds mustache, though it was slick with his own gore. One of his arms dangled, holding on by bare threads of sinew, bone poking through the skin as if it were parchment. The radio still somehow worked. It played *Here I Go Again* by Whitesnake.

I clutched my stomach and threw up on the tar next to a loose hubcap. I fell onto my hands and knees, cutting my palms on glass shards. Violette helped me up, and we made our way back to the store, her shaking as badly as me.

"How was he?" Frank asked when we returned.

"He's dead," Violette said, taking her arm out from around me once I could stand on my own. I supported myself with a table, though my arm wobbled. All I could think about was the dead man in the car outside. What he looked like. What he smelled like. I knew it would haunt me forever.

"Are you serious?" Frank asked. "What're we going to do? That's so messed up."

There was a silence. Violette didn't know what to do any more than the rest of us did, but she felt responsible for us, for the man, and somehow probably even for the commotion downtown. I sat down at the nearest table and pulled little glass shards from under the skin on my palms and fingers. Molly brought me some paper towels. My hands were shaking like crazy. My heart beat so fast that I expected to throw up again. The constant throbbing of my heart filled my skull.

"What did the cops say, Molly?" Violette asked in a shaky voice, her timbre belying her otherwise cool appearance looking out the window at the wreck across the street.

"I was on hold," she replied. "The operator didn't even talk to me. I can try again. My phone hasn't been getting a signal for a while." She pressed a button and held the phone to her ear.

Frank pulled his phone out of his pocket. "I'm going to try my girlfriend and make sure she's okay."

"Shouldn't we just go home?" I asked. "Nobody is here. The firefighter wouldn't even stop. Something bad's going on. I don't think anyone's going to come in and get lattes."

"Seriously," Molly said, still clutching the phone to her ear. "I'm still not getting anything. I'm going to call my mom."

I didn't have a cell phone or anyone to call, even if I did.

"We can't just leave," Violette said. "We need to find out what's going on first. Janet would have my hide." Janet was the district manager. Violette turned and walked back toward the office. I was wiping the blood from my fingers, and now that the last of the glass seemed to be free of my palms, I got up from my chair and walked to the sink behind the bar. I rinsed the cuts in cold water and pressed a wad of fresh paper towels between my palms, hoping the pressure would staunch the blood flow. For the moment, it seemed to work, though the blood seeped through the wet towels more than I liked.

As I continued applying pressure, I looked out the window in the smoke's direction. A few other cars had stopped, the passengers inspecting the wreck of the tan Chevette outside. Frank and Molly were each talking in a separate corner of the café, and Violette was still somewhere out back in the office. A woman burst into the store. She was pretty, with blue-black hair, wearing tight black jeans and a white, form-fitting *Alice In Chains* tee-shirt.

"Help! There's an accident out front," she shouted, brow furrowed in panic.

"Yeah," I said, walking over to her, throwing the bloody wad of paper towels into a nearby trashcan. "He's dead. We tried to help." I noted to myself that I sounded callous just then. Maybe I was in shock.

"Call the cops!" she said, waving her arm in the wreck's direction in a sweeping gesture.

I looked away from her to the cuts lacing my fingers and palms. The tremors remained, though not as severe as earlier. I felt weak, my legs as useless as sponge stilts. The world seemed suddenly surreal. Was I dreaming? *None of this could actually happen, could it*?

The young woman ran back outside, frustrated. The door slammed behind her. I watched her go, in a sort of daze, watching her approached the ruined Chevette. I could see, and hear through the glass, her cries for help. A few other cars sped by, barely missing the woman who ducked behind the wreckage. More rescue vehicles sped toward whatever mayhem was ensuing in downtown Saco. The new first responder vehicles were those from the adjacent town, Scarborough. This was now a multi-town emergency, whatever it was.

A naked woman in her forties ran into view on the street, a sheen covering her body like sweat. The dampness extended to her hair, matted down like a marathon runner at the finish line. The skin hung from her frame like it didn't belong. Snot poured from her nostrils into her open mouth, intersecting with a pool of saliva. The twin pools of disgustingness ran down her chin onto her bare, sagging breasts. Her tongue waved back and forth as she came to a stop and noticed the Alice In Chains woman calling for help on her cell. The nude woman ran full speed, tackling the other with the force of an NFL linebacker. The two went down in a heap behind the wreckage.

"Oh, shit!" Frank said, holding his hands to his ears in dismay.

Molly gave up trying to reach anyone and rose, watching. Frank looked over at me, eyes wide in alarm. I couldn't move. Frank opened the door and ran into the street toward the scuffle. I ambled to the window, unblinking. Molly stood at my side and we both just watched.

The naked woman had the younger girl in a bear hug. We could see the younger girl was screaming, kicking her feet, trying to roll sideways. The naked woman was licking purple-hair's face, which left long and viscous mucous trails dripping from the younger woman's cheeks and eyebrows.

Frank approached the two women and tried grabbing the naked one's shoulder to shove her off. His hand slipped away, bringing trails of oozing mucus along for the ride, and the naked woman just went on licking the screaming girl. That tactic failing, Frank tried to grab the naked one around her neck with his arm. He kept slipping because of the disgusting ooze but eventually caught hold. She just ignored him.

"What the fuck," Molly said. "She's licking her! Why is she licking her? Oh, my god!"

I stood there frozen, unable to do anything but stare. My head felt like it was inside a box full of swarming bees.

The younger woman finally stopped struggling, though her eyes were open wide in horror and tears as she went limp. Ben also seemed to fall, limp, onto the ground behind the naked one. His head lolled back, and he stared at me through the glass with confusion and terror. Mucus covered his body and the front of his shirt fell along with his sleeves. The Alice In Chains tee on the young woman fell away as well, curling into little bits of material that dropped onto the asphalt like falling snow. Soon, Layne Staley's face disappeared long with the band logo until I was staring at the younger woman's naked breasts. There was not thrill behind that, only horror.

Violette ran past us holding a large pipe that we used to prop the back door open when bringing out the trash for the night. She ran outside, leaping over the immobile Frank. She hit the naked woman in the back of the head with the pipe, splitting her skull wide open and spraying blood across the wrecked vehicle in an arc of crimson.

Molly screamed in horror and ran out the door, away from the Latte Lair.

I walked out behind her and let the door to the coffee shop close behind me. I stared down at Frank, who took panicked breaths, his chest heaving up and down. His clothing had fallen away enough that he lay naked on the remnants. The younger woman appeared in the same condition. Both seemed alive but with faces twisted in terror, their fingers and legs curled up tight as if suffering seizures. Red and purple welts rose on the skin over their chests, faces, and arms.

Violette breathed hard, staring at the naked dead lady she'd just brained with the pipe.

"Zombies," she said. "She was a fucking zombie. It all makes sense!"

"What?"

Ignoring my incredulous response, she crouched down over the naked woman who had been wearing the Alice In Chains shirt. "She's still alive. Still breathing."

"What's wrong with them?" I asked. "Why aren't they moving? Hey, Violette… Zombies aren't real. You just killed that lady. Damn!"

Violette grabbed me by the shoulders and looked me in the eye. I noticed she was trembling. I recoiled.

"Shane. Wake up. Seriously. You need to snap out of it."

"Snap out of what?"

"You need to help me."

The buzzing in my head faded, now filled with the much more pressing reality of gunfire in the distance, coupled with more sirens. The smell of smoke filled the air. Vehicles had ceased speeding down the road in either direction.

The oddest thought occurred to me. "I don't think Richard is coming in today."

Violette stared at me a long time before letting go of my shoulders and walking away. She disappeared into the store and soon returned with some yellow rubber gloves we used while cleaning the bathrooms. She threw me a pair, which I put on. They irritated the cuts on my hands, causing me to wince. She handed me a large rock we used as a doorstop when receiving deliveries. Back door pipe, front door rock. We were a classy shop.

"Can you do this?" Violette asked. "You're my best shift manager. I know you have what it takes. We need to brain them. We need to knock their brains out. This is a true zombie situation, Shane."

"Man," I said. "I dunno. With a rock? I only get paid ten bucks an hour. Honestly, this is bonkers. You're bonkers. I don't want to go to jail."

Violette sighed, grabbed me by the shoulders, and moved me backward about five steps. I let her, all the while feeling stuck in a dream. Maybe I'd had a stroke and was under sedation in an ambulance or a hospital fighting for my life. That is what my brain came up with to cope.

Frank and Alice no longer in chains, or clothes, breathed in heavy, shuddering breaths. It unnerved me. I was coming back into myself and felt less like I was in a dreamland fog. The reality of what was happening was difficult to accept. My mind tried to reject the reality even while the same brain urged me to flee. I wanted to run, somewhere, anywhere, but there with the two living cadavers laid out on the street, naked, glistening with droplets of goo. We were careful not to get too close, to avoid slipping in it. It had a horrible odor approximating a mixture of rotting cucumbers and almonds. The stink permeated the area.

"Violette," I said. "You really think that woman was a zombie? She didn't bite anyone."

She didn't answer right away, instead pacing back and forth while I ran my hands through my hair. "What else is it? What else could it be? You saw what she was doing."

"What if she was just on bath salts or something?" This wasn't completely out of the question, because there had been a similar case down south a few years before where a man high on bath salts attacked patrolling police officers who shot him to death. He was naked, too.

"I don't know, I don't know. I. Don't. Know," she said, unraveling a bit. "We need to get help, but I have to stay here, in the store, at least for now. I can watch them, from inside."

I didn't like where this was heading.

"You live pretty close to here," she said, reminding me. "I'll lock the store and wait for you inside. You go out and get help or see what's going on, or both. Come back when you know for sure and then we can decide what to do."

"Are you sure?" I asked. "I don't want to just leave you alone."

"The store will be safe, I think. Your bike will be easier to get around with than my car, though, and these two need some medical help. I'll keep trying the phone."

I nodded and went out back into the break room to get my leather coat, gloves, and bicycle. It was a grey hybrid off-road and street bike. A Schwinn. Violette came with me and unlocked the back door so I could get out that way. We checked to make sure no surprises were on the other side, and then I rolled my bike out into the sun. If not for the chaos, it would seem like any other day I was leaving from work to go home. I briefly indulged in feeling the sun's rays on my face and tried to ignore the smell of smoke and the sounds of chaos from downtown.

"Good luck, Shane," she said. "Come back safe. Don't trust anyone."

I started pedaling, and with one last look back at the Latte Lair, I turned onto Main Street, toward home. My heart pumped faster as I headed further toward the rising column of smoke. What was I getting myself into? Little wisps of the smoke were rolling through the streets, being carried along on the autumn air like patches of soot-smelling fog. Leaves rustled and blew across the road and under my tires, with little crunches I could barely hear over the sirens and gunshots. I picked up the pace and rode another two blocks, passing abandoned cars here and there with owners nowhere to be found.

The local school, Thornton Academy, appeared on my right. It was a high school (but looked like a college campus) which comprised several academic style buildings and a large green lawn wrapping around the entire property. I stopped my bike and looked over at the front entrance, which was set in from the road a few hundred feet. There were bodies on the steps. All of them naked, or close to it. More bodies littered the lawn.

A man in brown tweed and a derby cap ran from another *zombie*. My stomach churned; the same sort of excited and anxious churning produced whenever I watched a lion chasing a gazelle on a nature program. Run, man, I thought to myself. The guy in tweed kept looking over his shoulder at his pursuer with terror on his face. It was a stark contrast against the blank and shark-like coldness in the eyes of the "zombie" pursuing him. As I stood there, I didn't realize that some others were heading my way.

They almost got me.

Hearing a frantic gurgling combined with a hiss, it felt like the earth dropped out from under me. I whipped my head around, eyes popping open in dawning horror at the sight of two nude dudes running in my direction. Fast. Violette was right. This was like the set of Dawn of the Dead, and I was an unnamed extra.

I pushed off with my feet to get a head start, then stood up so that I could pedal faster. I pedaled like I was Lance Armstrong. As I started moving, I clicked the gears on my bike all the way to seven and pushed hard. I didn't look back, but I could hear their naked footfalls slapping on the sidewalk behind me. Something yanked on my leather coat, almost knocking me off balance. The zombie failed to get a good grip, probably because of its gooey secretions. I looked behind me to make sure I was clear.

I was not. They were fast. *Too fast.* I must have been going about twenty-five or thirty miles per hour, but they weren't far behind me. I came to a three-way intersection and turned right. There were more bodies, more empty cars. People ran through the town square. It was mayhem.

Everything seemed to move in slow motion as naked zombies tackled several people in the same fashion as what I witnessed back at the Latte Lair. A police officer fired rounds from his pistol at an approaching group of zombies barreling toward him. I recognized the officer who sometimes came through our drive-thru at work. He dropped two zombies with well-placed gunfire, their brains spattering out the backs of their skulls in violent eruptions. He hit others, but the bullets seemed to pass right through their gelatinous skin. A stray bullet hit a man in the thigh, and he fell, screaming. As the man clutched his leg, he forgot about his pursuer, which allowed the zombie to tackle him. They both writhed on the ground like a constrictor and mouse in a dance of death.

The officer emptied his magazine and ran to a nearby cruiser. Three more zombies pursued him. I rolled my bike forward as the zombies behind me caught up. I pedaled across the intersection to Elm Street, which led to my apartment a couple of miles away. The officer attempted to open the cruiser door and get in, but two zombies grasped his limbs, trying to bring him down. He fought, causing them to slip off, with one falling on the ground, the other against the cruiser.

I biked past. If I stopped, the zombies would catch up to me, too, and it would be the end for us both. The officer brained one zombie with his baton. The other two dragged him down to the pavement. He pepper-sprayed another in the face while hitting it with his nightclub, but it kept coming. He screamed as it pinned his arms to his side. The zombie licked his face and mucus dribbled into the officer's screaming mouth.

"Help!" he yelled at me, spitting out the mucus as I pedaled past. "Hey, you, help me! Help me!"

Soon he stopped screaming and his features went taut and stiff like Frank's had. The other three zombies kept after me, so I just kept on pedaling. I was hyperventilating with fear. All I could hear was the wet slapping sound of the pursuing zombies and their throaty gargle-hissing.

I rode another two blocks before getting to the bridge that linked Saco with Biddeford. My heart stopped. A throng of police officers and cars blocked the road. A battle raged. Bullets tore through the mass of naked zombies trying to breach the blockade. Bullets struck the ground near me. If I wasn't careful, one might hit me, and it'd be all over. Taking a sharp right, I headed back to the Latte Lair. It was useless for me to attempt getting across the bridge, and at least my workplace had been safe.

"Shit, shit, shit, shit, shit!" I said as I turned down Scammon Ave, which would loop me back to another side road that would lead me back to where Violette waited. A blue Corolla roared past, almost hitting me when I neared the corner. It struck two zombies, crushing them under its wheels before the vehicle erratically sped off down a side street. The zombies then stood up and ran at me, some of their limbs now torn and hanging, mangled by the car tires.

I took a route far to the left, avoiding them as best I could, despite some still pursuing me. They almost reached my bike, but I pulled forward at the last second. I was tiring. My legs and lungs were burning, and I was shaking and covered in cold sweat.

Taking another right turn, I was back in the town square. The cruiser and the officer were still there, except the officer was now alone, naked, and covered in stringy mucous. He was curled up like Frank was. *Fuck*, I thought. *Please don't let that happen to me. I don't want to die!*

I rolled past and noticed a horde of zombies smashing at the glass of church windows nearby. People must have been taking refuge in there because I heard the crack of pistols being fired from inside accompanied by lots of frenzied screaming.

Flames flickered further down on Main Street, where the smoke came from earlier. As I biked back toward the Latte Lair, I noticed the zombies behind me had fallen away. Maybe they'd found other prey. The thought made me sick to my stomach, and sicker still to feel somewhat relieved.

With a roar, three fighter jets flew overhead, drowning out the gunfire and the sirens. They were so low to the ground that they knocked me from my Schwinn onto the ground. Scrambling with fear, I re-mounted the bike as they flew past, toward the fires. The jets circled the center of town before arcing back into the sky for another pass.

Shit, shit, shit, shit, I thought. *Shit! I'm going to die! I'm going to die!*

I rolled into the parking lot of the Latte Lair and jumped from my moving bike, letting it fall onto the garden area in front of the store. I pounded on the windows. Frank, the Alice In Chains girl and Violette were all nowhere to be seen. My stomach knotted up. I pulled on the doors in desperation.

"Violette," I screamed, pounding on the glass with my fists and yanking on the doors. "Violette! Open up! We have to get out of here!" No answer. No movement. Then, I heard a low gargle from my left and saw naked Frank and the Alice in Chains girl staring at me from behind the wreckage of the Chevette.

Looking around, I found a large rock and faced them with it.

"Pearl Jam is better than Alice in Chains!" I yelled. The rock was heavy in my hand. I was hoping I'd at least take out one of them when they attacked. There was no point in running. I grew tired, and they were too close.

After a tense couple of seconds, the couple rushed me with surprising speed. I readied the rock. Frank reached me first. I dropped to the ground and rolled into his legs, causing him to stumble over me and fall on the ground. I rolled over, raising the rock above his exposed head.

"I'm sorry, Frank!" I said and struck. Frank's head burst open and a scent like a salad that had been sitting in the sun for too long assaulted my nostrils. I expected to be attacked by the Alice in Chains zombie. When the attack didn't come, I risked a look.

Violette stood over the Alice in Chains zombie, her pipe dripping with more goo. I didn't need to look at the zombie's head to know what had happened while I struggled with Frank.

As expected, my pants dissolved from the ankles up. Luckily, they stopped dissolving a few inches above the knee on the right leg and just at the knee on the other. Violette shot me a look. She didn't need to say anything more.

"Thanks for the help," I said. "I thought for sure she was going to get me."

"Yeah, well, they almost got me," she replied. "As soon as they started getting up, I hid and waited for you to get here."

The flames grew brighter downtown, and smoke filled the air.

"Well, what did you see in town? Did you even make it there?"

"Yeah. Lots of these zombies. You were right. Lots of people dying. They have the bridge to Biddeford closed off. What are we going to do? This is insane."

"Maybe we can make it to Scarborough," she said, looking in that direction. "I saw jets go by from the roof. That's not good."

"Yeah, they knocked me off my bike," I said. I glanced at my elbow, scratched from my fall to the asphalt. It was such a mundane way to be injured during such dangerous chaos.

"Well, let's get moving," Violette said. "Who knows if we can even make it very far. They might have blocked off Scarborough too."

I shrugged. "Better than staying here."

As we made our way through the parking lot to Violette's car, I said a silent goodbye to my Schwinn. That little bike had saved my life. We both entered her car and rolled away from the Latte Lair. As we drove down the street, we saw Molly wandering through the forest on the side of the road. She was naked, glistening, and still carried her phone in her hand. She was now one of the afflicted. Violette and I looked at one another but said nothing.

We sped toward the access ramp that would take us to the highway, flying through two traffic lights and past a gas station in flames. Through the rear-view mirror (right before we made the turnpike) I saw the jets fly toward downtown Saco followed by a ball of flame as they fired missiles into the town square. We felt the rumble of the explosions as they rocked the asphalt, and the car. For a moment, we thought we'd flip over, but we didn't, and we kept on driving on smoking wheels.

I didn't know where we were heading, but we at least had a chance. That was something. That was more than everyone else had gotten. Ahead, the exit sign for Scarborough beckoned. Violette paused, looked at me, and then drove us forward into the unknown.

PEET'S COFFEE

SANTA MONICA, CA

A nother chain, though this one is in a much different part of Santa Monica than the previously mentioned chain. This one located where one change of a digit at the tail end of a zip code can astronomically raise the price of rentals, retail space, and especially home ownership. Santa Monica runs from Main Street to Twenty-Sixth Street. The further one gets from the beach, the more affordable life becomes, by local standards. "This place ain't cheap," as one of my many roommates from back in the day said, back when I needed roommates to survive out here.

Many homeowners rent near the beach but when they are ready to buy a home, they move to other places. The Valley comes to mind. This Shop is located close to the beach on a pleasant street a stone's throw from Malibu. There are plenty of great restaurants and small shops to visit if one gets bored with the beach.

The Baristas are friendly, quick to move lines and know many people by name. The clientele is a mix of locals, entertainment industry types (many retired with lots of great stories to tell of stars past), writers, attendees of the nearby yoga studio, businesspeople, and yes, even in the highly expensive zip code, people do still own homes, so realtors also frequent here.

There are realtor shops on either side of the fancy street in both directions from this coffee shop. The realtors rarely ever appear to be in their offices, instead are out and about showing places or maybe stopping for coffee. It is not uncommon to witness realtors at the coffee shop meeting with clients.

The one thing people will notice if they happen upon the realtor offices is how over priced the market is in the immediate area around this coffee shop. The realtor's do not waste people's times, the homes available are on display in the windows along with the asking price with intentions of keeping the looky-loos at bay, those who hope somewhere deep inside that maybe, just maybe there is a hidden gem, somehow undiscovered that might fall within a certain price range.

There is not.

What there is, for some unknown reason, are a few homes that have remained in the realtor windows for multiple years. The prices never changing, the homes never sold. The locations listed are beyond desirable, making one wonder why are some houses orphans?

What do I have to do to get you into a house like that? Oh, that's right, I'm not a realtor, simply a writer, so that's how I can get you into a home like that. Let's find out together why some houses are better left alone. Please follow me...

OLD BONES

PAUL CARRO

The old Sutton house landed in the sweet spot of two desirable zip codes, a prime intersection where Tony Avenue met Old Money Street. The house in question sat on the more desirous taxation side of an invisible border. Strange how an arbitrary line in the sand (or pick any other earthen material) could change the classification of homes, towns, or even people. Society labelled people uptown or downtown with connotations ascribed to each depending on the community, Bob thought.

He served as the realtor for the property in question. Bob wondered what would happen if a woman gave birth in the famous tourist spot where four states intersected. Would the child have quad citizenship? Bob thought about a lot of things, given how much time he had on his hands. He already found enough time in his day to raid the master bathroom's medicine cabinet. It did not take long for him to find that which he desired. More like needed. Mouthwash. He looked around to make certain no Suttons were in view before drinking straight from the bottle.

After a quick swish, Bob spit, feeling he might follow up with some premium hurling. An earlier liquid lunch swam the channel of his esophagus. An alcoholic concoction which appeared just as happy traveling north as south. He felt it rising; the tide moving where it damn well wanted to, despite his Herculean efforts to hold back the tide.

"Are you okay?" A voice asked from somewhere behind him.

Bob looked up into the mirror. His reflection had seen better days. He wondered, *Jesus, is this what forty looks like*? *What happened to the college athlete*? *The stud*? Long gone based on the individual staring back. The man in the mirror appeared older than memory served, heavier around the waist and scruffy faced. The reflection stared back through eyes once upon a time called baby blue. Now the accurate word would be bloodshot. His hairline, already thinning as well as greying, rose in a lick near the back of his head. Bob wondered how anyone let him go out in public looking like that. Oh yeah, he did not have anyone.

Bob attempted to straighten a tie which appeared intent on dangling crooked. He pulled it taught, only to have it fall back to its questionable position. He turned to face his accuser. She of the many questions. Or at least the one. Pointed at that.

"Jill, right?" Bob asked.

"Juliet. Seriously, are you okay?"

"Something I had at lunch," Bob said truthfully. Vodka tonics.

Juliet, as if sensing, moved in on him. He smiled just enough to let the smell of mouthwash seep out. Good old vodka, the drinker's version of scent-free deodorant. Boring but gets the job done. She sniffed. When she did not get the desired scent, she eyed his hands—another telltale sign. He gripped the edge of the sink to keep them from shaking.

"A woman gets that close, she's usually looking for something," Bob said.

"What? Fuck no," Juliet said, launching herself away from him.

Good, he could breathe again, though each inhale provided fuel for a stomach intent on evacuation. He even avoided the snappy comeback. Hard to be quick on one's feet when one could barely stand on them.

"Six of us, how the hell does he leave it to all six of us?" The woman griped, already moving on from the state of her realtor.

She meant her brood. The Suttons. Old Man Sutton went and died and left the home equally to all six kids. He must have done a number on them. The siblings were the equivalent of six opposite personalities trapped in one head. As the realtor, Bob spoke to each of them at least once. Stunning how different people sharing at least partial DNA could be. They had one thing in common though, none of them much seemed to like any other Sutton.

Juliet was the oldest of the brood at fifty. The woman was reed thin with hair down to her butt, glasses, (of course) though curiously she also wore sunglasses pulled up onto her hair above her forehead. Bob could never figure out if she somehow pulled them down over the other glasses or how the whole thing worked.

With the thought fresh in his mind, he considered finally asking her, but the stomach protested. He breathed and waited for it to settle. Unwilling to chance a likely spewing, he refocused on the familial beef while smiling and nodding. Finally, he felt the gorge tamper, settling back into the safety zone. He turned to her, finally feeling better. A bit of a zip to his zap returned. *Who cares what the mirror says*? *In my head, I am still twenty*, Bob thought.

"That decline a minute ago? You sure now, sweetheart? Your sister Nadia has been laying it on thick around me. I thought maybe I hold out for you, give you first shot, what with you being the…"

She looked to him, waited for the word oldest to slip past the dodgy lips of the man in front of her. She folded her arms in advance. To his credit, he swerved.

"Most worldly," Bob said.

"Nadia, huh? Wants to get with you?"

Bob nodded. It was easier to get women back in the day. Show up on a football field then show up at the after party and that was where the real scoring took place. Nowadays, he had to work it harder. Take his shots where he could. He saw Juliet falter, saw her pitted against a sibling she loathed, and suddenly Bob's day was looking up. She stepped up, straightened his tie for him.

"Oh, you poor thing. You actually believe those words you say," she said. "I bet you were pretty once. One cannot be this cocky if they did not have game at some point. But oh, my little friend. You have no idea how that ship has sailed."

Bob felt his chances slipping away. Glancing down, he noticed at least the tie looked better.

"The thing is that you can read me well. If I believed my sister was desirous of you, I may have mercy banged you to get back at her, except her name is NICKY. You cannot even lie properly. So now that we are clear, I want no part of your inappropriate remarks as my employee. How about you do your job and sell my damn house so I can get my sixth of my inheritance!"

She stormed off. Bob suddenly found her a bit more attractive than when they started the conversation. Of his abundance of flaws, an attraction to the unattainable was one.

"Hard to sell when the house comes with so many nuts," Bob yelled back. She flashed an over the shoulder middle finger before bounding down the hallway. He looked in the mirror, ready to high five himself for his zinger, only to discover his reflection failed to find the retort witty. In fact, the silvered glass doppelganger looked like it wanted to puke.

Bob had not expected Julia, nor any Sutton to be on premises, which was why he came to the house when he did. The stopover for "lunch" was problematic in hindsight. He needed to prep the home for a weekend showing.

The house was an ideal piece of property, yet it had not sold in nearly two years. He desperately needed a commission, as his self-owned realty company had hit the skids in recent months. He lost his lease for his office and had to let his assistant Marsha go off to a competitor across town. Terrible mistake that. Seems many of his best clients were fond of Marsha. Since Bob's promises for her to make partner never panned out, she took it out on him by absorbing a large cross section of his client base.

Clients liked Marsha a lot. There was plenty to like. She was whip smart, knew her stuff, was passionate about selling homes. All the things that Bob had in him once upon a time.

No longer.

Time caught Bob in its icy grip and damned if it ever planned to let go. Time was the worst type of parasite. Once it had its hooks in, it refused to depart until bringing youth and beauty to its knees.

"Christ, I can do this. I can sell this house," Bob said, without believing it.

To sell the Sutton place would mean he finally had a grasp on life again. To sell it would allow him to become… Who did he want to become? Anyone other than the man who looked back at him.

Unable to reflect on his reflection any longer, he looked out the bathroom window. The time on market made no sense. Even the view from the shitter was glorious. While the front of the house was quite traditional, the backyard was something to see. The yard was large enough to host but also roomy enough for kids to play. It was spacious compared to other homes in the neighborhood.

Bob imagined how nice evenings would be in such a space, how freely the beer could flow. (It would be beer if he had a day off. He reserved vodka for workdays.)

The backyard comprised two sections. The part Bob could see through the window was a wide-open space boxed in by a hedgerow and trees combo. A picnic table sat nestled in one corner, the balance left open for children to play. The area remained fully enclosed except for a vine-covered lattice archway. That was where the view from his vantage point ended. The archway led to the larger section of backyard immediately off the house.

Unable to see any further but wishing to comprehend his inability to sell the place, Bob pulled out his cellphone for a closer look. Bringing up pics viewed countless times, he scrolled until he arrived at an image of the rear of the house. He enlarged it with a swipe of his fingers.

The image on his screen was a night shot, which only highlighted the elegance. Just outside of the triple glass French doors was a patio. Square sets of marble sat in patterns atop the sea of perfectly trimmed grass. A formal stone dining table held court on one side with generous seating. It offered the same motif of farm to table communal restaurants that were all the rage.

Beyond the dining area, atop other square slabs nestled among green, rested a massive sectional couch. The couch back was a durable white wicker matching the exterior colors scheme. It sat covered in an overabundance of cushions and pillows of varying sizes splayed across its entire length. The couch sat opposite an electric fire pit flanked by two sturdy outdoor chairs. String lights hung above the entire area, supplying a warm glow to the place.

He brought up another pic, this one a daytime shot. Each image, whether on his phone or on the website, highlighted the uniqueness of the lovely home. Sun lit a front yard which while smaller than the back was itself crisply green. A nice shade tree housed a child's swing. Forgetting the interior of the house (which Bob could not, because he had memorized every nook and cranny) the property alone should have already sold given the two five asking price. That was modest by area standards.

Yes, the place was stunningly beautiful. And Bob hated it. His personal white whale had taken on the shape of the American Dream, which somewhere along the way morphed into an American nightmare. It was as if the home wished to remain an orphan. Something constantly scared off buyers. God knows it could not be him. Bob had sold real estate for decades. *Decades*? *Christ, I really am forty,* Bob thought as he closed the pic on his phone.

Such a revelation deserved a drink. Bob locked the house. Juliet remained parked out front, gabbing on her phone. Bob smiled and waved. Juliet turned away, never leaving her conversation.

·· • • • • • • • ··

Bob pulled up to Mick's Place, an old school bar with a simple wood sign dangling off a metal pole like an English pub. A construction zone across the street hampered efforts to park. A brand-new mixed unit housing high rise was almost complete and towered over the pub. He circled the block three times before finding a meter.

As he walked past a restaurant on his way to the bar, Bob noticed a communal table matching the one at the Sutton Place. The thought of the home caused a shiver. He needed that drink.

The California sun vanished immediately upon entering Mick's Place. It was as though the business itself was a reverse black hole with a polarity that no light could enter versus escape. Fake candles lined the walls, supplying a barely visible yellow glow that matched many a patron's pallor.

After dropping onto his usual bar stool, Bob raised a finger. Mick nodded and prepped a Vodka Tonic. 'Two Drink Charlie' sat at the end of the bar. The regular was a surly man of indeterminate age (sixty to two hundred would be a fair guess) who hunched over one of his two-a-day pitchers of beer. Charlie kept to himself, never speaking to anyone.

Despite the man's eternal presence, Bob always shook his head at the sight, hoping never to become that guy. Lately, though, he wondered who he was exactly. Not the young stud anymore. That thought came on more frequently in recent months. More important than realizing who he was, he wished to determine who he wanted to be. Trying to think of any role models left him short.

"A little early today," Mick said, dropping the drink.

"Your point?" Bob asked.

"I just made it."

"The point, or the drink?"

Mick shrugged, walked away to serve a woman who leaned across the bar. Appearing over drinking age by only a day or two. She wore a pair of shorts long enough to cover what needed covering but short enough to be interesting, Charlie thought as he sipped his drink.

The young woman's leg bounced up and down excitedly as Mick checked her ID before dropping the beer in front of her. Another young woman in similar garb returned from the bathroom. Mick repeated the check and the pair retreated to a nearby booth with their drinks, tapping on cells the entire time.

Mick returned to Bob.

"You tell them it's early too?"

"Spring break for them. That ship has sailed for you. Besides, they mentioned how they loved the décor. When's the last time you mentioned my décor?"

"Last time you changed it? Nineteen eighty-five is my guess," Bob answered.

"Ouch. That would hurt coming from them. A lot more students coming in lately, good for business. The term for my place is vintage."

"I'm a realtor. Vintage is for clothes. This place is a dump."

"When did you become an angry drunk?" Mick asked before walking off to restock bottles along the back wall of the bar.

Bob bristled. He was joking with Mick, of course, but felt poor Mick had taken it personally. Bob realized he was overly snide with the man, but would not apologize. There was a time when Bob would enter places with the same leg bouncing energy of the woman in the corner. Of course, there was a time when one drink could get him buzzed. Bob waved his empty glass to Mick.

Mick eyed a wall clock and shook his head before making a fresh drink for Bob. The clock watching did not go unnoticed. Bob checked his cell and identified the bartender's concern. He had arrived earlier than normal, and he finished the first drink too quickly. Still, there were no homes to show until tomorrow. He had three back-to-back starting Friday culminating in Sunday's open house at the Sutton Place. Yeah, drinks were in order.

Mick dropped the glass. Bob went to work, giving his drinking arm a workout while considering his future. He again questioned who he wanted to be. For now, he remained content to be the guy at the bar who was not Two Drink Charlie.

· · · ●●·●●·· ·

Prongs of an open house sign stabbed deep into the soil. Bob affixed fresh balloons to it with practiced efficiency. Food came next. A bag of Chips Ahoy and a case of small water pods.

Friday showings were never as well attended as weekend events, but the home only recently went on market. Bob had no expectations of anyone making a move on the place. The thought relaxed him. No pressure. Not like the Sutton place, which he would have to show again in a matter of days.

Bob barely had time to prep the place when a young Asian couple shouted out from the doorway, startling Bob, who dropped a cookie on the floor. He kicked the broken treat underneath a kitchen cabinet and turned to the pair.

"Hello, I'm Bob. Sorry that I'm in your house!" Bob tossed a line that had not worked for years. It landed as subtly as a ninja star. Reading the sudden chill in the room, he extended the tray of cheap dessert.

The young couple gripped hands, looking at one another, speaking a silent language. Instinct kicked in for the realtor. The trick was to keep things moving so potential buyers had little time to think. Bob draped arms over their shoulders in an involuntary threesome and led them toward the carpeted stairway.

"Second floor, you just have to see it. Too many one-story houses in Los Angeles you ask me," Bob said.

"Earthquakes," the young man said.

"Pardon?"

"Preponderance of earthquakes in Los Angeles is why there are so many single-story homes," the young woman completed the thought.

Sweat beaded on Bob's brow. His hands went cold at the thought of losing them so quickly. They were not even speaking the same language, and it had nothing to do with anyone's nationality. Bob was simply out of step.

"They're not ready," a voice said from behind them.

A striking woman in her thirties, tall, with deep red hair pulled back in a tail, stood in the doorway. She wore a green sundress, which hugged her body nicely, showcasing curves in all the places Bob liked. It was clear the woman was in excellent physical shape. She pulled off a pair of sunglasses to reveal eyes greener than her dress.

Bob had never been one to fancy redheads, but the woman before him was stunning, right down to the subtle freckle pattern across the sides of her nose. He made a mental comparison of the college coeds from the day prior and found those younger women wanting compared to this beauty.

She met his gaze and did not look away. Bob felt a stir of excitement. He sensed a connection much like the ones he felt when younger, when love at first sight was possible.

Or at least lust. He smiled awkwardly at what he assumed to be another potential buyer.

"Welcome?" He kept his arms around the young couple the entire time. "I was just about to show them the second level. Care to join?"

"You're wasting your time," the woman said. "The young woman, what is your name?"

"Sook Lee," the woman answered.

"Sook Lee has had it with apartment dwelling. Let me guess, being trapped with the sound of video games at all hours has lost its charm?"

The young couple squeezed hands, smiling at the thought.

"She hates it. I'm Ken," the young man said.

"Hello. I'm Michelle, pleasure to meet you. Now where was I? Sook Lee wants out, needs space to move around, but Ken believes homeownership is a money pit. It would have to be an ideal situation to invest in a house, because that is what a home should be, an investment. Am I right, Ken?"

"Yes. We work remotely. Either of us can easily move any time. Why buy?"

"It would be nice to have more space though," Sook Lee said.

"I hear you. There is only one room you need to see then."

Michelle took the lead and pulled Bob's arms off the couple.

"They don't like it when you do that. Save it for after you close a house," she whispered to Bob, then nodded for the couple to follow.

Bob opened his mouth, but she placed a finger to his lips before ascending the stairs, followed by the couple. The realtor stood dumbfounded even as he took in the woman's scent. Strawberry adjacent but not from a starter perfume or lip gloss. Though Bob found the woman intoxicating, her presence in *his* house confused him. He raced after the group and found them gathered around a window in the master bedroom.

"If you know the area, you have seen all the construction nearby," Michelle said to the couple.

"Used to be a mall," Ken said knowingly.

"Correct. It will be a mixed-use space when it reopens in a year. One of the biggest tech companies in the country signed a ten-year office lease. Once it opens, the property values in this area will skyrocket. This is the lowest it will ever be which makes it perfect for flipping. Every employee of that place will need homes. If they find one within walking distance? Well, name your price. You could make a killing on the investment," Michelle said.

Bob stood dumbfounded as if watching himself in a different type of mirror, one where he was decades younger, much better looking than in recent years, and in a strange turnabout—female. He opened his mouth again, but the woman gently shook him off. He took the hint.

"Yeah, wow, this would be a brilliant investment," Ken said.

His wife crushed his hand, smiling. "It has character. I could do a lot with the place until we sell."

"Might even want to renovate so by the time all those tech workers move into the neighborhood your asking price will skyrocket. The structure is sound, it has good bones."

"Good bones?" Sook Lee asked.

"Surface is just that. One can scrape it away, change it, polish it, but it all means nothing if the foundation is not solid. The gloss is useless without good bones."

Michelle looked at Bob as she explained the concept. He wondered if she felt that way about him. Did she see the better man underneath? Someone better than one who drank promise away over time? Better than one who gave hope so many dark places to hide it might never be found again?

"I'm in," Ken said.

Sook Lee screamed while hugging her husband then mouthed *thank you* to Michelle.

Michelle sidled over to Bob. "How did my job interview go?"

"Tell you over drinks?"

Michelle smiled enigmatically. It pleased him when she accepted the offer.

· · · ●●●● · · ·

"Sister, younger cousin, or niece. Any other possibility explaining your presence is beyond me," Mick said to Michelle.

Michelle smiled her gracious smile, contagious enough that Bob and the bartender reflexively smiled along.

"Mick here likes to break balls," Bob said.

Michelle cut to the chase. "So, are we work partners?"

"I don't really have an opening but if you can repeat what you did today then, sure, you're hired. You licensed?"

She nodded.

"The usual for you, I assume," Mick said. "And for the lovely woman?"

"Club soda, same for my boss," she said.

"Wait, what? You making drink decisions for me? Who works for who?"

"Whom." She turned, straightened his tie. "We need to toast my new job, but you need to meet with that couple this afternoon for paperwork and still have houses to show this weekend, so club soda. The drinking is less charming than you think."

Charlie dropped the fizzy beverages with aplomb. "I don't want to lose a customer but sometimes it is good to lose them, know what I mean?"

Bob reached for his glass with shaking hands. Michelle clasped them with her own and squeezed. It surprised him how quickly the tremors stopped, but it did not keep him from flushing red in embarrassment. The low light became his best friend. She found his eyes, despite the darkness.

"You got this," she said.

"Why? Because I've got good bones?"

"Very good." She raised her glass, clinked it with his. "To new beginnings."

He drank, wincing at the shock of finding no alcohol in a bar glass, like a toothpaste orange juice combo. She sipped hers slowly, eyeing him over the glass. It was not a look he was familiar with without an alcoholic haze.

After the bar, they swung by his place. Bob's ex got their house in the divorce. He settled into a one bedroom, one bath house near the Marina, intending it to be a stopover, a place barely above a rental. Besides, he spent most of his time in his office. Until he lost his office.

A porch with a screen door fronted the property. The porch acted as a buffer to a home not much larger than the porch itself. A metal metal plate taken from the office door before he lost the lease hung crooked on a string at the entrance. The screen door tilted at roughly the same angle as his tie.

Michelle followed him in as he scrambled to spruce up the porch ahead of her. The small desk housing an old Dell provided the only clue that the place was an office. While a generic wheeled chair occupied the tiny space between wall and desk, guests had the luxury of choosing between one of two mismatched seats. A urine yellow newspaper article praising his business from almost twenty years ago hung in a frame on a wall.

Michelle frowned. *Still beautiful when she frowns*, Bob thought. He pulled a chair out for her, but she shook her head.

"You need to go meet the couple for paperwork. Let me take care of things here."

"Look, Michelle, I appreciate what you've done. I want this to work, but you can see I can't really afford to, urk…"

She cut off his breath by gripping his tie and jerking it tight. He struggled. Was she trying to choke him out? Her strength was incredible, he thought. Then she came up with it, ripped it free like a snake. She fixed his collar, unbuttoned his top two buttons.

"No more ties, they make you look…"

"Distinguished?"

"Older." She ran her fingers through his hair, pulled it at its roots. "I'll style this later. This commission will get us started and there will be more soon. I just need to get up to speed on your portfolio. What is the password? Vodka?"

Bob eyed the woman as though gifted with superpowers. "How did you? Never mind. It is 'vodkatonic' actually."

She smiled knowingly and settled in behind the desk, waving him away. "Now go. I've got this."

Bob exited to his car. Sober for the first time in days, he felt almost drunk. Everything was moving so fast. How had he let the woman rope him into hiring her when he could not even afford an office? She had scored him his best and fastest commission in some time on a home not expected to move for months.

There was one more open house before the Sutton house shit show as he came to think of it. He would test his protégé at the Rothman house the next day. But no matter how she fared, the Sutton open house loomed ahead. If she were some a fraudster, that house would reveal all. This he believed about the albatross in his portfolio.

Sook Lee and her husband waited patiently at a local coffee shop. Michelle insisted on the location before she ever even saw Bob's house. It was as if she knew what the place looked like. Though how could she? Then it hit him. He never told her his name, yet she knew. His underlying worry about a con job in progress suddenly swam to the surface of his thoughts. She was in his home, had convinced him to leave, had his password. Bob excused himself, stepping away from the couple to dial his cell.

"How did you know my name?"

"I know everything about you, Bob. And about your business. I do my homework."

"Well, you would know you signed up on a sinking ship, so what is your game?"

"To right the ship," she said. "You've got good bones, Bob. We can work with what you've got."

The 'we' struck him as odd, but he let it go as he noticed the young couple through the window. They appeared too animated, perhaps a fight brewing. He needed to save the sale, so he hung up on the woman and rushed back into the coffee shop. Bob realized Michelle would not have answered if she were simply looting the place. He called the landline on his desk, and she answered. The woman was not on the run.

His meeting with the couple went phenomenal. Bob was on fire, feeling back on his game. Even the absence of a tie helped him feel looser. The fact he felt no gorge rising was a plus. Sook Lee even laughed at his jokes. Ken smiled knowingly, nodding at Bob for shepherding them through a tough decision. Bob got the paper trail rolling, then drove home.

Michelle had departed by the time Bob arrived. It was just as well she was not there to hear him drop an F bomb. His new employee transformed the pigsty into a stunning sight. Fumes of fresh paint filled the air in a space which now resembled an office. The desk was a welcoming blue. A wet paint sign hung on its front with a snitch of masking tape. Sexier matching took the place of his former mish-mosh chair assortment. A bamboo love seat occupied a far corner.

The jaundiced newspaper article no longer hung on the wall, replaced by a clean online reprint hanging in a decorative frame. A new file cabinet anchored one wall. Several plants dotted the room. A blue and orange surf and sand motif filled out the room up to a few buoys and a fishnet attached to one wall. It transformed the place into a seafaring motif. While the paperwork with the couple occupied him for hours, the amount of work she accomplished in the meantime shocked him.

Moving beyond the porch, he entered the house, disappointed to find there was no difference on the inside. But why would there be? There was one noticeable difference. Her scent lingered in the air, a sign she at least entered his home. Bob went to the kitchen and opened the refrigerator. He cursed at what he saw, or more accurately, did not see. The beer was all gone. Panicking, he checked the cabinets. No more vodka, either.

Bob blanched red, brighter than the alcohol usually made his cheeks. Who was she to touch his things? That was out of line. She worked for him, not the other way around. Then he looked back toward his living room and noticed something. Once upon a time when Bob dreamed of returning to his former healthy shape, he bought a treadmill. It was one of the few things he got in the divorce. Since he moved in, he never once used it. In fact, it had become his hamper of sorts. It remained eternally covered in dirty clothes. Until now.

On it, he found a note. It apologized for the alcohol and mentioned he had two more open houses. He cursed again but took the hint. After a quick change into sweats, (when did even they get tight?) he ran three miles on the treadmill. That night he slept more soundly than in years.

The next day, Michelle was at the open house when he arrived. It was refreshing to find balloons already in place. Bob stepped into the Foster's house and followed a pleasant aroma. As he stepped into the kitchen, Michelle pulled a tray of fresh-baked cookies from the oven.

"It's the smell that gives them a feel of nostalgia. Fresh baked or nothing at all. No more store-bought snacks ever again, deal?"

"Like no more alcohol?"

"That's your choice, this is business."

Before Bob could get into it further, someone arrived. It was an older gentleman who Bob would have latched onto as someone fiscally sound, but Michelle pulled Bob aside and made it clear the man was only there for voyeurism and snack purposes. Neighbors were naturally curious how the other half lived. The man set off her wasted time alarms, so she remained polite while offering the guest little of her time or charm. It shocked Bob how quickly the man departed, cookies in hand, never once asking for a price.

Several potential buyers came and went. Seeing people not bite after meeting Michelle comforted Bob slightly. It relieved him to discover his new hire was not a wizard. Before the day was over though, she latched onto a couple who were collectively on their second marriage and looking for a new start together. Bob took them back to his office and made a tentative deal.

Closing two properties (paperwork and finances pending) a day apart stunned Bob. When had that last happened? At twenty-five? Bob wanted to celebrate and briefly considered hitting up Mitch. Instead, he changed into sweats and ran on the street rather than on his treadmill.

Passing sale signs on houses while jogging (back when he used to run) used to cause significant anxiety. That was why he originally switched to a treadmill. But now he felt calm, peaceful. With no destination in mind, he ran as if heading toward who he wanted to be, after all. Though the speed at which he ran the jog exhausted him was disappointing, he fought through it seeking a second wind.

That night he slept soundly.

The next morning it was time to face the Sutton House. A sense of dread overtook him. The place was cursed. He worried the misery of the place might rub off on his new employee, and she too might lose her mojo. Bob believed the place could cause his and hers misery equally. Would the place split the partnership, cause them to become two ships passing in the night? A winning streak over. Partnership null and void.

His fears only grew when he pulled up to the absence of an open house sign. Michelle's car was in the driveway. She should have set it up before going inside. What happened? Entering the home, he noticed something else missing. There was no warm cookie smell. Michelle's scent lingered, confirming her presence. Someone passed by an open doorway down the hall. Client or employee?

"Hello?"

Bob followed the movement and felt a breeze. Another flash of movement caught his eye as something white fluttered past. A ghost? He gave chase, worried for Michelle's safety.

One of the rear patio doors remained open. He slipped through. The beauty of the yard stunned him. Not even nerves could change the fact. Its beauty did not falter due to circumstance. He heard a sound and spun. Michelle stood in the doorway, one arm against the frame, wearing a flowing sundress. Her position, angled in the sunlight as she was, revealed what lay beneath. Nothing but skin. No lingerie at all.

She advanced on him until standing as close as Juliet Sutton earlier in the week. Unlike that miserable encounter, Michelle's intent was clear. The woman grabbed both sides of his face and kissed him. Softly at first before turning animalistic.

Bob slipped into another world as the beautiful woman (employee?) pushed him back with ease. They continued to kiss until his legs hit the edge of the outdoor sectional and they fell, her atop him. Bob struggled to remove his clothes, feeling the awkwardness of a teenager tinged with an excitement he had not felt since that same awkward period in life.

Once partially unclothed, Bob leaned back while she straddled him. Not a word spoken. He groaned, closing his eyes while experiencing pleasure beyond anything he ever felt. Despite a long sexual history, something about Michelle's moves stood out. Almost too much. Perhaps he was just rusty, so attributed the newness of the act as the reason for how great it all felt. But then his head shot back involuntarily as an intense pleasure rocked his world.

Below his waist, he felt as if... What? As if her flesh were devouring his, absorbing him.

Abnormal intensity caused him to open his eyes, hoping to identify the source of such feelings. The only thing he saw was an incredibly stunning woman straddling him. He was not rusty. She was that good.

The woman imbued him with a vigor long forgotten. In brief flashes when his brain could function, Bob struggled to understand how such a woman overlooked his flaws. He soon abandoned all thought and gave in. Time dissolved while in her embrace. Bob was uncertain how long they had been making love by the time he heard a scream. Not from Michelle.

"Oh my God!" Juliet yelled.

Bob scrambled for his clothes, struggling to cover himself. Juliet stood a foot away, apocalyptic, red faced. Michelle remained calmer than him (an easier feat because she remained clothed). Somehow, the woman's sundress remained in place. Bob wondered how that was possible, based on how much flesh he felt pressed against his own. Then he felt self-conscious, worried he was not at his best if their go around failed to disrobe his lover.

Michelle rose to face the homeowner. Bob fought to find his way back into the business side of his brain. It had been more than a decade since someone went on a romp with him in a show home. Bob struggled to articulate an excuse. Michelle turned to him and smiled.

"I've got this," she said. "Ms. Sutton, your house is off the market. I have found your buyer."

Juliet raised her hands as if to suggest she was short of the information needed to understand. The homeowner glanced at Bob, who finally pulled himself together.

"This is Bob's new house, he's buying it, congratulations on your sale." Michelle stated.

"I am?" Bob asked.

"Of course, we talked about this and how your other quaint place can become a proper office, and you can finally get this place off the market. We've already started building memories here, wouldn't you say?" She winked, and it was Bob's turn to go red. He was putty around her.

Juliet nodded. "Fine, okay. Done then. Good lord, this whole experience."

Bob reached out to shake her hand. Juliet grimaced before storming off.

"I'm growing on her. Normally she just gives me the finger."

"Things are looking up for us then," Michelle said.

"Us?"

Michelle answered by pushing him back onto the couch for round two.

··•·•·•··

The year passed quickly for Bob, who found himself in the whirlwind of a new life. His business was growing. Michelle became his partner in life and business. He proposed to her after only three months of dating, if they could call it that. She moved into the Sutton place a week after the open house and never left. He moved in soon after and they made it official when she replied with a single word. Yes.

Some evenings after love making (on the rare occasion he still had any energy) Bob quizzed her about her history, fishing for information about other men in her life. She replied there were some but never elaborated, leaving him to worry a jealous ex might storm their new castle.

The pair married in Vegas, a quickie wedding where a drunken young couple (sure to regret their own slurred vows) served as their witness and vice versa. While Bob embraced a sober lifestyle around his paramour, he assumed they would indulge in Vegas. But no, she kept him on the straight and narrow except in the bedroom.

Even after marriage Bob found himself unable to articulate how different love making with Michelle was. Her entire body felt electric, alive, moving in ways seemingly implausible. Stamina returned to his life as he began eating better and running daily. The couple often exercised together. Bob beamed with pride when men checked his wife out. To her credit, she never batted an eye around them. Bob began playing the lottery behind his wife's back, a fool's errand, a waste of money for sure. But based on the luck in his relationship, he believed it might carry over to a power-ball.

Life was taking shape, transforming from lost and lonely into a rewarding feeling of success greater than Bob could have wished for. He still stopped by Mick's place, because the bartender was his only friend and he needed to brag to someone. The new Bob always ordered a club soda and tipped heavily. The bar became a favorite of millennials living in the mixed unit buildings. As the two men talked, a coed occasionally sidled up and flirted. Bob paid them no mind. Mick dropped him another glass.

"You know, Mick, my worst day sober is better than my best day drunk. Who would have thunk, huh?"

"Don't get to say this to many people in my line of work, but I'm proud of you, how you white-knuckled it into submission."

"More like someone whipped me into submission, huh?"

Mick shook his head, dropped beers for a college couple.

"How she married into that sense of humor, I'll never know. At least you're not a mean drunk anymore," Mick said.

"Yeah, sorry about all the things I used to say about this place. Look at it now, booming. You know why?"

Mick shook his head.

"Place has good bones, Mick. Your place had good bones."

Bob dropped his glass and walked out, ignoring the smile of a coed on his way.

Upon arriving back home, a familiar odor greeted Bob, that of meal preparation. Pot roast. He loved the potatoes and carrots that came with it. The smell was luxurious and filled their entire home. *Maybe I should start cooking this at show houses instead of cookies,* Bob thought.

Stealth was once unattainable for once upon a time *bull in a china shop Bob*. In his leaner, cleaner frame, Bob's footfalls were nearly silent as he approached the kitchen. The sound of his wife prepping the meal filled the void. Michelle liked her carrots crisp, so added a second batch late in the cooking process for her pot roast. Bob loved all her unique quirks. He rounded the corner to the sound of snick, snick, snick, a knife on a cutting board.

"Hi, honey!"

His entrance startled Michelle. She leaped in fright accompanied by a sickening thunk. *Awful, it sounded awful,* Bob thought. It was as if she went from slicing carrots to steak. A tough, gristly cut of meat, resistant to the blade. Bob's face went pale at the sight of his wife's finger severed at the knuckle! Michelle screamed like an animal, her cry bordering on a ferocious growl. Michelle suddenly noticed his presence.

She turned toward him, flashing teeth like a rabid beast, howling in pain. The scream was so different from that of the woman he knew, or any woman. What at first sounded like growling turned into a screech, like a dying cockroach amplified. A sound Bob knew well from stomping on so many in his disgusting kitchen prior to marriage.

Michelle scrambled to the kitchen sink, turned the faucet on full blast, and ran her injured hand underneath. Bob finally emerged from his fog long enough to approach his wife, grabbing her from behind, trying to bring the affected arm into view. She shrugged him off and continued the water therapy.

"Honey, are you…"

She turned, smiled.

"Fine. I'm fine."

"You're not fine. We need a hospital. I watched you cut your finger off. I think you are in shock."

"Whatever are you saying, dear? Close call was all. You're seeing things. Maybe you are the one in shock. Understandable if you believe you saw such a horrible thing."

"I did see it!"

He forcefully pulled her hand from the running water, shocked to find her fingers intact. He examined the hand, which was wet but not bloody. Not even a scratch. She pulled back against his forcefulness.

"Ah, looking to get a little rough tonight? Have a little fun?"

Bob attempted to step away, shocked at the turn while still worried, but she loosened his belt. Bob looked to the carrots, confused, but could not fight her efforts any longer. Lifting her over his shoulder, he stormed into the bedroom.

The lovemaking was wilder than normal. Bob did his best to keep up, but Michelle appeared ravenous. At one point, her screams of passion segued into clicking whines. Bob flashed back to the kitchen, flustering at the memory. Whenever Bob tried to slow their antics down to check on her, really check, she retook control, growling in the more familiar way. Once they finished, Bob slept soundly. The pot roast would keep.

An itch woke him. Bob found himself wrapped tight in the blankets, knotted up (when had he pulled away from Michelle?) in a manner matching his solo sleeping days. He quickly kicked off the covers, triggered by the thought of being alone again. Bob never wanted to return to his former life. Long had he wondered who he wanted to be. In his new marriage, he found it. She made him into the man he wished to be.

Waking alone made him uneasy, serving as a painful reminder of a lonely past. All those days in Mick's place in the haze of alcohol, Bob never dared admit how much isolation haunted him. Though Bob rarely missed his first wife, single life brought with it an emptiness he feared would chase him to the grave.

After kicking off the cocoon of covers, Bob broke out into a sweat as the images of his wife severing a finger played out in his mind. He wanted to wake her, to inspect the injury once again, but his wife already left. If she rose earlier than him without disturbing him, she had to be fine. But he could not shake the shakes. He trembled at the thought of something happening to Michelle. The tremors in his hand another reminder of his boozing days.

The itch that initially woke him still bothered his leg. He reached down to scratch the offending right calf, only to find something attached to his skin. Scraping it off, he lifted it for inspection. The tiny was a deep black with a yellow streak down its center. A fingernail?

It could not be. He placed it on the nightstand. It could not be. Surely the item was something entirely different. A piece of stray plastic from God knows what. Bob inspected Michelle's hand. She was also beyond fine in their bedroom after the incident. Looking at the clock, he leaped to his feet. It was almost noon.

Bob spritzed in the bathroom sink and rushed to the kitchen, where he scrunched his nose. Something foul filled the air. Normally Michelle's scent greeted him everywhere in their home, but now he fought his gag reflex. Something potent, ripened to the point of rot, surrounded him.

Could it be the pot roast? The slow cooker should have been fine with the overnighter. Bob allowed a quick sniff to detect the origin point and followed. Walking slowly to the sink, he glanced inside, finding nothing except a dislodged strainer from garbage disposal. Did that occur when Michelle flushed her hand? Bob peered down the open drain and spotted the blades clear of obstruction. Still the smell staggered him.

Perhaps she had burned the food and unwisely disposed of it in the sink. Bob held his breath, poured a portion of the dish soap down the open drain, then flushed it with water. Bubbles formed, clear at first, but soon turned a sickening greenish black.

With the flip of a switch, the drain cleared, emptying the sink and minimizing the stink. Mostly. The stench lingered enough to require the cracking of a window. Then he left for work.

They kept the old home to use as a formal realtor's office. Michelle oversaw renovations to the office, resulting in a beach house vibe. "Get them to buy their first home while planting the seed for a summer home," Michelle told him in relation to the chosen motif.

A client's car sat parked in the driveway. That meant his wife met a client at the office and drove them both to a property. Bob's day was open for cold calling. He booted up the computer to prepare for a day of awkward phone calls. Brakes screeched outside and a man yelled. A second screech of the brakes accompanied a second round of protest from an upset individual.

"I said, let me out!"

The voice was that of a man. Bob parted the curtains to find the individual storming his castle. The man burst into the office, rushing past Bob.

"Bathroom?" The man yelled more than asked, rushing forward, as if sensing where it was.

Bob pointed it out anyway. The man made it just in time to vomit into the sink. Bob glanced out the window again and spotted Michelle behind the wheel of her Mercedes, head drooped over the steering wheel. The client emerged from the bathroom, pale, wiping his mouth. Walter Higgins was his name. Bob remembered meeting the client at some point. The man pointed toward the front door.

"You need to get her checked out," Walter said.

"Mr. Higgins, what happened?"

"She, she is just not right is all."

"My wife?"

Walter nodded, fighting off a second round of gagging.

"Please, tell me what happened."

"First, she is clearly drunk. And not the lightly buzzed version where she might pretend to come on to me," he said.

The words shook Bob. The man openly suggested a desire for Bob's wife, unconcerned over how that might upset the husband in the room. Walter appeared so traumatized that he remained in a world of his own, unaware of who exactly he was talking to. It could have been anyone. The man needed to vent. Rather than choose which question to begin with, Bob started with a declaration.

"That's impossible, my wife does not drink."

"Are you suggesting she forgets almost an entire vocabulary while sober? That's not entirely accurate. She started speaking, but it wasn't words. It was all garbled and gurgled. Maybe a foreign language. Then it happened."

"What happened?"

"She got sick."

The pronouncement shook Bob. During their courtship and marriage, Michelle never once fell ill. Maybe that meant she was due, he thought, surmising she suffered a stomach flu. Hurling was as contagious as yawning. It was the reason bartenders kicked out sick patrons so quickly. Dealing with the mess was an afterthought. Stemming the tide of chain-reaction contagion it could induce was the real driving factor to throw bums out. Mick kicked Bob out plenty in the past.

Bob assumed his poor wife ate whatever ended up in the sink at their house. The stench was stomach churning. It must have hit her while showing a property. Walter, a man of seemingly low constitution, was susceptible to sympathy sickness. Though concerned for Michelle, Bob understood she would expect him to save the sale above all. He attempted to charm the distressed client.

"Mr. Higgins, I am so sorry. My wife has been under the weather," Bob lied. "It was wrong of me to send her with you to the home when I should have taken you there. Why don't you give me your impressions of the place and I can take over from here?"

"My impressions? My impression is the place looked like a crime scene with all the blood, can't believe I let the bitch drive me back, but how else could I get to my car?"

The man started toward the door. Bob grabbed his shoulder. Normally he would have raged over the name calling, but there was a more pressing concern.

"What do you mean, blood?"

"Haven't you been listening? She got sick, man, real sick. Threw up everywhere, like geysers of blood."

"What? That is impossible, she's never sick."

"Never drinks, never sick. Do you even know your wife? I need to go," Walter said. He looked to Bob, then sternly at his arm. Bob got the message and let go. Walter started off, only to stop in the doorway. "It wasn't just that. She threw up some bones."

Walter finally exited. Bob stepped out onto the porch as if on someone else's legs. His world went white around him, and he feared he might pass out. Nothing made any sense. His wife, the most beautiful woman in the world, the one who had rescued him from himself, had somehow frightened a man so much that the client yelled at her one last time about being crazy before peeling out of the driveway.

Bob approached his wife, who still sat in the driver's seat, her head lolling about as if sloshed. Bob stepped closer.

"Michelle?"

Michelle's head danced around as if seeking the source of sound. Upon noticing Bob, she smiled, her face tilted askew. "Oh, hi, Honey."

"Are you okay?"

She nodded in a bob and weave. "Sure thing. Made a little mess is all. Need to go clean it up."

Michelle backed the car out, jerked to a stop, then pulled out all the way. The car swerved as it vanished down the street. Bob gave chase, but quickly lost her.

"Michelle!"

A young couple pulled in behind Bob's car.

"Hi, Bob! We are here to see Michelle. We have an appointment," the young man said.

Bob ignored them and rushed into the house, searching for his keys. Nothing made any sense. By the time he found them, the young couple stood on the porch.

"Is she here?" The young wife eyed him with confusion.

"No, uh, she's sick, sorry, need to reschedule," Bob said. He rushed to his car and climbed in.

"We had this appointment for a week," the couple said in unison.

Bob leaned his head out his window. "Look, can you move your fucking car, please!"

Rather than wait, Bob drove over the yard and turned around to get past their car, narrowly missing its front end. The couple stepped off the porch with arms raised.

"We're going to mention this on Yelp," the young man yelped.

Michelle planned to show four properties that day. It never occurred to Bob to ask the client which property the incident happened in. Bob dialed his wife twice. Straight to voicemail. Any other woman, any other time in his life, and Bob would have waited it out, believing she was fine. Maybe a little sick was all. Except Michelle was perfect. Michelle was who Bob wanted to be. His efforts to emulate her in all ways had changed his life for the better, bringing him out of a soulless gutter.

The first two stops were a bust. He only made cursory searches of the properties since her car was not on site. Both were blood free. (And bone free?) The third house looked to be the magic number. Her car was not in the driveway, yet there were tire marks leading from the driveway into the street. Had she burned rubber? His wife?

Rushing into the home, he called Michelle's name. An overwhelming odor stopped him cold. The scent of bleach filled the air but could not eliminate a powerful stench. Lifting his shirt over his nose, he moved past the foyer, deeper into the house.

"Ah, Hell!"

A horrific smell hung so thick in the air he felt as if he walked through curtains, the stench fluttering around him like drapes as he approached the kitchen. Walking through the open doorway, he crossed an arm Dracula style across his nose, trying to lock in on the fabric softener scent of his sleeve. Bob never bothered with dryer sheets previously, just one more beautiful thing Michelle brought into his life.

Bob approached the sink and encountered a replay of his morning. The garbage disposal appeared to be the source of the smell, the same as earlier, with one major difference. Looking down into the drain, Bob noticed something white.

Collapsing his fingers, he squeezed his hand into the narrow opening, reached down far enough to grip something. He retrieved it, revealing a small chunk of bone, possibly brachial. It appeared slightly larger than a chicken bone.

Peering deeper, he spotted more whiteness. Before he could conduct another search and rescue, he leaned onto the wall to balance himself and accidentally hit the disposal switch. He cursed as a chunking noise ground away any evidence. He powered it down, but the drain had emptied.

Bob ran to his car and sped home, dialing his wife the whole time. She never answered. Her car was not in the driveway, so he drove to every haunt he could think of. As he did so, it occurred to him every destination was a location from his past, not hers. He realized Michelle was a mystery. During their marriage, he avoided prying into her past, and now it cost him. He had no way to hunt her down.

Eventually, he returned home to wait for her. He left the TV on for hours but did not watch, not really. At midnight, exhausted mentally and physically, he went to bed, hoping he might soon wake from the worst of nightmares. A crash downstairs woke him. The clock showed the time to be 3AM.

There were multiple vases and decorative bowls in their home, plenty of things which could have made the noise if dropped, bumped into in the dark of night. Their alarm had not sounded, which meant only one thing. Michelle was finally home.

Thump. Scrape. Thump.

Leaden footsteps trudged loudly up the stairs. Bob stirred, rising against the headboard, sitting upright. Had an intruder broken in? No way that could be his wife, he thought. The steps were too heavy. Every other step sounded like a dragged foot rather than a delicate step. Like someone carrying dead weight.

A hall light turned on. An intruder would not announce their presence. It had to be Michelle. But how to explain her thunderous approach?

Thump. Scrape. Thump.

The room shook. Someone banged into the bedroom wall from out in the hall. Drunk? Was his perfect wife drunk earlier and more so now?

"Michelle?"

Bob remained on the bed, frozen in indecision. He crawled from beneath the covers, settling onto all fours on top of the bed, eyeing the door, waiting to identify who was about to enter.

"Hi, honey," Michelle said from out in the hall in a gurgling voice.

"What is wrong? What happened? Something is wrong, I'm going to call a doctor!"

She erupted into a childish giggle. Unsettling. Her shadow crossed the threshold, highlighting her shape, still beautiful in silhouette, though she leaned too far as if on unstable feet. The shadow grew closer. Another thump against the wall. Was the wall the only thing holding her up?

"No, no, no. No doctor today. I'm fine, some bad chicken was all," she said, her voice quivering like Jell-O.

Bob should have been off his feet, should have rushed to her side but given her perfections, he remained lost, uncertain how to approach a woman in such a vulnerable state. He had yet to turn on a light, instead relying on the pool of light spilling into the bedroom from the hallway.

Michelle finally stepped into view, standing there entirely naked. Bob's groin stirred at the sight, enticing even while shrouded in uncertainty. Yet why did a chill rustle up his spine? She walked forward dead legged, dragging one foot along. The sound from the stairs.

"What's wrong with you?"

She laughed like the disposal crunching bones at the other home.

"I almost took a man tonight," she said, stepping closer still. "Imagine that? Our perfect life and I take another man?"

"That's it, I'm calling a doctor."

Bob reached for his cell. The darkness messed with the facial recognition. Before he could even open the screen, a hand gripped his wrist. Forceful, powerful. White and dead. She moved too quickly for someone in her condition.

"I'm fine!" It was an order, not a declaration.

Bob jerked in fright, yanking his arm free. Michelle stumbled back, her dead leg twisting. She timbered backward onto their hardwood floor, landing with a massive thump. The sick slap of flesh might well have been a cut of raw meat being slapped against a butcher's block.

She landed out of view of the ambient light of the hallway, so Bob used his cell for additional lighting. Leaning over the edge of the mattress, he jerked in fright as something small scuttled across the floor, disappearing under the bed.

He aimed the light back at his wife and screamed. The beam landed on a gaping hole where his wife's nose used to be! The size of the hole versus the scuttling object matched. (Had it crawled under the bed?)

Bob struggled to understand the horrific change to her facial structure. Even as he watched, her skin seemed to move. A bubble formed near the fleshy edge of the cavity in her face. No, not a bubble. Something struggling to break free. A piece of skin, no larger than a cockroach, detached and scrambled toward the bed. Soon her face came alive with motion.

Another piece of skin made for the underside of the bed, followed by another, and another. More and more, until her entire body came alive with movement. Bob leaped off the bed and almost stepped on a piece of finger, or perhaps a toe. He raced for the door when he felt a searing pain in his right foot.

Glancing down, he watched as a cockroach sized piece of her skin ate its way into his foot, attaching itself roughly flush with his own. He turned back as hundreds of pieces rushed him, his wife's body nowhere in sight, at least not in one piece.

Hot jolts of pain shocked every part of his body as his own skin came alive with movement. The white section of an eye, with a hint of her green, ate its way into his blue. Bob could not defend himself, as nothing worked any longer. Not even his vocal cords.

He could not scream when a swarm made work of his genitals. Bob felt the weight (as meager as it was) of his penis vanish, replaced by a feeling he could best describe as a void, though the searing white hotness possibly clouded his perception. Movement fluttered over every inch of his body, leaving him without control of anything other than his terrified thoughts. His mind raced, remembering how badly he wished to become someone else. Then it hit him how Michelle suggested he had good bones. Certain bodily functions returned, starting with a voice.

Bob cried out. But in no time at all, his screams sounded very much like his wife's.

CARPE DIEM COFFEE & TEA COMPANY

MOBILE, ALABAMA

COVID hit us all hard. When I agreed to this anthology, the world was in a much different place than it is now. I was still in Maine and knew I would visit the south to get away for a while eventually but what I didn't know was that I would stay there for a year or more, living in Alabama with my friend Frank and his wife while COVID raged around us.

While I was working on some of the other stories, I was also going through lots of personal drama and life stuff, including a divorce. Every night for a while, I worked on this story in the café of Carpe Diem. This shop is a little unassuming two-story building right across from Spring Hill College in Mobile, Alabama. Inside, it feels very homey, and is what appears to be a former house converted into a shop. There is a fireplace complete with decorative overlays, and hardwood floors and very comfortable furniture. The owner is very involved with his business, kind, hardworking, and there all the time. College kids congregate there during evenings, trying not to fall asleep as they sit on the softest chairs imaginable.

The original idea for this story came to me while I was actually on my way to my uncle's wedding and my GPS turned me down a road, which looked like no one ever travelled on before. The actual story is much weirder than the one presented here, but not quite as bloody or tragic. I blended truth, fiction, and metaphor for my life events over the past couple of years into this tale, and it hits close to home for me despite being just a fun little horror yarn. Number one lesson: Don't always trust your GPS.

YOU CAN'T GET THERE FROM HERE

JOSEPH CARRO

My wife and I drove toward Brownfield, Maine, heading to my uncle's wedding in the same car he'd sold me two years prior, a silver 2009 Nissan Versa. It was beat up and on its last legs. When I'd first brought it home, there'd been a problem with the exhaust. The mechanic I brought it to was down to earth and suggested I let him "tape it up" suggesting it would "hold for quite a while, maybe a year or two." I took his advice so I could save some money and had it patched up. Since then, it sometimes came loose. That was my uncle Don for you, selling his own nephew a lemon. Family was family, however. At least that's how I looked at it, sighing as I thought about how disconnected we'd all become in our adult lives, spread out over the country in random spots. It felt like everyone was just trying to escape the harsh childhoods we had and forge new existences through which we could ignore the past.

According to the GPS, we only had a couple of miles left before we'd arrive at the old barn and meeting hall the wedding was to be held in. The Big Red Barn was a popular destination for live music. Bands, especially folksy ones, used the Barn to promote their bohemian image. They would use the spot for artsy album covers or Facebook ads set against the marketable backdrop of rural Maine. Most locals would prefer to be caught dead rather than listen to that kind of *Millennial music*, so it was no surprise that many folks in the surrounding neighborhoods showed open disdain for the Barn's outsider clientele.

Brownfield was a small town with a history of antagonism toward *flatlanders*. Being a flatlander meant one was a Mainer in name only, someone who hadn't experienced the authentic, rugged lifestyle that came with being born and raised in certain parts of the state. And thus, they didn't belong. To them, there was no difference between a tourist from Massachusetts and someone who lived in Maine but lived or acted as a flatlander.

My rear was already sore from the drive because I'd forgotten to take out my wallet before sitting. I frequently forgot to take my wallet out on long drives and suffered for it, no matter how many times I promised not to do so again. I shifted my weight to the other side while promising myself to take the wallet out next time.

I wore a tailored blue suit from my wedding because it was the only suit I owned and, thankfully, was comfortable. Amy and I married in a different expensive tourist town—Cape Elizabeth—only a year prior. We lived in an overpriced one-bedroom apartment in Portland, which was becoming too expensive for us. Soon we would likely have to pack up and find an apartment in my hometown of Lewiston. Lewiston was much cheaper than

Portland. Slowly but surely, all the bohemians and artists were being pushed away from the city and into outskirt towns like Westbrook or Lewiston because of an influx of Massachusetts money driving up already expensive real estate. I'd lived in Portland for the past decade with Amy, and we considered ourselves part of the last vestiges of Portland's carefree original residents.

Amy was in the passenger seat busy with her phone, (when wasn't she?) trying to connect to Instagram. She wore a bright yellow sundress and her long black hair fell in strands over her designer glasses. Tattoos emulating black lace covered the backs of her hands. I didn't consider her tattoos well executed, but her artist was popular among her friend's group, so I said nothing because I loved her, and they weren't my tattoos.

My wife was an Instagram influencer who spent a lot of time taking photos and posting stories from our adventures around New England. She called me her "Instagram Husband" because I always took photos of her against interesting walls or backdrops. Sometimes we'd spend hours taking photos in various locations throughout whatever random city we took a day trip to. As a result, her life looked luxurious and adventurous, at least more so than it was. Of course, I rarely appeared in her posts, and she seldom ever gave me credit for the work I did for her posts. She was a *Boss Babe*.

I never gave her any flack. Partly because I loved her, but also because her obsession with social media allowed me time to indulge in my obsession... watching eighteenth century cooking videos on YouTube. I couldn't make a bookcase from pine planks, but I could crank out a delicious meat or fish pie for dinner in a Dutch oven served with a whipped syllabub for dessert. I had always wanted to start a food truck. Portland's hipsters would likely flock to a food truck that produced colonial fare made with locally sourced ingredients.

Neither of us spoke as I turned the wobbling car down a dirt road branching away from the paved section we'd been traveling on. From out of the trees emerged ghostly silhouettes of ramshackle clapboard houses, abandoned vehicles. Two disheveled and burly strangers stopped what they were doing to watch us as we passed. They stared intently as if unused to outsiders turning down their road despite it being so close to the Big Red Barn. Creepy they were.

"Oh my god," I said, which caused Amy to look up from her screen, startled. "We're going to get murdered." I was only half joking.

One man in dirty overalls wiped his massive, greasy hands with an oilcloth and spit on the ground as we drove by. Amy stared in his direction from the passenger window.

"Ew, they're staring at us," said Amy.

"Yeah, there's a 'Hills Have Eyes' vibe going on here," I said, keeping my own eyes on the narrow dirt road ahead.

"Like, have they never seen an actual city person before? Hill people, I swear."

We passed a makeshift clothesline stretched between the beds of dual rusty trucks. Wet pants and flannel drying in the chill fall air. I laughed at Amy's comment and hummed the banjo tune from *Deliverance*.

"Don't even joke around like that," she said. "If I hear one note from a banjo, we're turning around and I'm just going to send a wedding gift to your uncle if he's even still alive and not getting murdered right now."

"I mean, you can't fault them for staring. All these lonely forest men deep in the Maine woods with no women around for miles, and here you come zooming through their neighborhood in all your glory looking like a beautiful yellow sunflower from Heaven."

"*Stop,*" she said, laughing. She hit my right arm as I moved into second gear to slow down and then into first to stop. The dirt road ended abruptly.

"Heck, I'd stare at you, too," I said.

"Yeah, but you're a pervert. That's why I married you." She smiled and gave me a mischievous side ey. This time, I laughed.

From there, the road turned into what I can only describe as a carriage trail strewn with large, jagged rocks. The surrounding trees choked the path, their skeletal limbs jutting out into the road as if nobody had traversed it in years. My GPS showed a solid blue line heading down that same direction for only two more miles, where it ended with a digital red flag denoting our destination.

"Babe," said Amy, voice full of apprehension. "You're not thinking of driving into that, are you?"

"I dunno. It doesn't even look like it's an actual road. But the GPS says otherwise. Maybe it's just an access road and looks worse from here than it is?"

"Babe, nobody has *ever* driven down it. Look at it!"

She was right, of course, but it was two forty-five and the wedding began at three PM, sharp. Turning around would make us late.

"I'll just drive into it a little. Maybe it'll lead us to a main road in a few minutes. We only have two miles to go. It's just two miles!"

She sighed in frustration but didn't protest further. I started driving again. Tree limbs reached out and scratched the doors of the vehicle, and the car bounced back and forth as the tires rolled over the rocks.

This went on for several agonizing minutes and I pictured the outside of the Versa covered in deep, long scratches. A small boulder I didn't see until the last minute scratched at the car's undercarriage with a screeching crunch, causing me to come to a halt once we cleared the obstacle.

"*Motherfucker*!" I cursed. "I cannot believe the GPS wanted us to go down this trail! Don't they do updates to these things? And it still says we have a mile to go, and I don't think the car can take much more of this." I was madder at myself for taking the route than I was at the GPS, but I refused to admit my mistake out loud just yet.

"Well, we've come this far already," Amy said, looking back through the rearview at where we'd come from. "Maybe the road is just up ahead like you thought." She looked worried but tried to smile to assuage my anger.

I nodded and pulled ahead some more. Amy patted my leg in support, soothing my anxiety. She knew me like the tattooed backs of her own hands.

After a short distance, we reached a spot where the path wheeled downhill into even darker woods ahead. It was now minutes past three, with only one measly mile left to go. We were already late. I stopped the car.

"My phone still has no service," Amy said, sighing. "What about yours? You try texting your sister?"

I pulled my phone from my pocket. No service. I searched for my sister's name in my contact list and sent her a message anyway. 'LOST. LOL.' I tossed the phone onto the center console of the car. It may as well have been a brick for all the use it was out in the Maine wilds.

"Did it send?" Amy asked, hoping.

"Nope, nothing. I think we're not going any further this way. I can't see what's down the hill. At least where the car is now, we can still turn it around. If I pull forward some more, we won't even be able to back up. It's too steep."

Twenty minutes past three. We were missing my uncle's wedding, lost in what seemed to be Hill People country. I grew frustrated. I'd always been bad with directions, so relied on the accuracy of the GPS to relieve me of that burden. Now I found myself stuck in the woods like a moron, dressed for a wedding I wouldn't even make it to.

"Look," I said, gripping the steering wheel and turning off the engine. "I'll get out, run down the hill, see if I can find the road or spot some sign of the Barn."

The GPS screen taunted me with a straight line toward the destination, only one measly mile away.

"Babe, is that a good idea?" Amy asked, looking back down the carriage road.

"I don't know what else to do," I said, taking one of her hands and rubbing it with my own.

"We're already late, and if I drive any further down the trail, we might get stuck. That hill looks mighty steep from here. There are so many freaking rocks and stumps. Where the car sits now, we can still turn around and head back if I don't confirm a road ahead."

She nodded, understanding our predicament. She liked it no better than I did, but she understood how important it was for me to make my uncle's wedding. He was like a brother to me, and we grew up together, but over the past few years we'd grown apart some. I didn't want to increase that divide.

"Plus, I've really got to pee." I flashed her my best smile.

It was her turn to laugh. I couldn't help but smile when she laughed. She was so beautiful, which was why I tried to make her laugh as often as possible. I leaned in and kissed her, feeling the warmth of her lips against my own. Then I broke away and looked ahead, taking a deep breath as if I was about to plunge underneath the crystal-clear waters of Sebago Lake back home.

"Don't get mauled by a bear," she said, half joking.

"I hope not to," I said, stepping out onto the trail in my shiny black dress shoes. My heart hammered in my chest at the thought. This was wild country and coyotes, bears, bobcats, moose, or even worse... *people* could attack. I calmed myself somewhat by remembering hunting season wouldn't start for another month, so I was at least safe on that front. Back in college, I suffered a collapsed lung. While in the hospital, I shared a room with a man attacked by a moose in the woods. The moose had really worked him over. I hoped not to meet the same fate.

I looked back at Amy. She smiled, giving me a small wave, then blew me a kiss. I blew her one back and began my walk down the steep hill toward The Barn.

The forest was alive with the sounds of wildlife. As I moved further and further from the car, I gave a last look back before rounding a bend in the path. I smiled upon spotting her in the passenger seat, her yellow dress sticking out like a summer flower among the fall colors. She still tried to access Instagram. Then, as I rounded the bend in the trail, she and the Versa disappeared from my view as I became immersed in shade by what remained of the fall forest canopy.

I likely looked like an idiot, walking through the lonely woods, wearing a blue suit for the wedding, which I was now almost a half hour late for. I kept picturing the man from earlier who spit in the dirt at us, and what he might think. He'd laugh at me if he could laugh, that is. The man looked as though he never laughed a day in his life.

It bothered me how *angry* he looked. I pictured him wiping his hands with the oilcloth, sneering, spitting at the ground again. *What kind of idiot wears dress shoes in the fuckin' woods? Fuckin' idiot kids. Fuckin' morons, that's who. This is why the country is going to shit. Car probably runs on avocado oil.*

The day was hot for fall even in the shade, so I took off my blazer. Draping it over my shoulder, I jaunted toward a rise in the trail. At one point, I thought I heard a movement in the trees, so I stopped and listened. I tried to pick up the sounds of music from the highway or sounds of trucks careening down the asphalt to more civilized territories with their shipments. I listened for literally any signs of human life besides my own but found only silence. It was an oppressive quiet, so I coughed to ensure I hadn't somehow gone deaf. The sounds of wildlife had ceased, but the act of clearing my throat echoed off all the trees around. A wild cacophony compared to the quiet.

I lurched my way to the top of a small hill and my heart sunk when I noticed a fork ahead. The path seemed too narrow for my car to fit into and my hopes for making the wedding were dashed. In frustration, I unzipped my fly and pissed, wondering whether a bear or moose might smell my urine and think I was challenging it for its territory. I developed a primal feeling of vulnerability as I exposed my nether regions to the wilds, so I zipped back up as fast as I could. As I did so, I felt my pockets and realized I'd taken the keys with me. If something HAD happened to me, Amy could not drive away. Stupid. I pictured her in the passenger seat of the Versa, realizing this same thing and panicking. I started the trek back.

Our trip down this dark, unused carriage path was *through*. No more bears, no more hill people. We'd have to turn around, head back, and try to find some other road to at least make it to the wedding reception. There I would explain to my uncle what happened. He was more of a salt of the earth guy than I was, had a better head on his shoulders about cars and things like that, so possibly he'd get a kick out of my misadventure. If he wasn't too angry with me.

Walking back, I worried over the path appearing different. At first, it was only a slight change, like a flower here and there. But then, I realized there were rocks I felt I would have noticed earlier. I spotted an old carriage wheel in the overgrowth, proving it had been a carriage path at some point.

A feeling of being watched crept its way into my thoughts and soon I was looking over my shoulder while walking back toward the car. I turned the bend and spotted the vehicle just where I'd left it. I breathed in relief. The path merely appeared slightly different on the way back. But my heart dropped into my stomach. The passenger sat open with Amy nowhere to be seen.

I called out. "Amy? Babe?"

No response. What felt like an icy wind swept through me. My hands trembled. My voice cracked. "AMY?!"

I thought I heard a muffled cry from behind the car, so I crept around, this time picking up a large rock from the path. I poked my head out around the trunk, eyes wide with anxiety. My fingers gripped the rock, and I raised my arm behind my head, prepared to strike.

Amy squatted in the woods a few feet away from the main path. "Privacy?" She shooed me away with a free hand.

"Oh, thank Christ," I said, dropping the rock and moved back toward the passenger side. I wiped my brow with my sleeve and put my blazer back on, airing it out by flapping the hem with both hands. I'd sweated fiercely.

"Sorry, babe," I said. "I thought you'd run off or hill people had taken you."

I waited a few seconds for a response. When she didn't reply, I gazed out at the treetops. The sun would set soon.

"Are you mad at me? I'm sorry I took the keys. I didn't think about it until after I was already a ways down the trail. Bad news, though. The car won't fit through the trail. It gets tight down about a half-mile or so. Maybe more, I can't remember how long. It seemed like it took forever."

Still silence.

"Babe?" Sometimes, she wouldn't talk to me for a long time if angry with me. But this felt different, and she hadn't seemed furious when she'd shooed me away. "Babe, look," I said, turning around and risking interrupting her privacy again. I stopped mid-sentence, gazing at the spot I'd just seen her, my mouth hanging open in confusion.

She was gone.

"Amy?" I vacillated between anger over her playing a prank while I was late for a wedding and worry. "Babe? This isn't funny."

All around me, the forest erupted in noise. Branches snapped, trees and bushes rustled. I heard footsteps nearby, the surprise of which caused me to stumble and fall next to the car. I let out a little holler and backed myself up against the passenger side of the Versa. From my new vantage point from the ground, I noticed something sticking out of the front right tire. A knife. The handle appeared carved from a deer antler. I pulled it free, and the tire let out a large hiss in protest. I looked at the back right tire, and it looked to be deflated. My heart hammered in my chest. I grasped the knife and stood up, using the open door for support. Once on my feet, I slammed it shut.

"Babe! Where are you?" I shouted, running to the spot where she'd been crouching. The grass was wet from her urine. Where was she? "Amy? Amy, where are you? Babe? *Babe*!"

Something tapped my shoulder. I spun expecting my wife but found a man shorter than me by about a foot (I was six-two). He had short black hair, almost completely buzzed. His face was sallow, sunken, his eyes were dark circles, and his chin disappeared into his neck. He smiled, revealing an absence of top teeth. His mouth looked like a horrible black void. He had tattoos on his neck, but I couldn't make out what they were.

I stepped back, holding out the knife for protection. I darted my head around, looking for accomplices. The hill people.

"Who the *fuck* are you?" I asked, trying not to betray how terrified I was. "Where's my wife?" My fear was turning into anger. My hand shook.

He smirked, and it was probably one of the smuggest smirks I'd ever seen. My rage erupted and stepped toward him, brandishing the knife. Something struck me hard in the back of the head. Everything flashed white hot like the sun. My mouth filled with the taste of pennies. As the world dropped out from under me, I saw the toothless man smirking until I fell into a void darker than his mouth.

· · • •• • • · ·

I woke to thunderous pain and the smell of the earth and grass in my nostrils. Sitting up with some difficulty, I gasped for air, fighting the overwhelming urge to vomit. Then I finally did, clutching the grass between my fingers as I dry-heaved. Shivering, I suddenly realized I was naked. A moan escaped my larynx like a rogue ghost. I hacked and coughed, struggling to breathe in. My head swam, throbbing worse than any migraine.

Darkness.

Had night fallen or was I dying? After I gathered what little thoughts I could through the pain, I realized it was late at night or even early in the morning. I touched trembling, soil-covered fingers to my scalp and winced. My head was split open and bleeding. My fingers came away wet, covered in blood.

"Amy?" I stood, bracing myself against a tree. My voice was hoarse, my throat sore. Had they strangled me? An icy feeling roamed through my body as a panic attack set in.

Stumbling forward, I dropped to the ground. Pain overwhelmed my body. I screamed upon discovering an open wound on my left side, under my armpit. I clasped my trembling fingers around the stab wound, which bled freely. Some of the blood was cold.

Of course. It made sense. They knocked me unconscious and left me for dead after robbing me. But there was no telling what had happened to Amy. Ignoring the pain and clutching the wound as best I could, I shambled forward. I had enough sense not to shout for Amy in case the attackers were nearby. Each step felt like hot shards of glass, and I limped with my left leg. My knee felt dislocated. My left side throbbed. Probably broken ribs. My breath sounded willowy. Though barely able to see in front of my face, I knew I was still in the forest. I tried to remember all the nature documentaries I'd seen about surviving alone in the Maine wilds, but none of that came to mind in my current state. I was empty, my anxiety taking hold like the grip of a giant's hand around my frame. Most of all, though, was the growing concern over my wife.

Ignoring all the pain and discomfort from the scratching tree limbs, loose rocks and sticks, and other hidden obstacles before me, I made my way in a direction. I did not know where I was going, but it felt right. There seemed to be more of an open route, so I went with my gut, hoping it would lead me to help, or my wife, or my car. My eyes had adjusted to the darkness, and I used what little light I could to guide my movements. I discovered that my left eye swelled almost entirely shut, so I relied on my right to do most of the work. In my shock, I failed to notice several other wounds and injuries. One of my teeth was missing, my lips were swollen and raw, my jaw was stiff, the pain growing in intensity. My head buzzed like it was full of angry bees and throbbed with a massive pressure that made me want to vomit. More than once along my dark trek, I did so.

I walked for what felt like hours but could have been only one or two. Or maybe even just a half an hour. I couldn't say. Eventually, through what must be an act of some higher power, I broke through the tree line onto a path. My bleeding and bruised feet found some relief on the worn trail, free of things scratching and poking them. Initially, I tried to cover my manhood while walking through the brush out of some innate sense of impropriety, but eventually abandoned the modesty, only shielding it from low-hanging branches when I could. Being so exposed, in my mind I saw myself as some wild animal. I was hungry, thirsty beyond belief, and in immense pain.

Shambling in the night down the path, not knowing whether I was going the right way, I used the moonlight to light to search for anything familiar from my trek earlier. (Was it even the same day?) If I could get to my car, I might have some sort of chance, maybe. I wasn't sure what I would find there, but anything would be better than this.

I hobbled along the trail through the darkness, surrounded by creatures stirring in the forest, including the dull low wail of coyotes roaming in a pack. When I was a child, the sound terrified me, but in my current condition, I almost howled along with them. *Amy was dead.* I'd already set my heart against it, though I still hoped to find her alive. My spirit had waned at the thought, but then anger flared up inside me, a rage I didn't know was possible. I clenched my fists tight until my nails dug into my palms, drawing blood.

My breath grew ragged as the initial shock of my condition wore off. I felt wounds I hadn't before and found myself lightheaded. I stopped in my tracks. Just ahead, a pair of gleaming eyes shone in the moonlight, feral and predatory. Its head stooped low to the ground, and it crouch-walked toward me. A coyote. They'd smelled my blood trail, and where there was one, there was more.

I turned my torso and sure enough saw black shadowy forms of four other canines moving around me, positioning themselves around their prey. They rarely attacked humans but understood how wounded and weak I was. They likely sensed that I neared death and hoped to hasten me along. My body would make a good meal because my human attackers had already tenderized and torn me open in spots. I tried to position myself better by moving toward a large tree, with plans to place my back against it.

One nipped at the backs of my legs, and I screamed in anger, causing the pack to back off briefly, but they quickly pressed in closer. I smelled their animal musk. They were good at following their instinct, striking one at a time, causing me to focus my attention on my attacker while the others tried to bite from my flanks and rear. I tried not to stumble as I moved toward the tree. If I stumbled even a little, they'd attack, finishing me.

I screamed at them until I couldn't scream anymore. With a free hand, I picked up a heavy stone with a wicked-looking point on the end and threw it at the nearest. It bounded off one of the coyote's heads with a loud crack, and the beast yelped and howled, throwing its legs out behind it in desperate kicks. It writhed on the ground, spinning in circles, kicking up dirt. The others snarled and fell back, uncertain. It gave me time to reach the tree. I placed my back against it, then waved my arms in front of me like a madman, shouting as best as my hoarse voice and aching throat allowed. Loud phlegmy coughs in which I spit out blood punctuated my shouting. My mouth tasted of copper and my chest made a horrible sucking sound.

My legs and calves were on fire, and I could feel fresh blood oozing down onto my ankles as I struggled to stay upright while retreating slowly. The dark forms of the remaining coyotes paused in the middle of the path, eyes glinting. It seemed they were measuring the situation. The coyote I'd hit with the rock had stopped moving. I backed up slowly, grimacing whenever I stepped on a stick or large rock.

Then relief. The remaining coyotes decided to make a meal out of their fallen brother and leave me to my sorrowful retreat. As I ascended the path, they dragged the dead coyote into the darkness of the surrounding forest. I sighed, hands, arms, and legs trembling. I spit more blood onto the path.

I don't know how long I walked after that, or how far away my attackers had carried me into the woods. They did not even give me the decency of a shallow grave. I shambled forward like a zombie, no doubt leaving a grim and bloody trail in my wake. The woods were alive with the sounds of wildlife. Crickets, toads, and owls all created a cacophony, which drowned out some of my grunts.

As I rounded a bend in the trail, my feet struck a large piece of wood jutting onto the path and I lurched forward, dropping to the ground, landing hard on my knees and face. My head struck a rock, and everything went dark as I sailed down into the void and floated there for a while.

I woke to the sound of birds singing morning song. My head was sticky with blood, and I threw up. Now that I could see my limbs and flesh, it was more disturbing than I initially thought. I was ashen, cut, scraped, scratched. My torso had long slashes, and the stab wound still bled through the partial clotting. My feet were almost entirely raw, my calves torn where the coyotes had ripped away some of my flesh. Several of my toes were black and purple. I could only guess what my face and head looked like. Under my knees was an old wagon wheel. The same one I'd seen yesterday. My heart raced. I looked behind me and there was a gruesome red trail of blood and bloody footprints draped across the rocks and dirt of the path.

Pushing myself up, I cried out in pain. That I'd made it to the wagon wheel gave me a second wind. I stood on shaky legs and moved forward with purpose, almost running. My labored and uneven gait reminded me of when I was a kid at Sebago Lake State Park and would try to walk around on heated sand without shoes, lifting my feet every few seconds to spare myself from pain. I kept my eyes on the path ahead, looking for my car. I still refrained from shouting Amy's name, knowing she was likely dead or gone. If I were to find the man with no teeth or neck, I'd know just what to do.

I came around another bend in the path and looked ahead. The spot was right there, but the car was gone. *Of course.* They'd left me for dead, stuck me with the knife, and moved the evidence. I seethed with a newfound well of anger. No car window to reflect my face contorting with rage, but didn't need it, I could feel it. I moved past the spot where my car had been and examined the area. Tire marks, footprints. I followed the prints, which soon disappeared. I couldn't tell if any were Amy's. But the tire marks made a vast circle through the clay and mud and doubled up where I'd driven from on the way to my uncle's wedding the day before. I wondered if anyone had come looking for us yet but guessed nobody would for many days.

Walking on, I headed to the one place I thought might harbor my would-be murderers. I pictured the men working on the truck I'd seen the day before, sneering as their friends and accomplices brought my car out of the carriage path, pictured them rifling through my belongings, burning what they didn't want to keep for themselves. I imagined them dismantling the car for parts and laughing about how they'd left me in the woods. Just another *flatlander*. Then I pictured them torturing or killing Amy. Soon I emerged from the trail and stood just a few yards from the ramshackle house with the red trucks I recognized.

I made no pretense of stealth, moving on wobbly legs, naked, beaten, robbed, humiliated. I turned the doorknob to the back door. It clicked open, and I entered the kitchen. My phone sat on the kitchen table. Amy's too. I picked up my phone and tried to power it on, but it was out of battery. I dropped it and checked Amy's. Hers was out of juice as well.

Finding dead batteries somehow confirmed my worst fears. I had nothing left. I spotted my car keys hanging on a hook near the sink. My shaking stopped reaching for them when I noticed the knife that I'd brandished against the hill people. Probably the same used to stab me. I grabbed it without hesitation, then moved through the house, searching each room.

The downstairs was small and comprised the kitchen and a big living room area with a cheap looking off brand TV from Walmart. There were couches with camo coverings. There was a set of wooden stairs leading up to a second floor, the lumber unfinished, just bare wood. I left bloody footprints everywhere I stepped and never considered trying to dress myself again. It was pointless. I felt I was dying and wished to take them with me when I went, if possible.

Within minutes of searching the house, I heard the rumble of a vehicle outside. I glanced out the window and saw a large blue SUV. Two men got out of the vehicle and grabbed work gloves and dusty shovels from the back. I closed my eyes and waited in the kitchen with the knife.

The front door opened, and one man entered. It was not No-Teeth. This man was taller, bigger, older. The same who I'd seen spit on the ground before we entered the carriage path. He failed to spot me because I remained still. He coughed and placed the shovel against the wall, then started singing *A Boy Named Sue* by Johnny Cash. I approached him from behind. The front door remained open. The Spitter turned on the television, having to glance at the remote up close no doubt because he was getting older.

With no sound escaping my lips, I reached my blood covered hand around the man's neck and slid the blade hard across his throat in a sawing motion back and forth, feeling the flesh and cartilage underneath give way under the pressure. The big man screeched and elbowed me in the face out of pure surprised reflex, sending me sprawling backward into the wall and to the floor. However, the damage was done.

He turned to me, eyes bewildered and wild as blood sprayed in sheets down the front of his chest. He attempted to stop the bleeding with his large, oil-covered hands, but it was useless. I sat on the ground and laughed through my blood-covered teeth. I didn't see recognition in his eyes until I displayed the knife and pointed to it. Then his ancient orbs opened wide, and he tried to step toward the door but dropped to his knees, all the color leaving his face. I spit blood at him as I struggled to stand up.

I took a slight stumble, my eye already swelling shut from where he'd struck me with his massive elbow. The Spitter was gasping on the floor for air like a fish waiting to be placed in the bucket. The top of No-Teeth's head moved around the side of the building toward the kitchen door with his shovel and other gear. I moved toward the kitchen door and waited.

After a few long minutes, (*was time even a thing anymore?*) I closed my eyes and pictured all the small moments I'd shared with Amy. Those were all I had now, at the end. These men, and especially No-Teeth, had taken everything from me.

I pictured my first Christmas with Amy. She and I gifted each other the same movie. *Step Brothers*. It was our favorite. As she opened mine, I opened hers and we laughed, then shared it on Instagram and Facebook. I pictured the time when she worried about her father and some legal troubles that he was in. She'd spent a couple of hours crying into my arms as I'd stroked her hair. I pictured the time I'd proposed to her outside our locked apartment door as she struggled to find her keys. We'd just come back from dessert at our favorite nearby restaurant, The Great Lost Bear, and I knew I was going to propose to her and didn't know when. Why not right then? Amy teared up and said yes. I remembered all the times we'd cooked together in the nude, poked fun at each other for laughs, and had day trips to Boston. All of that was gone.

When I opened my eyes, No-Teeth was entering the kitchen. He spotted the bloody footprints right away. The bloody handprints on the cell phones and even the bloody mess in the living room where The Spitter lay.

"What the FUCK?!" He yelled as he turned to run out the door but never made it.

I was right behind him. His small eyes opened in fear. I felt certain he realized it was a mistake to leave the knife in plain view as I used it to stab him over and over and over. He made tiny squeals like a horrified child and blood poured out in rivulets. He made a weak attempt at shoving me aside, which worked in that we both slipped on the bloody floor and dropped. I laughed while he crawled along on his belly, leaving a wide berth of blood.

His legs kicked out like the coyote I'd hit with the rock a few hours earlier, his body flooding with adrenalin and endorphins, trying to stay alive. I jabbed the knife into the back of his right knee, causing him to cry out, then I used the embedded knife to push myself onto his back. I flipped him over and he punched me repeatedly.

It didn't do any good because I'd already accepted my fate. I couldn't see through my swollen eyes, covered as they were by blood. Blindly, I grasped at his face, searching for his eyes. An eye for an eye, isn't that what they said? After locating them, I stuck both of my thumbs into his sockets. He screeched when I broke through them with my digits. I thought of Amy and the life he'd stolen. He flailed and tried to slip out from underneath me, but I was drifting off to unconsciousness and became deadweight. After what felt like I long time of me stabbing No-Teeth and punching his motionless form as best I could, I succumbed to the darkness.

· · • • • • • • · ·

I woke some weeks later in the hospital. Eventually, someone discovered the carnage. Police searching for me and for Amy found my Versa in the woods, at least what remained of it. After that, they discovered the house. They took me by helicopter to Maine Medical Center in Portland. I answered their questions so many times, as best I could. They couldn't find Amy. Nobody could. She was just… gone. The last time I'd seen her, she was peeing in the woods.

The only reason they believed I had nothing to do with it was the fact that my wounds predated the two hillbillies, and I was almost dead. But I'd killed the only two people, it seemed, who knew what happened to her. I never got to say goodbye to the woman I loved. She just… disappeared.

After a couple of weeks in the ICU where my family and friends came to visit me, my doctors released me into a different section of the hospital to receive physical therapy. At first, my family was just relieved they'd found me alive. But soon, they realized I'd become somebody else. The old me died in those Maine woods along with Amy. I became a ghost of my former self. They tried bringing me gifts, cards, and everyone and their mothers called me or messaged me on social media. My brain just shut all of that out. I felt like a spirit.

The police searched the hill people's home after everything and discovered video of the men beating another bound woman. They identified the woman as the pregnant former wife of No-Teeth. They never found her, either.

I was a compliant witness, and I tried to help the case. When I could finally walk, the detectives brought me to the woods again, and I showed them where I had driven the car. I showed them the wagon wheel and where the men had dumped me. The police did a thorough search of the area. All they could find was a scrap of the bright yellow dress Amy wore that day, the cloth now browned and faded from the sun and the elements. The captain told me they were confident they would find the women's bodies soon, but none of that mattered to me. She was gone, as gone as I was.

Soon, I left Maine, saying goodbye to that life and to my family and hers, though they'd already stopped talking to me. Nobody liked the empty shell I'd become. I left it all behind, and I set my sights on the south for no other reason than to get as far away from the ghosts of my life as I could. Maybe there I'd be able to find peace. *But it would always haunt me that I never got to say goodbye.*

10 SPEED COFFEE

SANTA MONICA, CA

This little coffee shop sits nestled below a medical building and across from a hotel restaurant they might as well name The Bermuda Triangle, since every business that sets up shop there disappears quickly. Strange how a hotel in a busy tourist city like Santa Monica cannot maximize their captured audience. Perhaps a hotel restaurant has a unique difficulty of building return customers, regulars, since by nature their guests will vanish usually within a week's time.

Transitory. Transitory could describe the coffee shop across from that hotel. The place is a waystation, a stopover for those in the bike culture. People with bikes pricier than some cars stop for their caffeine fix and to show off physiques wrapped in Spandex. With parking at a premium in Los Angeles, this spot has bike parking for days in the guise of multiple bike racks well positioned, with lots of space to secure one's prized set of wheels.

The place closes early, before sunset each day, which makes sense. Biking after dark in Los Angeles is its own horror story, right up there with the most frightening of King, Koontz, or Lansdale.

Yes, they designed the place to get in, get caffeinated, then get out, back onto roads all before the sun sets. There is less danger in daylight. Caffeine aids brave bike riders who must navigate alongside a sea of speeding metal boxes called cars. Recently cities invested in bike lanes, but if anyone in a parked vehicle opens a door at the wrong time, the biker finds themselves in a world of hurt.

Biking has plenty more dangers outside of Los Angeles. There are few roads ever designed with bikers in mind. Good luck riding the dirt roads anywhere across the country. Great for some cool skids when one hits the brakes hard, but only fun when done on purpose. In an actual emergency, stopping in a timely fashion on such surfaces is not an option.

Then there is the lighting situation. Today there are headlamps, bike lamps, cellphone flashlights, all cost prohibitive in the eighties. Bike riders were less affluent during that time and rode beat up hand-me-down two wheelers for fun versus function. For most bikers, lighting was out of reach. Yes, they designed this coffee shop's hours around the very issue that existed once upon a time. Once darkness settled in, there were no streetlights to guide one home or keep them safely on the blacktop they rode.

This shop inspired me for this tale. That of a young man who wishes he had a stopover like 10 Speed Coffee, somewhere to escape to, or at least some light to guide him home.

THE CANDY HOUSE

PAUL CARRO

C ooper put the pedal to the metal, trying to make up time. His snot-nosed sisters threatened to rat out his planned day trip if he did not perform their chores before he left. His parents would have at least five conniptions if they knew he planned to bike all the way to the city to catch a movie rather than spend the day with friends like he promised.

Tattletale scum-buckets he called his two sisters. They did not seem to mind while playing with their stupid Barbies while he did the dishes and cleaned the bathroom. He believed one of them turded without flushing on purpose before he took over their bathroom duty, except he could not put it past his father.

Luckily, his dad already left for work, leaving one less person to deceive. His mother was visiting the next-door neighbor, having coffee and doing whatever grownups did. He felt grownup at fifteen, mostly, except an inability to drive landed on the hard bummer side of life. The indignity left him feeling less than a man.

Movies were Cooper's life and would be his destination for the day. Tether Falls was diminutive population wise but was dang immense when talking square mileage. Some houses were up to a quarter mile away from their nearest neighbor. Many parts of town remained undeveloped altogether. It was nineteen eighty-five, though. Times were changing. People were purchasing plots on which to build summer homes.

Maybe population growth would eventually allow Tether Falls to build its own movie theater, Cooper fantasized. Such a thing would save him from all the pedaling. The nearest theater was in the city of Westbrook, many miles away. By car, it took the better part of an hour. By bike, on the back roads (his only option) it was about three.

Cooper had to (just had to!) see the new movie Ladyhawke. The blockbuster had it all from what he gathered from his older sister's friends. The ones who frequented movies on dates. It starred Matthew Broderick, the awesome actor from Wargames along with Michelle Pfeiffer, the super-hot blonde from Grease 2. *She was no Olivia Newton John in leather,* Cooper thought, *but boy Michelle was all kinds of alright.*

For the final icing on the cake, the movie had a soundtrack by The Alan Parsons Project! How cool was that? He could not fathom how their music fit into an epic fantasy but was eager to find out. Only thing would have been cooler had been if John Williams scored the film.

Cooper had an Alan Parsons' song somewhere on his mix tape he played while pedaling. Cooper always wore his Sony Walkman while biking. Each completed song brought him closer to his destination.

"Gonna be your man in motion. All I need is this pair of wheels. Something, something, something—St. Elmo's Fire!" Cooper sang along to the song on his tape.

He was getting better at editing out the DJ introductions of the songs he recorded off the radio. He learned the sweet spot of when to hit record on his tape recorder. It meant missing a few bars of the tune, but it felt more like a record without the blather of a DJ. It pleased him to have his favorite songs for the ride, many of them straight from movies. Soundtracks were hot. Radio stations knew a good thing when they had it. They played all the cool stuff, like songs from John Hughes movies, and even the cool disco Star Wars song.

The eleven-mile stretch began near Tucker Road, then led to a long stretch of River Road before segueing into several side roads leading into the city of Westbrook. Cooper had a beat to shit Schwinn ten speed that he purchased at a yard sale. The brakes were highly questionable. Rust stains ran the length of the cables leading to his tires, but the wheels were sturdy, and the tires remained inflated, so no problems there.

The gears were another story. There were plenty of hills along the way, so shifting as needed would be ideal, except doing so caused them to grind horribly. The noise signaled an imminent dislodging of the chain. Getting that back in place was difficult and time-consuming. It was bad enough riding for so many miles. To be forced into walking, even for Ladyhawke, was unbearable. For that reason, Cooper left the bike eternally in fifth gear.

Arriving in time for a matinee was the key to his plans. Any screenings after that meant riding home in the dark. The thought of such a journey frightened him. He had done it a few times and vowed never again each time. (Only to mess up and therefore repeat the undesirable task.) Riding at night in the country was nightmarish. There were no streetlights once out of the city and the already narrow roads grew more so when one could not see the pavement.

Homes were not plentiful on the route and most ditched their porch lights after a certain hour. Forests lined both sides of the country roads and did their best to blot out any beams of moonlight that could have aided him on his treacherous evening ride. Sand ditches lined the roads and bled onto pavement, so he used that as his guide.

When forced to ride at night, he pedaled slowly. Once tires crunched into dirt, he steered back toward the road's center until eventually drifting back. Rinse, wash, repeat. The whole nighttime fiasco even added hours of commuting time because of the cautious pace.

The poet Robert Frost was a local. Cooper often thought of the town's streets as the 'road less traveled' Frost wrote about. Cooper hated poetry, hated English class, but boy did he love movies. He planned to move to Hollywood someday to make films and even had a cool idea of how to bring Indiana Jones into the James Bond universe.

"Jones, Indiana Jones," Cooper said loud enough to hear himself over the headphones. A song from Rocky chimed in, something sung by Rocky's brother. Who knew there was that much talent in one family? Cooper's mind wandered during his trips. But that was by design to keep himself occupied as he neared a worrisome part of his route. There was no avoiding it. Not far ahead was the one thing which sometimes made him wonder if he should even make the trip.

The Candy House.

The damn Candy House.

The Candy House was a house painted in an odd mixture of brown hues touched off with rose and pink accents. Curved trimmings extended off the roof ledge like frosting on a cake. The same frosting trim hung from a porch rail running the length of the house. Cooper felt imagined the place was the same as the house in Hansel and Gretel, where a witch would lure hungry children. Once kids entered, the witch would go all Julia Childs on their asses.

The house contained three stories and sat well off the road. A long dirt driveway bisected an immense front yard. The strangest thing about the home was that it remained abandoned. Locals told tales of the owners encountering something so frightening they departed without their belongings. Supposedly, even leaving an unfinished meal on the kitchen table.

Plenty of older kids interested in making a name for themselves planned to enter the abandoned structure. Yet none ever made it inside. Strange that Cooper thought. There were plenty of rabble rousers in town. There would not be a Tether Falls Correctional Center otherwise. Despite all the promises to enter the abandoned spot, no one ever found the cajones to enter. The furthest any got was the front door. Each person who tried abandoned ship without ever explaining why. Their silence only added to the mystery.

The house was just ahead. *Pedal fast is all,* Cooper thought. He needed to make up time anyway, or chance missing the early show. The house would soon appear on his right. There were other houses near the candy house. The isolated nature amplified Cooper's discomfort. If other homes abutted the place, perhaps it would appear less menacing. Just another home, one odd enough to annoy the neighbors. The impending fright fest revealed itself through the trees, (which always seemed dead, shed of leaves even during the summer months). Cooper spotted the pinks of the trim.

He remained in gear, wishing he could shift higher, but dared not lose the chain. He focused on the road, trying to ignore the horrific home even as it rolled up on his right. Suddenly, a guttural groan filled his ears.

"Shit!"

Cooper slammed the brakes and skidded on sand, gliding sideways into a stop. The skid caused him to face the very thing he hoped to avoid.

The Candy House.

With no time to lose, he brushed off his fear, busy with a rescue mission. Cooper hit the stop button on his Walkman and ejected the cassette tape, which had become gnarled in the machine. *Footloose* slowed to a crawl until it sounded like a demon took over the vocals on a favorite song from a favorite movie.

He pulled the tape out carefully, the crinkled magnetic tape stretching like spaghetti. It took the full reach of his arm to lift the cassette high enough to release it from the cannibalistic machine.

"Stupid batteries must be low."

They were always low. Cooper could buy the higher priced batteries, which would last longer except he spent most of his money on film and developing for his Vivitar camera. If he ever planned to direct movies, he needed to start somewhere. On his budget, all he could do was still photography. He staged scenes with his Star Wars toys, filming them in closeups as if they were real actors. It wasn't super eight, but the stills placed together told a story.

Cooper zipped open his fanny pack in which he kept his camera, among other items. He planned to drop a roll of film off for developing in Westbrook. He checked for extra batteries but found none. Worse, there was no pen. Lacking a better option, he stuck his finger in the rotator hole of the cassette, turning the wheel to rotate the tape back in place. A laborious task. A pen was much quicker than a finger.

Working as fast as he could, Cooper soon realized he forgot all about the house. Glancing up, he noticed something odd. A bicycle leaned against the front porch. It looked old. A single speed with twenty-six-inch tires. Cooper was good with bikes, so he could identify that much, even from a distance. The J shape of the frame seemed old school, like the earliest days of bicycles.

It looked to be in remarkable shape after being exposed to the elements in Maine. If no one lived there, it meant the bike must have sat outside for years. His own rusty cables gave testament to what a single winter outside in Maine could do. He wished to snap a picture of the bike because it reminded him of something. What that was, he could not remember.

Cooper finished with the tape and found himself overcome with a sense of being watched, though he failed to identify an observer or a location. Then it hit him. Up. The house comprised three stories. He was being watched from on high, or at least felt he was.

A pickup blasted past, blaring its horn, narrowly missing his rear tire. Someone riding shotgun tossed a Budweiser can at him. It missed and plinked along the asphalt.

"Get out of the road, Dingus!" the wordsmith in the passenger seat yelled while also shouting in sign language via a raised middle finger.

Cooper's heart raced at the near miss, and the home started freaking him out again. It was only the unique bicycle that kept him from riding away already. Cooper dropped the tape and Walkman into his fanny pack and tore off, racing away, happy to leave the Candy House behind.

· · · ● · ● · ● · · ·

Sure enough, Cooper missed the early showing, which meant at least part of his ride home would be in the dark. He cursed his sisters again for their delay in his plan. To fill the time before the next show, he stopped by the drugstore to drop off his film for developing. While there, he also purchased new batteries. As Cooper handed off the film for processing, he thought of the bike from earlier.

"What's your cheapest film for my camera?" He held the Vivitar up to the eighteen-year-old clerk.

"For that piece of junk, they only make cheap film."

Cooper deflated. It was the best camera he could afford. The best directors had to make do with what they had, right? He remembered they seldom showed the shark in Jaws because of budgetary constraints. Still, it stung.

"I just need to take pictures of a bike is all, saw an old one on my way here."

"Does it have a chick on it flashing her tits?"

"What? No," Cooper said.

"Then I'm not interested in anything you're saying. Here, we have a sale on this off brand. Knock yourself out with your bike pictures."

Cooper left the store only to realize the movie was about to start. He rushed to the theater and during the previews loaded the new film since it was dark enough to do so. Before the previews ended, he also replaced the batteries in his Walkman.

· · · ● ● · ● ● ● · ·

"That was the best movie ever!" Cooper yelled on his way home. The sky had not fallen dark yet. The summer sun took longer to set than in fall, so he was lucky there. Still, full dark was imminent for part of the trip if he did not get a move on.

He wished to buy the soundtrack to *Ladyhawke* but figured the record would cost a fortune. At least twelve ninety-nine. He would have to find a job over the summer since his birthday already passed and Christmas was super far away. No way could he wait that long for it.

The sky settled into grey as dusk settled in. Traffic was minimal in his town but plentiful in the city. Most vehicles already turned on their headlights, making it difficult for him to see whenever one passed him. Those same lights warned him he was running out of daylight.

His tape appeared okay on the return trip. While the batteries were new, the tape had yet to cycle through again. The machine had not eaten it yet, so that was a plus. He would know its status for certain when it reached the same song devoured earlier. The Sony Walkman Gods would either claim it for eternity or allow it to pass. The candy house was fast approaching, so he turned off the tape. He stopped well before the house, both to prepare himself and to steel his nerves.

Cooper knew the bike from somewhere, so wanted to take a picture. The bike's pristine condition still nagged at him. He placed his Walkman in his fanny pack and readied the camera. After snapping a picture, he would ask his father about it. His Dad was old, maybe even had the same bike when he was a kid.

Kicking off toward the house, Cooper grew increasingly nervous as he pedaled slowly. It was only because he was pre-occupied with rescuing the best mix tape ever that he forgot his fear of the candy house earlier. Though afraid, he vowed to be as brave as Matthew Broderick in *Ladyhawke*. All he had to do was man up and take the picture, then run. He knew the bike from somewhere. Looking at a picture from the safety of his own house would allow him time to remember. It was impossible to focus while freaked out by the frightening place.

He pulled over near the Budweiser can from earlier and felt a sense of being watched again. Night was fast approaching, so Cooper lifted his camera and snapped a photo. The flash went off and would be meaningless from such a distance. The house sat too far off the road, its dirt driveway twisty, significantly long. Still, the fact the device auto flashed confirmed night was near.

After taking the picture, something caught his eye high in the house. On the third floor, he swore something flashed in a window. He also felt certain that was where he was being watched from. A curtain appeared to drop back into place. Was someone up there?

Cooper took one more picture, again glimpsing an echo flash from within the house. This time exactly one floor below on the second story, where another drape fell into place.

He thought he glimpsed a woman before the third-floor curtain fell. This time, he was certain. But no way could anyone get down a flight of stairs that quickly in the time he took the second picture. *One way to find out,* Cooper thought.

With shaky hands, he raised the camera and took another picture. There was a first- floor window below the other two. It relieved him to find no echo flash from that window and no motion behind the curtain. That meant the earlier versions were mere tricks of light.

The first-floor window proved all was okay. There was no woman in the window. There was no one in the house. Then he realized why.

Cooper looked at the old bike and screamed!

The woman sat on the bike! It no longer leaned against the porch but faced him. The rider's arms raised high on the handlebars! Now he remembered why the two-wheeler looked so familiar. The woman resembled Miss Gulch from the Wizard of Oz.

Miss Gulch was the neighbor who became the Wicked Witch of the West in Dorothy's dream. Miss Gulch rode the bike before turning into the witch and riding away on a broom, an image that always haunted Cooper. The woman resembled Miss Gulch right up to the empty cage basket on the front. She rose on her haunches and pedaled. Despite the driveway running uphill, she effortlessly gained momentum, riding straight toward him.

As she rode closer, it became clear she was not Miss Gulch after all but looked very much like an actual witch. All the way to a face covered in heavy grease paint colored dark green. The woman flashed a wicked smile, exposing white teeth outlined by black lips that matched eyes as dark as coal.

Cooper turned his ten-speed in the homebound direction. His ten-speed, even in fifth gear, would lose the crazy woman on a one speed in no time if he hustled. Cooper cranked the pedals and skidded from dirt to pavement. A glance over his shoulder revealed the woman never even merged onto the road.

Something clacked against the bike's frame, startling Cooper so much he almost put the bike down. He quickly identified the source of noise. With no time to store his camera away, it remained in his grip, dangling from a nylon strap. The noise made as it struck the frame unnerved him, but he wanted to ride a safe distance away before stopping to store it away.

One more glance back relieved him further. The woman was not behind him, if she ever existed at all. The place spooked him so much he could have made it all up in his head. One thing was real, though. The bike which appeared to be a replica from the movie. That was why it looked so familiar.

Something crunched in the trees to his left. Cooper looked off the side of the road and his eyes shot open with surprise. About forty feet away, the witch rode her bike through the heavy forest! Despite pedaling across loam, mulch, and branches, she kept up with him.

He watched her in profile as she somehow trudged through the woods with no difficulty. She wobbled occasionally, but likely because of her high arm stance. Somehow, she rode the forest floor while mirroring his own flight. She wore a black hat, much like in the movie, along with a black robe of sorts on which the shoulders puffed out. The only difference from the film appeared to be her eyes. Those horrible eyes.

They were deep wells that well could have been twin black holes rotating within orbital sockets. With no whites anywhere, Cooper found it hard to determine exactly where her focus was. But every time she turned her head, it was as if she looked directly at him. Her snarl remained constant, the guise of one determined to outrace him.

Where was a passing car? There had to be one coming soon. Where were the bozos in the truck? Cooper wished for traffic. He planned to ditch the bike and leap into the first vehicle that came along.

Looking ahead, the road ran straight for at least a full mile. The next turnoff would not appear until arriving at the church (with the large cemetery in the rear). If he made it there, perhaps he could make it safely inside and pray away the devil on his tail.

With a cackle, the witch threw her head back in the air, delirious with the chase. She would soon catch him. While remaining parallel to him, she angled nearer the road, heading into an intercept. Already she was less deep in the woods than when she started. Each time the woman appeared close to hitting a tree, she somehow managed her way around.

Then Cooper spotted a ray of hope. A house appeared in the distance, blocking the woman's path. Finally, a home! Cooper knew many people in Tether Falls but could not think of any who lived on this stretch of River Road. The house would force the witch to go around since it was right in her path. The woods opened onto a front yard before converging back into forest again right after the home.

He sped up. Though increasingly tired, Cooper hoped to cause her to slip up, to mess up at the approach of the house. She was so focused on him, maybe she had not even noticed the oncoming structure. They were almost there. He felt as if a rope held the two of them together based on their mutual speed. But a game changer lay ahead for one of them. Cooper still had a straightaway while the evil woman had a two-story Victorian directly in her path!

Cooper leaned into it, pedaling faster, ready to lose her at the structure. She stared sat him hard, unaware of what loomed ahead. He would lose her in just a moment. The witch crossed the lawn. Dew had arrived with the onset of dusk, and water whipped up behind her as she sped across the green of the side yard. Strange how she kept steady, did not slide on the slick surface.

He rose off the seat, pressing on like at the end of Breaking Away. This was his chance to lose her. She approached the house and never even slowed, running straight into the side of the building. Cooper laughed.

Though terrified and much in need of a pee, he felt relieved. The old bat had ridden straight into the side of the house! He lost her. Or thought so until he heard the cackle from inside the house, louder than ever. The horrific laugh sounded over the crashing of pots, pans and glasses. People inside screamed, frightened by whatever they witnessed.

The rider emerged from the opposite side of the house without ever slowing, still on his tail! All the lights turned on in the home accompanied by yelling from the homeowners. Pure chaos inside.

How? How was she still after him? She rode the forest floor as if it were clear asphalt. Cooper gripped the uneven handlebars. The right curved grip of his ten-speed still had its original black foam wrap, but he long ago replaced the other with black electrical tape.

A buildup of sweat soaked and loosened the tape until it slipped off, causing one hand to lose contact with the handlebars. The bike shook while the handlebars wobbled. A bull trying to lose its rider. Cooper slowed while fighting to regain control. Gripping the exposed metal caused his hand to ache as he battled to hang on.

Tears streamed down his face. He needed the witch to crash into that house, but she did not. He could not ride at the current pace forever. While he struggled to continue, she simply grinned through it all. Instead of looking ahead, she focused on him with the understanding he would soon run out of gas. She angled her trajectory ever so slightly toward the road.

Cooper eyed his gearshift. If he shifted into higher gear, he could outrun her. He understood the risk, but figured he had no choice. Reaching down, he flipped the lever, shifting all the way.

Ka-thunk.

Pain jolted up his leg as his foot slipped off the pedal and struck blacktop, twisting painfully even while the bike continued forward. His pedals lost contact with the chain when he shifted.

"No, no, no!"

Cooper felt the bike give up the ghost, which caused the witch to cackle harder. So close now, so close. He got both feet back on the pedals and cranked out several rotations. The grind of the chain sounded like a chainsaw unwilling to start. The woman was gaining on him, and he was slowing down. Then suddenly it took!

He grunted at the extra effort the higher gear required. He had not used the tenth speed in some time. Despite the difficulty, he was moving again, and faster. The witch sped up as well. Cooper opened his mouth to scream but burst into sobs.

Rivers of snot rolled from his nose, while tears flowed from his eyes. How could this happen? Why wouldn't she stop? Where was everyone? He needed help. He was so, so tired.

Cooper spotted the church in the distance. His church. The one he used to attend Sunday school at. It was as far into that side of town as he ever went with his family. He never ventured into Candy House territory unless sneaking away for the movies. Now he prayed he could reach the church.

The witch cackled wildly and seemed to notice the approaching curve. Not only was the church looming, but a wild turn in the road followed by a steep incline that ran downhill.

On the witch's side, another house sprung up, but she barreled through that one as well. Children screamed inside. More glass crashed as she went through. A car alarm went off, blaring in the night. The road became hard to see. Asphalt merged into shadows. He could not afford to slip off the road. The bike would not absorb the same punishment hers appeared capable of.

"Go away!" he yelled.

Cooper finally stopped crying, too exhausted to shed more tears. He was ready to give up. His legs burned and cramped.

The witch laughed and closed in. He felt more than saw her angle toward him, ready to intercept. The ever-present knocking of the camera continued, an annoyance that any other time would have drawn his ire. The device could only take so much abuse though. Cooper felt the camera shift, the strap fraying, threatening to give.

He could not care about that now. The bend approached, and the witch launched herself toward him. She used the upcoming curve to ride at him. She would catch him before he could get off the bike and into the church. His best chance was if he could ride straight to the door and rush in. It all depended on the church being open. *Churches stayed open for those in need, right*? He needed it to be open. Desperately needed it.

The witch was closer, almost on him now. His tenth speed meant nothing. She would not stop. He had only one chance. Shooting toward the front of the church, he felt the curve work against him. It boosted his speed when he needed to slow enough to stop and run through the doors. Cooper felt his hand slipping off the metal handlebar. He was going to lose it, going to bite the dust if he tried to slow!

She was so close! He went into the turn and let gravity take over. The bend swept him up so that he almost rammed the front of the church, but he avoided catastrophe by leaning into the turn. The sharp turn swept the camera up in the centripetal force, causing the strap to snap. He felt the tug as the camera ripped itself from his grip.

He heard the camera smack the ground and bounce away at the same time the witch reached him. Cooper ducked as her arm swung wide above him, the black cloak looking like a raven's wing. He heard its swoosh as it missed what may have been an attempt to sever his head. Cooper leaned into the handles, riding the hill, feeling his speed increase even as the world seemed to move in slow motion.

Then the strangest thing. The cackle followed the trajectory of the camera. He looked back and could no longer see her. The Wicked Witch was maybe not dead, but gone. Cooper rode the hill, allowing it to bring him home.

· · · ● ● ● ● ● · ·

Cooper's family worried after he refused to leave his room for an entire week. He claimed to be ill and truthfully was. Dehydration from the ride took its toll. He drew a fever and vomited repeatedly for days. What Cooper refused to tell anyone was the real reason he puked was because of the flashbacks. In his mind he still heard the cackle, watched the raven's wing swiping wide above his head, and saw the green face with the ebony eyes.

That Sunday, he asked his parents to take him to church. He froze upon arriving at the parking lot, remembering how close (so very close) it all came to ending right there. While it haunted him to return, he needed the comfort of strangers. His parents were happy to see him leave the house but surprised at his desire to return to such a familial Sunday tradition.

After the sermon's end, the preacher addressed housekeeping matters. The man mentioned upcoming suppers, Sunday classes, charity work and eventually something that shook Cooper.

"We found a camera in our parking lot last weekend. We assume it belongs to a parishioner. The strap broke, you may not be aware you lost it. If it is yours, please come forward," the preacher said.

Cooper did not and never would. He realized that was what the witch sought. She did not want her picture taken. Maybe she could only go so close to the church. If the camera remained in the building, she would have no way to get at it, or get at him. He prayed the priest never opened the camera. Inside where the film went in, Cooper had long ago affixed a strip from a label maker with his name on it.

If someone missed the obvious, he prayed no one from the church would develop the film, hoping to locate the owner. Cooper feared if the camera ever left the safety of the church, it might free the woman from the house once again.

Luck only takes one so far and his luck ran out that night. Deep down Cooper understood that if ever there was a next time, the witch would win the race.

AFTERWORD

One last thing.

This project began prior to the pandemic but finished during it. Like many things in life, it was delayed because of the world event. There will be future volumes with stories written in new places, inspiring new horrific tales. That is if we can find new coffee shops. If we learned anything is that one must show their love and support of businesses big and small if they wish to see them still open tomorrow.

Many shops referred to here have not reopened and I am uncertain whether they ever will. Both big and small suffered and I miss them. Do what you can to keep them around because we now know even something as ubiquitous as the local coffee shop can die. Now that is truly scary...

ABOUT THE AUTHOR

JOSEPH CARRO

Joseph Carro is a freelance writer, editor, and blogger who also has an unhealthy obsession with cosplay, steak, and the supernatural. He received his MFA degree from the Stonecoast MFA program, and he is a barista in his spare time. He lives in Alabama with his depression.

Follow Joe's blog at: https://awaywithwordsjc.com/

ALSO BY PAUL CARRO

THE HOUSE

"The day began when sheriff Frank Watkins discovered two bodies and three heads..."

Horror has found a home!

Nine strangers with nine secrets so dark they plan to take them to their graves. One house is willing to accommodate them all.

The House is now open. Enter if you dare!

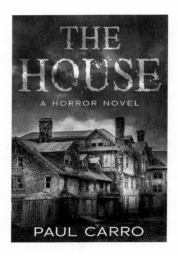

Roots of All Evil

Decades after a shocking cult murder rocked an unsuspecting farming community a woman goes missing.

It appears evil never left, in fact, a crop born of the blood of an innocent has finally born fruit.

As two families come together to search for the missing mother, they vow to go to the ends of the earth to find her. When a sinkhole opens on their property they learn they may have to. For hidden in the darkness below their feet is a world of madness and horror with an army of creatures hungry for flesh.

The town soon learns it only takes one bad seed to raise a little Hell!

About The Author

PAUL CARRO

Paul was born and raised in Maine and was published at an early age in an anthology of Maine authors alongside one of his horror icons. Paul moved to Los Angeles after college and worked for years in TV and film in multiple capacities but never in the horror genre. To rectify that, Paul (a lifelong horror fan) returned to his literary roots starting with his debut novel *The House*. He followed that up with *Roots of All Evil* and coming soon is *The Salem Legacy*. When not hiding in the dark of a movie theater getting his horror on, Paul can be found hiking all over the state with occasional stops at the beach.

For updates on upcoming projects visit: https://paulcarrohorror.com/

Made in the USA
Middletown, DE
26 August 2023